Barkhordar-Nahai, Gina
Barkhordar-Nahai, Gina
SUNDAY'S SILENCE

11/01

Sunday's Silence

Sunday's Silence

GINA B. NAHAI

Harcourt, Inc.

NEW YORK   SAN DIEGO   LONDON

www.HarcourtBooks.com

Any resemblance to actual people and events is purely coincidental.
This is a work of fiction.

Library of Congress Cataloging-in-Publication Data
Nahai, Gina Barkhordar.
Sunday's silence/Gina Nahai.—1st U.S. ed.
p.   cm.
ISBN 0-15-100627-X
1. Appalachian Region—Fiction. 2. Murder—Investigation—Fiction.
3. Fathers—Death—Fiction. I. Title.
PS3552.A6713 S86 2001
813'.54—dc21   2001024957

Text set in Fournier
Display set in La Figura and Requiem
Designed by Cathy Riggs

First edition
A C E G I K J H F D B

Printed in the United States of America

FOR *H*.

WITH LOVE

isten.

I will tell you a story you will not easily forget—one you cannot turn away from, or deny, or leave behind in the folds of my hands and on the edges of my lips.

It is the story you have searched for all these weeks, the one you resolved to uncover no matter what the cost to yourself or others. You have traveled the world looking for an answer only I can reveal, and now you are here, armed with a long-ago fury that has cooled and hardened and turned into rigid certainty, seeking the truth, intent on proving it to the world.

You have come to destroy me—you who can save me with your silence. You have come to destroy me, and all I can do to absolve myself is to offer you my words as I have offered you my skin, to take your hand and guide it over my memories as if they were my flesh, as if I could seduce you with my tale instead of my passion.

Is Truth more urgent than Desire?

So come closer. I will show you what you have wanted to know since the beginning of our time together. For when I am done, you will believe that which seems impossible to you now—that you and I are one and the same, regardless of all of our differences, that you cannot undo me without destroying yourself, that hearing my story has made you—my confessor, my judge, my enemy—it has made you my accomplice.

Listen.

Summer 1775

SHE WENT TO find him when he most longed to see her, walked through town in her white cotton dress and her bare feet, and all along the way men stopped and stared at her as if to wonder if she were not a figment of their imaginations. Adam sensed the men's agitation before he became aware of Blue's presence, heard the murmurs of their hearts and their faint, embarrassed gasps as she traveled past them like a breeze in the heat of the two o'clock sun of a Sunday afternoon in August. Then he recognized the stirrings of an old sadness, felt Blue move toward him with the beat of his own breath, and by the time he went to the door and saw her, he knew he should never have come back.

She looked like rain.

She stood before him with her purple eyes and her innocent's smile, a storm of golden-red hair against her tulip-white skin, her body long and lean and unself-conscious, her arms bare and cool and hinting of desire—and he realized that he knew nothing about her at all, that he had spent days investigating the woman without gaining the slightest understanding of her.

"I wanted to see you," she said.

They stood in front of the Lamar-Church Boardinghouse in downtown Knoxville. An old colonial mansion built on one of the original sixty-four lots that had comprised the city in its early days, the house had been abandoned for close to forty years—victim of the urban flight that overtook Knoxville after the Great Depression and that lasted well into the mid-1970s.

For forty years the house had sat, unoccupied, along a deserted street, its windows smeared with dust, its steps crumbling with age and covered with kudzu. Around it the city had slept in shells of empty department stores and locked offices, houses overrun by colonies of mice and giant cats, cobblestoned alleys frequented by naked ghosts and orphaned children, railroad tracks that transported only freight cars, and a station where no train ever stopped. Then the city's leaders had embarked on a plan to invite life back into its center. The boardinghouse had been sold for a pittance to the first and only bidder, and money had been loaned for a renovation. Investors had been invited to take over stores and businesses. Streetlights had been installed. The train station had been revamped. A year after it had opened its doors, the boardinghouse was still among only a handful of buildings that held a semblance of life downtown.

That Sunday Adam shared the hotel with three other guests—college students from Amsterdam on a year-long cross-country tour of the United States. One of the boys had heard Blue come in and was now standing at the window of his room overlooking the street. Even without turning to see him, Adam could imagine the look of stupefaction on the boy's face, the way his eyes watered as they strove to swallow Blue's image whole, the way he whispered to his friends "come-to-the-window-and-look-for-yourselves-this-is-definitely-a-sight-to-see, the-one-we'll-remember-when-we're-old."

Adam had been in Knoxville for ten days already. He knew where to find Blue, of course. She had lived in the same house in Fort Sanders since she had moved here from a far-off and exotic land twenty-four years ago. Her husband, a man everyone knew as "the Professor," had brought her here with no fanfare and with little explanation of her background. In Knoxville the last few days, Adam had followed Blue's trail around town and talked to people who knew her, looked up her records at the county courthouse and the DA's office, searched the archives of the local press for references to Blue and her past. He knew he had to call on her—to look her in the face and determine for himself the truth or falsehood of the rumors surrounding her. Yet every time he came close to seeing her, he was overcome by an instinctive sense of danger, a feeling that he would lose objectivity the moment he set eyes on her, and so he had kept his distance, from hour to hour and day to day, until she made the first move.

"You've been asking about me," she said.

The smile had spread from her lips into her eyes, and spilled like heat onto everything she looked at. Adam watched the edges of her mouth, the soft dimple in her right cheek, the curve in the nape of her neck. Her dress, cut at the top in the shape of a V, was almost transparent. Through it he could see the bareness of her breasts, the line that ran from the center of her chest down over her stomach, the tips of her hipbones against the sheer fabric. She was like a creature from another world, he thought—a child's drawing of a woman, all those vivid, improbable colors, the red and purple and blue that belonged more to trees and to fish than to humans. She must have picked up a box of crayons, he thought, once when she was three years old and her world was filled with promise, picked up the colors and painted herself into what she thought a woman would look like.

Blue shook her head to move the sun out of her eyes. Her hair fell in long, soft curls onto her back and shoulders, reflecting a thousand variations of light, giving her an aura of unreality. She walked closer to Adam and out of the sun. At the second-floor window, the trio from Amsterdam inhaled uneasily and remained glued to their spots. Aware of their desperation Blue raised her eyes at them for a split second, acknowledging their presence, accepting their eagerness. Then she looked back at Adam.

It occurred to him then that she was not afraid of him at all, though she must realize why he was here—because he had read about Little Sam Jenkins' death and come back to investigate how he had died, because Sam may well have died at Blue's hands—he had said as much to the sheriff in the hours before his death—because Adam was determined to establish the truth or falsehood of that claim.

She came even closer to him and stopped. He thought he could feel the warmth of her body spreading under his skin—like water moving through the earth, finding every pore, filling a long forgotten but excruciating need.

She was not afraid of him at all.

"Come inside," she said.

THE INSIDE OF the boardinghouse was dark and dim and full of shadows. Blue led Adam through the narrow hallway on the ground floor, the Dutch boys staring at her from the landing above the staircase. The hotel's owner, a transplanted homosexual from Michigan, had sensed the boys' excitement and came into the hallway to check its source. A costume designer by training, he had come to Knoxville in the late '60s to help the university set up its first theater arts program. He had counted on staying a month, maybe two. But the green of the Appalachian Mountains and the calm of the wide Tennessee River flowing silently through town had seduced him. The contrast between the humid Tennessee weather and the harsh, hard earth of Michigan had been soothing, and in the quiet, abandoned downtown of Knoxville he had found an anonymity that was comforting. Now he ran the boardinghouse and applied his talents to collecting small glass figurines which he displayed on every flat surface in the downstairs living room.

Blue went up to the man and took his hand. He smiled at her—a daring, knowing smile offered only to *her*, and withheld from Adam.

"How *brave* you are, my dear," he whispered, pointing out Blue's near nakedness, the heretical way in which she had let her hair loose and her feet bare. Among the Holy Rollers of southern Appalachia, women who showed their flesh, who cut their hair or dressed in immodest ways were considered Jezebels, damned by the church and shunned by its members. Holiness women wore floor-length dresses with long sleeves and no adornments, tied their hair back, refused to wear makeup or jewelry or even a watch. Until recently, Adam knew from his conversations with the townspeople, Blue had respected the conventions of the church and never flaunted her beauty, nor displayed her flesh and skin, as she had done the last few months. Then Little Sam had died and she had left the church and, with it, all the laws that had governed her outward appearance.

Watching her now, Adam thought that she was indeed brave—that this was what she had in common with the hotel's owner: they were both outcasts from their own tribes, rebels with little left to lose, alone but for the friendship of other fallen angels.

The owner gave Adam a sharp, disapproving look, then stepped back and let him among the colored glass.

The living room wallpaper was cobalt-colored suede. The floor was dark wood. The chairs were covered with yellow and red velvet. The table tops and mantelpiece displayed luminous shapes of animals carved in glass. Standing among them in her diaphanous white dress, rays of cream-colored light falling on her through the half-open shutters, Blue looked every bit as fragile, as light and magical as the glass.

She walked to the middle of the room and turned to face Adam. Her dress gathered around her like a puddle of white, setting off her purple eyes and revealing only her bare feet. She waited for Adam to come in, but he remained at the threshold—reluctant and cautious and aware of the dangers of getting too close to her. He stood with one shoulder against the frame of the door, at once intrigued and alarmed, drawn to and repelled by her. His body—tall and lean and indifferent—retained an old and almost forbidding tension. He still bore the frame of a man who has spent his formative years working outdoors, but he looked older than his thirty-nine years, more jaded. His face was broad and angular, scarred on the left cheek from one too many childhood beatings. His eyes, light brown like his hair, rested on Blue but refused to let her in.

She saw this and smiled.

"I've seen you watching my house," she said.

Her voice was rich and languid and laced with temptation. It spilled off her lips and into the lazy heat of the room, spreading itself against the air that was thick and heavy and still, settling onto the backs of the glass horses in the proprietor's collection, into the loops of the white embroidered linen on the armrests, the petals of the roses in the red-and-blue Persian rug.

"I see you asking questions of Mrs. Roscoe across the street. I hear you talking to my friend Anne Pelton in Pineville."

She had caught him off guard, upset the balance in which he was supposed to be the hunter and she the unsuspecting prey. Still, she did not seem hostile.

"I watch you from my bedroom window. You wait for us— my husband or me—to come outside, but you never knock on our door."

Adam reached for a cigarette in his shirt pocket and lit it. He knew this woman's game, he thought. In his years as a reporter, he had seen others like her—offenders with their backs against the ropes, aggressors who suddenly found themselves trapped, who realized their only chance at escape was to convince the opponent that they were harmless.

He blew a puff of smoke, watched it dissipate in tiny loops the color of Blue's voice.

"I'm working on a story," he said, his voice deeply detached. "Nothing personal."

She smiled again as if to say she knew better. He felt angry with her, dissatisfied with himself for having let her make the first move. He had to take charge of the situation, he thought, establish himself as the one in control.

He flicked the ashes from the cigarette onto the hardwood floor, inches away from the silk fringes on the Persian rug, and did not bother to hide them. He came into the room now and sat on a chair next to a bureau.

"I write for a newspaper," he said, intentionally patronizing her, treating her like the backward person with an undeveloped mind the rest of the world might have assumed she was. "You may get famous."

She remained untouched by his sarcasm. She was not about to engage in battle, he thought. He stretched his legs and leaned back in the chair.

"What's on your mind?"

Just then the costume designer from Michigan appeared in the room dressed in a green linen suit and a pair of suede loafers. Accompanied now by his yellow Persian cat, he carried a tray with a plate of chocolates and a single glass. At the doorway he stopped and regarded Blue and Adam.

"Might you have a drink, my dear?" he asked.

He was looking at Adam, but there was no question to whom he was offering the drink.

"Something sweet and easy," he taunted, "like *love* with a stranger."

When she reached to take the tray, Blue's hands turned toward the owner as if to a safe harbor.

The hotel owner breezed past Adam with theatrical flair.

"Use an ashtray."

She put the tray and the plate of chocolates on an end table, then looked toward Adam again.

"You want to know about Sam," she said without introduction.

Veins of regret ran through her voice. She was like water, he thought—clear and transparent and strong. Not at all what he had expected; not what he had hoped he would find.

"You've come to know if I killed him."

He liked her boldness—the way she said those words without flinching, the way her face and body remained cool under pressure. Suddenly he felt his anger rise.

"Did you?" he stabbed—"kill him?"

He did not expect an answer, but he waited for the question to do its damage, watched with satisfaction as the lines around Blue's eyes became tighter and her breathing slowed.

"Because that's serious, you know—intentionally killing a man. It's got consequences, out there in the real world."

He heard the anger in his own voice but could not suppress it. He was showing too much emotion, betraying a lack of objectivity that would detract from his work.

"That is, of course, if you *did* mean to kill him."

She came toward him then and knelt on the floor before his chair. They were almost at eye level with each other, he slightly higher. Suddenly he found himself wanting to reach over and touch the fabric of her dress, trace his fingers along the edge of her upper lip.

"All day long I hear the sound of your boots against the asphalt," she whispered, almost to herself.

She was looking at him as if to see if he were real, watching him as if he were a ghost come to life.

"I feel your voice in my head, see the whites of your eyes in the mirror where I look."

Her eyes were vast and calm and deep, not so much examining as drawing him in, and he felt as if he were afloat in something warm and heavy—the waters of the Red Sea where he had once lain in a state of perfect calm, closed his eyes and felt the sun on his face and told himself, this is what death must be like.

"I watch you and see the lines of our lives cast together like a wish, our colors running together till they merge, our bodies entwined in one another, seeking sameness."

When she spoke, her skin glowed with emotion. He wanted to touch her hand, to close his eyes and fall asleep listening to her voice.

She had not come to seduce him, he thought. She had merely followed a vision that intrigued her—the man who stared at her bedroom window but did not approach—and she had wanted to see it up close.

He knew nothing about her at all.

HE HAD BEEN in the correspondents' bar at the Intercontinental Hotel in Beirut, killing time and drinking the anise-flavored arak-and-water that was the local drink. He had been in Lebanon for four months—since April, when fighting had broken out between Palestinian fighters and Christian Phalangists. The Chicago desk, where the paper was headquartered, had counted on the war lasting a few weeks. It would stretch to upwards of fifteen years and lay the country in ruins.

In Beirut that evening Adam had sat in the half-empty bar, listening to the sound of the other reporters' conversation without taking part in it. Before Lebanon he had lived in Syria, then Egypt, Cyprus, and Turkey. He had written for the Chicago paper for twelve years, eight of them covering wars in places that took him as far away from America and her interests as he could travel. He had managed to stay away from Vietnam and Cambodia, did not touch Chile, cared nothing about Watergate. The other reporters—the ones with the college education, the ambition to win the Pulitzer, to become a recognized name and create a legacy—*they* wrote the front-page columns and did the interviews that made history. Adam wanted only to keep away from home and all its memories.

"Real Marlboro," the middle-aged man who poured drinks at the bar held a red box out at Adam. "Genuine American. My last one, but you're welcome to take it."

Adam smiled and told the man he preferred the local, hand-rolled tobacco.

"As you wish." The man looked disappointed.

He was dressed in a white suit. He had perfectly sprayed hair, manicured nails. He spoke English and French, German and Armenian and Arabic. Until a few months ago he had owned a travel agency on Beirut's West Side. Then the war had started, the tourists had stopped coming to Lebanon, and the man with the manicured nails had taken a job at the bar, working for tips and discussing politics with the reporters who passed through.

Adam asked the man his nationality.

The bartender smiled. "My mother is a Druze," he said. He waited a moment, as if hesitating to divulge a greater truth. Then he leaned closer to Adam, tilted his head sideways and whispered, "but I have been to Malibu, California, and that's where I would like to go again before I die."

As proof of his undying love for America, he reached under the counter and introduced a pile of old newspapers that he had tied in a neat stack with a string. He had gone to great pains to collect the papers, he said. Before the war Beirut had been an international city, with newsstands on every corner carrying papers and magazines in a dozen languages. Now he had to wait days for an issue of the *New York Times* to make its way into the city.

"This is how I keep in touch with the world." He smiled proudly, offering Adam the papers with a reverent hand.

The issue that sat on top of the pile was ten days old. Reluctantly, so as not to offend the bartender, Adam looked at the front page, downed another shot of arak, and turned to the inside sections. Sister Blue Kerdi of Knoxville, Tennessee, the snake-handling, strychnine-drinking, fire-breathing member of the Church of Southern Hope and Redemption in nearby Harlan, Kentucky, had been arrested for the murder of Little Sam Jenkins.

Adam stared at the paper until the lines became blurred. Relief streamed into his veins, like a rivulet of joy that sparkled as it traveled through his limbs and reached his extremities. He knew this relief, this bittersweet sense of joy. He had experienced it as a child the first time he had seen Little Sam Jenkins, then at every subsequent meeting. Later, when he had left the South and gone as far away from it as he could, he had felt the same joy every time he read about Sam in the American press or met someone who reminded him of the possibility, however faint, of resolving an enigma that had haunted him all his life.

Invariably, the sense of relief gave way to rage.

Little Sam Jenkins, a ninety-year-old preacher who was widely credited with having started the snake-handling movement in Kentucky, had perished after being bitten by an eastern diamondback handed to him by Blue. Having wrestled with snakes since he was thirty years old, Sam had received 446 snakebites during his career as a preacher. He had survived the previous snakebites with the help of the Holy Ghost, refusing medical attention on grounds it would prove his faith was weak, and he would have survived the last bite just as easily, he believed and many agreed with him, except that the woman who handed him the snake had *intended* to kill him.

Held at the jail in Knox County for a night, Sister Blue had admitted to violating a state law against snake handling, but refused to answer police and investigators' questions about her motives in giving Sam the snake. Under pressure from the sheriff and the local authorities, the DA had contemplated, but had ultimately refused to go forward with charges against Blue.

"It is not that I have any doubt about Sister Blue's intentions," he had announced to the local press. "But intention alone does not a case make, and it has been my experience, in over thirty years of prosecuting criminal cases, that matters relating to religious faith and its practitioners are sure losers in court."

Blue had been released without charges, but the stalemate and the resulting bad blood between the police and the DA had divided the town of Knoxville and brought chaos into Sam's church. The Tennessee state legislature had again passed a law declaring snake handling a misdemeanor, and Blue had voluntarily turned over her snakes to the sheriff. The matter of the preacher's death, it seemed, would be left unresolved.

Adam brought the glass to his mouth and realized it was empty.

"So this is how it ends," he thought. "He dies and takes the truth with him."

Without raising his eyes from the paper, he put the glass back on the bar, waited as the bartender filled it, drank down the arak, and murmured thanks. Conscious of the sudden change in Adam's mood, the man said something about the power of the written word. Carefully, Adam folded the paper and placed it on the bar, paid the bartender, then left.

Outside, night was falling, and the air smelled of humidity and salt. Two young boys with shaved heads and torn T-shirts played soccer in the lobby of a shelled building that had once been a car dealership. Behind them the sky was bright orange against the blue Mediterranean Sea.

The newspaper had mentioned nothing about Little Sam's history, Adam thought—nothing about the life that had been marred by crimes and contradictions, the people that Sam had saved and the ones he had destroyed. Perhaps, Adam thought, the reporter had not dug deeply enough. Most likely the church people and their stories were not important enough to the rest of the country.

He lit a cigarette and began to walk toward the Corniche, along the western coast. Once a busy promenade packed with street vendors and cafes, the Corniche had been rendered deserted and ruined by the war—a long and quiet stretch of golden rocks rising directly above the sea. Adam knew he should go back to the hotel and call the night editor waiting for his report back in Chicago, that he should get off the streets before dark, when martial law was enforced and the shelling and sniper fire began. Instead, he kept walking toward the arched Pigeon Rocks, where the cliffs were a sheer drop leading down to inlets that local fishermen used as a harbor. He stood above the inlets and watched the men—lonely, tired-looking creatures with sunburned skin and creaky boats, pants legs rolled up to their knees, their hands scaly and chapped and restless.

Twenty years had passed since he had stolen a ride on the back of a pickup truck that took him out of Appalachia and as far away as he could go. Yet across time and distance, a world of experience away from the church and the mountains that had surrounded him in his childhood, that had pressed against him and closed him in and blocked his view with their beauty and their harshness—across all the years during which he had tried to purge Little Sam Jenkins and the others from his memories, he had only managed to see them more clearly.

HE HAD HIRED a local man to drive him from Lebanon into Jordan, then waited two days for a flight to Frankfurt. Eight years had passed since he had set foot on American soil. From Frankfurt he called the Chicago desk and told the night editor he was going home.

"*What* home?" the night editor could not disguise his sarcasm. In all the years he had worked for the paper, Adam had never maintained a permanent residence or even a phone number. He listed no forwarding address, spoke of no family members. He made no friends, no attempt to establish relationships with other reporters or photographers he had worked with over time. Quick and bold and willing to go to any length for a story, he left a place as easily as he embraced it. He lived out of a single backpack—faded jeans and combat boots, shirts he picked up in any city when the old ones tore, a shaving kit. To anyone who insisted on inquiring about his background, he said only that he was from the South, the son of a moonshining father and a woman he—the father—had met in the back of a tent during a church revival in eastern Kentucky.

"What about Lebanon?" The editor had pressed. "You're on *assignment*."

"I'll be back there in a week," Adam lied.

When he hung up, the editor was still protesting.

He stayed up half the night at an airport bar. An American businessman on his way back to Detroit was drinking Johnnie Walker Black and talking about the firmness of the thighs of all the German women he had met in Frankfurt. "Must be the climate," he kept saying, with reverence more than lust. "Must be in the genes."

He said this to a plump German woman in a too-short miniskirt and a lambskin jacket she had bought from a Turkish immigrant on a seedy backstreet filled with smoke from water pipes and open barbecues. Adam watched her. She was not a prostitute, he decided, just a lonely woman out for the night, aware that her own thighs were far from firm, realizing that the American had barely noticed them—or her—at all, thinking that her loneliness made her invisible, regardless of the shape of her thighs or the shortness of her skirt, regardless of the quality of her genes or the extent of her need.

"To German thighs!" The American raised a glass of black label to the room and smiled.

Adam leaned back in his booth and closed his eyes. He wanted to erase the German woman's presence from his mind, to remove himself as a witness to her humiliation, spare her additional shame.

He thought about calling Chicago again, telling the night editor why he was going back, asking him to search the wire reports for any updates on Blue and Little Sam's story.

A snake-handling, Holy Rolling preacher from a godforsaken church in the Appalachian foothills, dead because he had picked up a snake someone else knew would kill him, buried in a field outside an abandoned shed in South Florida.

"You want to cover *what?*" Adam imagined the night editor gasp at the other end. "You left Lebanon for *what?*"

A snake-handling, Holy Rolling preacher who spoke of the love of Christ but indulged in war, who spoke of eternal life but flirted with death, who acted without shame, without remorse, without fear of man or God.

Many years ago, in the days of her youth and arrogance,

21

Adam's mother had seduced Little Sam Jenkins and borne his child. Afterward, she had followed Sam through fourteen states trying to establish the truth of his paternity. She had died disappointed, but not before instilling in Adam the rage she felt at Sam Jenkins for denying his son. Too young to understand the snake handler's motives or the mystery of his faith, too intimidated by Sam Jenkins to go near him, Adam had escaped Appalachia rather than pursue the answers that might have explained his own and his mother's fate. But the farther he had gone from the South, the more he had felt the weight of those questions, the certainty also that he had empowered Sam with his absence— that by removing himself as proof of Sam's indiscretion, he had bought the man impunity and allowed him to bury the truth with his lies.

This much he had learned from his own childhood in Appalachia, from the years, too, of covering wars and witnessing atrocities: the greatest sin of all was to refuse to bear witness.

HE BOUGHT TWO packs of cigarettes at the airport outside Washington, D.C., rented a car, and drove out. It was four in the afternoon when he pulled onto the interstate heading west. Adam had not slept for two days, but the thought of staying still, of spending the night in a hotel room before embarking on the journey toward Knoxville was unbearable. Before him the highway was long and smooth and still uncrowded. A warm, heavy wind—full of moisture, already tainted with the promise of dusk—blew in through the open window. Adam put his head back against the seat and tried to ignore the tide of anxiety that had hit him the moment he had looked out the airplane window and seen the colors of America against the horizon. He knew this road. He had traveled it countless times in his youth, in the days when Little Sam Jenkins was still alive and conducting services, the days when Adam followed him with his mother.

As a child Adam had watched the snake handlers with a mixture of awe and revulsion—a helpless mortal face-to-face with God's living soldiers on earth, drawn by the depth of their faith in the Lord but repulsed by the cruelty they showed other humans, the violence they inflicted upon their own bodies and that, in the end, they had inflicted on Adam and his mother. Later, he had examined his own memories and summoned every bit of knowledge he could muster. He had read about the Holy Rollers and asked questions where he could. Yet he had never managed to understand how a man as flawed and sinful as Little Sam, a man who wore his failings like the patches on his shirt—how such a man was able to establish his own cult within the Church of God and gather tens of thousands of followers across a dozen states.

———

From the airport to Virginia the freeway was wide and over-bearing and filled with commuters' cars. He drove until night fell and then he drove some more, the car moving of its own volition, lured by the tail lights ahead. Outside Fairfax he pulled into a truck stop and went into the café. A young girl, maybe fifteen years old, poured coffee into a mug before he had even sat down. She wore a faded black dress, an even more faded expression on her face. She stared at him as she poured the coffee, her eyes never leaving his face, her hand straightening the tip of the coffee urn just as the mug filled. A minute later she put a plate of ham and biscuits before him, filled a dirty glass with water, and vanished into the kitchen. Adam felt his stomach turn with the smell of the food and looked away. The scent of biscuits cooked in grease, of cured ham or fried potatoes or even plain, unrefined bread always reminded him of a child-hood of hunger, of the years he had slept wishing for food, the days when his only real meal was provided by church members who brought offerings to share after each service.

He smoked half a cigarette, paid without eating, without looking for the girl with the faded face, and got back into the car.

Through Virginia the highway narrowed, and the mountains loomed taller above the land. Adam drove in the dark, alone on the road but for the occasional truck. In his mind he could see the dense green cover of the mountains around him, the soil that was red and gold with strips of glittering black—coal seams, like dark crystal—the narrow, unpaved lanes that stretched from the highway toward the hills, into clearings where a few houses, a church, a cemetery, huddled together, forgotten by the world.

Little Sam may be dead, Adam thought, but his cult would

go on without him, entrenched within the community of believers as the coal seams in the dirt—narrow, deep, so hard it stuck to everything it touched. These same believers would protect Sam's legacy and perpetuate his beliefs. Like crusaders everywhere, they would be quick to declare martyrs and even quicker to accept converts, and yes, there was no denying the fact that no one, not the nonbelievers who dismissed the snake handlers' antics as mere deception, or the reporters who stalked them hoping to discover the smoke and mirrors Adam knew were not there, or even the doctors who attended church meetings armed with all the tools modern science had to offer—none of those people had ever managed to explain why the snakes often did not bite the handlers, why the fire that they handled did not burn and the poison they drank did not kill.

He drove all night, west toward Middletown, then south on Highway 11. Past Harrisonburg the mountains rose straight off the side of the road—walls of rock and trees that stretched into the sky and blocked out the moon and the stars. Beyond Christiansburg the highway veered west, and the valley grew deeper and more narrow. He headed toward Cumberland Gap—the narrow passage through the Appalachian Mountains that connected the states of Kentucky, Tennessee, and West Virginia. Sixteen hundred feet above sea level, this was the bridge across which Daniel Boone had blazed the Wilderness Road two hundred years earlier.

Long ago Adam had memorized, then tried to forget, every inch of this landscape, every color, every lonely, dust-ridden town along the way and yet, the first light of dawn struck him with all the wonder and magic of discovery.

The valley was a carpet of a thousand shades of green—vibrant, deep colors of stunning density and lushness—the earth a stark red, the air bright and glittering with sparkles of light. Where the road widened a bit, Adam could see dilapidated wooden shacks built on a slope with nothing around them but trees. Their porches were jammed with old shoes and discarded stoves, tattered clothes hanging on a line, broken benches and legless chairs. Even though it was morning, there were no people in sight, no children playing on the porches or on the side of the road. Adam realized he had forgotten how underpopulated Appalachian towns were, how, after years of living in crowded cities where every man's breath rubbed against the back of another's neck, one could draw comfort from being surrounded only by mountains.

Through the Cumberland Gap he found himself turning north, toward Kentucky. He watched the road widen a bit, the landscape dotted by simple wooden barns painted black, small cemeteries—their gravestones well tended, the graves bearing fresh flowers—bordering the road. Every few miles a church appeared alone against the horizon: simple, one-room structures built entirely of wood with an A-shaped frame and a steeple, with names like HIGHWAY HOLINESS CHURCH OF GOD, and the CHURCH OF LORD JESUS WITH SIGNS FOLLOWING. In between the churches, the highway was dotted with signs posted into the ground: ARE YOU READY FOR THE DAY OF RECKONING? they asked. Or: COME ON OVER AND BRING THE KIDS. SIGNED, GOD.

He drove through Harlan, Kentucky, then Pineville—coal-mining towns still bearing the marks of a devastation they could not recover from. Being here, Adam thought, it was easy to understand why Appalachia was so different from the rest of America, why little that happened on the outside could really penetrate the lives of the people here: there was a sense of life old but not worn, of nature invigorating its own, stubborn and inflexible, of living things growing but not changing—a world of majestic beauty that remained always the same.

Lynch, Kentucky, was a one-street town built on a mountain slope. The street, unpaved most of the way, was wide enough for one car. The few stores that bordered it were abandoned, their windows broken, their insides piled ceiling-high with giant, monstrous dust balls. Behind them were single-room shacks that had housed coal miners in another day. Now they sat empty, the coal miners gone or dead, the alleys around the houses still strewn with discarded toys and furniture.

Adam drove up to an old bridge made of rope and planks and suspended above a dried creek bed. Beyond it, he knew, in what was once the town of Corbin Glow, was a rusted freight car, derailed and long forgotten, split in half so that the top was open. He did not get out of the car here. He turned around and headed toward Knoxville. Down Highway 63 he stopped only when he saw the old chain-link fence surrounding an abandoned brick structure with darkened windows and kudzu growing all over.

He stepped out of the car and felt the humid air wash over him like sorrow. Squinting through the light, he saw the stone plaque that still hung next to the building's entrance:

TENNESSEE STATE HOME FOR CHILDREN.

This was it, he thought: home as he knew it.

INSIDE THE boardinghouse the heat had become palpable. The atmosphere was thick, like butter—a moist, heavy mixture of cigarette smoke and wood polish and humidity. After Blue left, Adam remained in his chair, stunned by the emotions she had evoked in him and by the memory of her presence. Around him the heat cast shadows on the walls and prompted ghosts to crawl out of their hiding places and walk the house searching for cooler spots—the narrow spaces between the shelves in the pantry, the smooth surfaces of the white satin sheets in the owner's bed, the bear-claw bathtub in Adam's bathroom. The owner's cat strutted across the Persian rug on the drawing room floor and licked the back of a glass dolphin with purple skin.

Past sunset, the Dutch boys changed into white shorts and tennis socks, and filed noisily down the stairs—headed for unknown destinations where they would drink American beer and dwell on Blue's memory till their senses dulled or the heat subsided. Behind them the owner walked through the house trailed by his Persian cat, and closed all the shutters to keep out the encroaching darkness.

"One must never allow the dusk to set in," he said as he lit the floor lamp with the painted silk shade above Adam's chair.

Adam acted as if he had not heard or seen the man. His indifference annoyed the owner, made him more determined to induce a reaction.

In Knoxville the last few days, Adam had put together the pieces of Blue's story without difficulty or much probing. The facts of the case were easily established and hardly in doubt. Ironically, their very simplicity was what allowed room for speculation.

Born outside the United States, Blue had come to Knoxville in 1951—the fourteen-year-old bride of a professor of extinct languages at the University of Tennessee. Himself of mysterious origin, her husband had first appeared in the city shortly after the second World War. For years he had lived alone in the house in Fort Sanders and attended the First Baptist Church on Main Avenue. Wednesday nights he had gone to the movies at the Bijou Theater, then dined alone at the S & W. He had been polite and civil to his colleagues and neighbors, but he had formed no relationships outside of work, and had never entertained a guest at home. One summer he had taken leave from the university and gone away for many months—to the East, he said, where language had first started. He had come back with a wife.

Thirty-one years her senior, the Professor had applied himself to the task of educating Blue and teaching her the ways of city women. He had taught the girl to speak and read and write English, brought her books by the dozen, bought her clothes at Hess' department store—the city's premier shopping spot— but he had not let her out of the house alone and had controlled her every move and every contact. Right then, their marriage had seemed bizarre—the first act of a tragedy about to unfold.

Sometime in late 1956 the Professor had taken an interest in the Church of God and Little Sam's movement. For a while he had attended Holiness services up and down the southern states. Distrusted and shunned at first, because he was an outsider and a foreigner to boot, he had been allowed to stay only when he introduced his young wife to the church: she was so beautiful, no man would willingly have deprived himself of the privilege of setting eyes on her during worship; and she had picked up a snake the very first time she had gone to church and at every meeting that followed. Fearless beyond reason, she had taken on every challenge the believers had presented to her—fighting snakes no one else dared touch, drinking undiluted poison and setting her body into burning flames, emerging unscathed and ever the stronger for her troubles—a fact no one could deny and that had, right from the start, guaranteed her a place among the members. Long after the Professor had lost interest in Little Sam's movement, his wife continued to attend services and handle snakes.

Blue's relationship with the church, however, had always been troubled. Little Sam had welcomed her at first, and for a while he granted her the benefit of his most indulgent attentions. He kept a close eye on her and blessed her in his sermons, and he would have laid hands on her, would have gladly anointed her with blessed oils and a holy touch but for the fact that she fought his advances with as much resolve and fury as she did the snakes. The more Sam tried, the harder she fought back and the stronger she seemed to become, until it was clear that Sam would never be able to tame her. Jilted, he had stepped back, then assessed Blue in a new, more critical light.

"See for yourselves," he began to tell the believers. "This woman lives in a big house in the city, indulges in luxury and great vanity. In church she never testifies, never faints or talks in tongues. She seems little interested in the sermons, even less interested in letting the Lord into her home and her life. She is, in short, the very image of evil and sinfulness. If the Holiness code is to be believed, if the strength of a man's faith is what protects him against earthly harm, then this woman should be ravaged by snakebite and vomiting blood and poison by now. She must be blinded by fire, paralyzed by fear, and yet...

"Yet she handles snakes more often and with greater impunity than any Holiness man or woman, and this could only mean one thing, could only point to one direction and it would take a blind man not to see."

Either the Holiness code was incorrect, Little Sam concluded, or Blue was the devil incarnate.

AT EIGHT O'CLOCK the humidity in the air melted into rain and began to fall in slow, heavy drops. Adam went to the window and opened the blinds. Church Avenue was empty. Across the way a light burned in the cluttered front of an antique shop that had been closed since Adam had arrived in town. A black woman in a lavender dress sat behind a desk looking at herself in the small mirror of a silver compact. She had left the door to the shop half ajar, placed the OPEN sign where it would be clearly visible to passersby.

Adam left the window and headed out of the room. A glass of "something easy—like love with a stranger," sat untouched in the light of the floor lamp.

Outside, the rain sounded like lead dropping against the asphalt on the street. He stood under the marquee and smoked a cigarette. The black woman in the antique shop had stopped painting her face and was having a conversation on the phone. She sat up straight behind her antique desk—a professional saleslady with impeccable manners, at work. All around her bits of junk and old furniture—broken chairs, kitchenware, a naked mannequin, books no one had opened in a hundred years—lay under a heap of dust.

The rain stopped.

Adam walked along Church Avenue toward Walnut Street. The railroad tracks ran parallel to Jackson, crossed Broadway, then veered in the direction of Gay and Locust Streets. The train whistled through town all night, catching him awake and smoking. Three old women wearing the bright orange color of the University of Tennessee and sporting purple-white hair drove past in a Cadillac.

Growing up, Adam had lived less than an hour outside this town, but he had been a world away.

He turned from Market onto Clinch Avenue and into Fort Sanders. From a distance, Blue's house looked dark, its shutters closed. The front yard was overrun by weeds, giving the impression of a place uninhabited by living beings.

Nine o'clock. Adam waited for the Professor to drive by.

He appeared at exactly ten minutes past nine, in his 1961 blue Chevrolet with white leather seats, its chrome bumpers covered with dust from the road. He had both hands on top of the steering wheel—the ten-minutes-to-two position taught to new drivers—and he leaned toward the windshield as he drove. He was so small, Adam could only see the top half of his face behind the wheel, and he focused on the road with such consternation, it was clear he was afraid of his own driving.

He eased the car up 19th Street, turned right on Clinch Avenue, and stopped in front of his house. He sat in the car for an eternity before stepping out.

He was small and thin, dressed in a gray suit and a fedora. He had the pallor of people who never see sunlight, the hollow expression of one who has resigned himself to great loss. He was unshaved but well groomed, his black shoes shiny in the night. He looked up and down the street. When he saw Adam, he looked as if he had been punched in the chest. Quickly he locked the door to his car and headed up the steps to the house.

Adam smoked his cigarette down to the very end. He thought about Blue moving through the quiet, darkened hallways of that house. He imagined the rooms from inside, the little man in the dark suit standing behind a closed window, staring out of the cracks in the shutters with fear all over his face. He remembered what Blue had said about watching Adam from her bedroom. Strange, he thought, how the Professor seemed to carry the guilt and apprehension that should have been Blue's— as if he were the concerned parent of a child determined to err; as if he feared a consequence that she, for her part, embraced.

Nine-thirty, and the town was already asleep. Adam turned away from the house and crossed the street. He wanted a drink, the comfort of being surrounded by people and noise. He thought he should go back to the hotel and take his car, drive out to the strip malls outside of town in search of a bar. Something tugged at him. He turned around in the dark.

Blue was standing on the sidewalk above 18th Street, her clothes wet from rain, her feet still bare. From a distance she looked drawn, tired, lost in a way that startled Adam—a woman who has waited too long for a train that never arrives. He realized she must have followed him from the boardinghouse, that she must have watched him as he watched her house and waited for the Professor to arrive.

She had *wanted* him to come here, he thought, *wanted* him to find her.

THE OWNER WAS waiting for Adam at the entrance to the boardinghouse. He had changed out of his safari clothes into a light Indian pantsuit with gold and coral embroideries. A shadow in the half darkness, he was sipping a martini when Adam arrived.

"Quite a night for a walk," he said sarcastically.

Upstairs, the Dutch boys had fallen asleep on their beds with their clothes still on. Adam saw that the door to his own room was open a crack—as if someone had already been there and wanted him to know they had. He went up to the door cautiously—following years of experience living in places where reporters were routinely targeted by government thugs or revolutionary zealots.

Inside, nothing looked out of place. His bed was still unmade as he had left it that morning and his few clothes spilled out of the top of his backpack on the floor, and the ashtray on the night table was still full of butts. But he had the unmistakable feeling that his room had been searched in his absence, that hands had reached under his mattress, through the empty dresser drawers, inside the pockets of his shirts in the backpack. The ceiling fan, which had been off when he left, had been turned on, making a clanking noise with every rotation. He reached for the switch and turned it off.

"It's going to be hot," the owner called from the hallway below. "Better leave the fan on and sleep with your eyes open."

Adam slammed the door and ignored the advice about the fan. The French doors leading to the balcony of his room were open, but the air did not move at all. He pulled his shirt off and lay faceup on the bed.

Beirut was a thousand years away. He missed its breezy after-noons, the stunning colors of the Mediterranean, the town built on the edge of a cliff. He missed being in a place from which he had no memories—an outsider, interested but uninvolved.

He thought about how odd it was that no one in Knoxville—none of the residents, none of the believers Adam had called on the last few days—had recognized him, how no one even suspected that Adam himself might be from the mountains. Growing up in an orphanage, he had been taught to shed his Appalachian accent, to behave and even to think like city folk. Maybe that's why, he thought, none of the people he had inter-viewed and dealt with had looked at him hard enough to recog-nize his roots.

And he thought how strange that he had glimpsed Blue for such a short while, but that she would manage to cast her colors into Adam's life forever—like the lavender bleach the Arab women on the streets of Beirut poured into their basins of water before submerging their clothes to wash by hand: one small pinch of color in a vast container of clean water, and it would run streaks of bright, vivid blue through the basin and change the color of everything it touched into a luminous, unforget-table white.

ADAM NEVER TOLD ANYONE ABOUT HIS BEGINNINGS. Partly, he was ashamed. Partly, also, he did not understand it well enough to explain it to others. Appalachia, he would realize in time, had had its own rules—the daily workings of a culture so unfamiliar to and so hidden from the rest of the world, it did not make sense anywhere beyond the mountains. That was Appalachia's curse, but also its strength: to understand it, you had to get closer, to cross the mountains, linger within the valleys. You had to watch time slow down, let yourself become mesmerized by the colors of the landscape—by the wild, pulsating quiet, the long and narrow roads of an ancient loneliness that no man or machine was able to conquer—until the day you woke up with the color of the rivers in your eyes and the sound of the waterfalls in your ears, and you knew, without having the words to define it, that you had become part of a world where reality had its own meaning.

Adam's father, Little Sam Jenkins, was a preacher who had loved God's children but felt he was not "cut out" to take care of his own. Over his lifetime he would take four wives and father more than a dozen children, and he would abandon them all, fighting and moonshining and preaching as he went along, living in poverty and homelessness but imbued with the spirit of Christ and the desire, above all, to spread the Word and through it, conquer the devil. For sixty years he had preached that marriage was holy and divorce a sin, that second marriages were not recognized by the Lord because they rendered a person "double-married." For sixty years he had cried at the miracle of the child Christ and played with the children of his congregants, telling the parents that children were blessed, that they should be cherished and nurtured and regarded as God's gift to the family. Yet he had left his own offspring without a second thought, and he had even denied paternity where he could.

Little Sam Jenkins was not a liar or a hypocrite. He believed in what he preached, believed in it with fervor and innocence— why else would he have taken up poisonous serpents, plunged his arms and face into burning furnaces, even promised to walk on water before hundreds of believers, all in the name of the Lord? Unlike some preachers of his time, he had no interest in worldly goods, demanded no compensation for his hard work, sought no earthly comfort, even in old age. Like most of them, he had trouble living by the laws he preached.

He had trouble, too, looking away from a pretty woman with bare legs and red-painted toenails, especially one determined to prove to him the futility of man's resolve before the lure of the devil, and that's why he had found himself in 1935 between the thighs of young Clare Watkins at the end of a ten-day-long revival in the coal town of Lynch, Kentucky, inside the very tent where, for over a week, he had talked in tongues and danced to the music of cymbals and guitars and wrestled with forty-pound snakes daring them to bite him. Little Sam had been bitten twice during the revival—once on the left temple and once on the wrist, but the snakes and their poison had not managed to stop or even slow him down: he had taken the bites and continued preaching without so much as a frown, refusing to stop and wipe the blood that trickled down his forehead and onto his cheek, or to pull out the teeth that the second snake, a six-foot-long copperhead with a sand-colored coat, had left in his wrist. He had continued to preach even as his head had swelled to the size of a watermelon and turned black as his shoes. Later he had temporarily lost use of his wrist.

"The Lord shall take care of me," he had told the church members, refusing medical care on grounds it would prove his faith in God was weak.

Then the revival had ended and all the Holiness members had driven away in their trucks and she had come up to him— Clare whom he had known all her life, and whose mother he had been married to for a brief and unmemorable time.

Clare's mother, Rose Watkins, had been one of Little Sam's strictest converts, handling snakes and talking in tongues and moving with the Spirit until she fainted and fell unconscious to the floor in every church gathering she went to. Her first husband, Cecil Watkins, had worked the coal mines of eastern Kentucky for twenty-five years before he was sent to the Kentucky State Penitentiary and hanged for killing a mine boss. In his absence Rose had devoted herself to the task of raising her children in the ways of the Lord—washing coal miners' clothes for twenty-five cents a load and reciting from the Bible, which she could not read but had memorized almost entirely from preachers' sermons. She had married Little Sam Jenkins less out of love than from a sense of awe and a deep faith in his holiness, and she would have considered her life a success, would even have forgiven Sam his quick departure and subsequent remarriage, except for the shame her daughter brought on her.

Clare, it was obvious, had inherited none of her mother's piety or propensity for self-denial, and she never missed an opportunity to allow Rose a glimpse into her base and ungodly soul. As a child she was always defying Rose—refusing to go to church and asking to go to school instead, threatening to run away from home and join her father in the "Castle" at Frankfurt, where he had long since been executed. She was twelve years old when Rose married Sam Jenkins, and she had gone to work on the preacher immediately—touching her stepfather with her hands in places she knew a man should not be touched, rubbing herself against him when she spoke and exhaling her sweet, soft scent into his lungs, later parading before him in those short skirts she made for herself over her mother's objections, and those silk stockings she obtained by tormenting the clerk at the company store in Lynch. In response Little Sam Jenkins bit his lip and preached piety in every meeting he held, but he never managed to look away from Clare, never stopped thinking about her even after he had left Rose and married an epileptic beauty with a small fortune and a Gypsy's curse, and maybe it was the force of his prayers late at night when he was alone with his God and not ashamed of baring his soul that had sent Clare to him when he was fifty-one years old and she was twenty-four.

At the end of the day, tempting death, praying to the Lord, or digging your face in between a young woman's breasts were all about achieving ecstasy.

And so that day in Lynch, Little Sam had watched as Clare had sauntered toward him in her short dress and her bare legs, her skin emitting a smell of danger, her lips pink and fleshy and moist with temptation, smiling as if to say this-is-your-moment-recognize-it-and-enjoy. Later he had stood still as she wrapped her right leg around his left thigh, opened the front of her shirt and placed his hands on her breasts, and at that point it was all he could do to keep himself from uttering the name of the Lord before he surrendered to a lifelong temptation with all the force and fury aroused in him by the snakes.

That was the beginning, and also the end.

Little Sam had taken from Clare the strength and vigor a man can feel only from fornicating with young flesh, and he had given her the sweet triumph of knowing she could corrupt God's most fervent prophet and he thought he was done—free and able once again to do the work of the Lord—but the Lord worked in mysterious ways and the Lord had not planned for Sam to be through with Clare just so soon, and that is why he saw her again, many months later at the McGhee Church of God in Knoxville, and this time she had a baby in her arms.

She turned up just as he was about to start a sermon, looking pale and drawn and not at all in the mood to tempt anyone, and the expression on her face told him she meant trouble. Little Sam counted on his fingers the months since he had held the re-vival in Lynch, and he counted, too, the number of children he already had and could not feed, and immediately he decided to focus his sermon on women who indulge in sins of the flesh. For two and a half hours he had walked the church talking about the fires of hell waiting to engulf those who created temptation in this world, and every time he had uttered the words *Jezebel* or *temptress devil* he had paused right by Clare so that everyone in the meeting could surmise without a shadow of a doubt that the target of his speech was the young woman with the short hair and the baby in her arms.

Through it all Clare had remained frozen in her seat, too stunned to react even as the church members sang and danced and handled snakes around her, and afterward she had picked up her baby and gone on her way without daring to approach Jenkins who was still reciting passages from the Bible on the subject of fallen women.

But she had come back, the next day and the day after, and every time he saw her he noticed that she was angrier—that she insisted on showing the baby to the believers, telling them his name was Adam, that Jenkins was his father. Little Sam had ignored her at first, then screamed that she should stop frequenting his church and spreading lies. The more he tried to shake Clare off, the more fiercely she clung to him.

She found him in every backwoods meeting he set up, followed him on foot or in a borrowed truck across fourteen states and into countless church meetings. It was clear she wanted him to acknowledge her and her child. What wasn't so clear was why she hoped he would own up, and what she expected to get from him.

She couldn't have wanted marriage, because he was already married and a rotten husband twice over. And she couldn't have wanted Sam's name, because he was wanted by the law and by creditors in more than one state. And she couldn't have been in love with him—what with his short stature and his cauliflower ears and a face and body that were scarred and ravaged from too many fights, a lifetime of sleeping in the wild, and, at that time, over three hundred snakebites.

Maybe, church members thought, she was motivated by revenge. Maybe she wanted Jenkins to restore to her the good name she had forsaken. Whatever her motives, however, Clare should have realized she was fighting a losing battle and given up long before she actually did: Little Sam may or may not have been the child's father as Clare insisted. He may or may not have fornicated with his second wife's daughter and refused to confess his sin. All that was irrelevant to Clare's predicament, because everyone who had ever heard of the girl knew of her loose morals and her reckless ways, and so they were not about to be swayed by pity or a sense of justice, to stand with her and challenge their preacher's truth.

She was, in many ways, living proof of what the Bible said and what Sam Jenkins professed: that the ways of sin lead to annihilation, that living outside of the Lord means embracing the devil himself, that the seeds planted by the mother will be reaped by her children. In Clare's case those seeds were damned and crooked as far back as anyone's memory could stretch.

HER FAMILY HAD been part of the group of whites who had settled the Appalachian Mountains in the mid-1800s. The oldest mountain range in North America, the Appalachians were named after the Appalachee Indians, and extended 1500 miles—from the Gaspé Peninsula in the Canadian Province of Quebec, to Birmingham, Alabama, in the South of the United States. Across the eastern part of Tennessee, through Kentucky, and onto the border of Virginia, they were called Cumberland Mountains, or Cumberland Plateau. Four hundred and thirty-five million years old, they were rich with minerals, especially coal, and they rose three thousand feet above sea level. But the soil that covered them was thin and rocky, and the streams that ran through them carved a maze of narrow, steep-sided valleys and created a rugged, unforgiving terrain.

The original white settlers of the Appalachian mountains had come from Ireland, Scotland, and northern England in the mid eighteenth century. Some among them were Protestants who had left Europe voluntarily, in search of religious freedom, adventure, or—since most of them were poor—wealth. Many did not survive the ocean crossing to the shores of America. Those who did, brought with them a love of privacy, a sense of being different, a dislike for organized religion and centralized government.

The more cautious of these settlers stayed in New England, where the climate and the soil resembled that of their native countries. Others—the more rebellious, the ones who did not fit in with the Quakers' neat appearance and sedate manners—traveled farther. In the West, they had heard, were valleys with temperate climate and rich earth. To reach the valleys, however, they first had to cross the Appalachian Mountains.

Many died in the crossing. Others stopped halfway, gave in to the mountains, and settled among the creeks and hollows, where life was hard and the climate was treacherous. They were the first of Appalachia's white settlers, but not its last.

Another group soon arrived, though not voluntarily. These were the indentured servants—white European slaves sold to American plantation owners by the British Parliament for seven-year periods. In search of a cheap labor force, the owners had imported slaves from Africa, to be sure, but when their numbers did not suffice, the growers had looked to Europe. Thieves and cutthroats and harlots who crowded England's prisons, orphans who lived on her streets, homeless thugs who were routinely rounded up by the police—all the liabilities of the state were placed on ships and sent away to America.

Clare's grandfather had been imprisoned in England for petty theft. In America he would serve out two years of indentureship, then kill his foreman with a blunt hog knife and escape into the mountains. In 1850 he would trek on foot from Pennsylvania all the way to the Kentucky-Virginia-Tennessee border. Harlan County, Kentucky, in the heart of the Cumberland Mountains, was inaccessible enough, he felt, to provide a secure hiding place from the forces of the law that might be looking for him.

The mountains then were covered with huge oak, walnut, hickory, beech, and maple trees. The earth was blessed with large coal reserves that would prove invaluable. But the surface soil was unfavorable for farming, and the climate was unforgiving. The few families who lived in the county did so as squatters, never owning the land they worked hard to cultivate. They built one-room log cabins into the side of a slope near a river or a spring, slept on a dirt floor, cooked on an open fire outdoors. Two or three households occupied a particular cove or hollow, separated from their neighbors and the outside world by the mountains, living on corn and potatoes, growing small patches of tobacco for their own use, raising hogs. They traveled on foot or on horseback along winding creek beds, formed local schools that met two or three months of the year and were taught by nearly illiterate teachers. And they would have lived in this way—content in their difficult freedom, battling climate and soil but not man—except for the coal and timber companies.

Franklin Delano Roosevelt's uncle, Warren Delano, was among the first of many speculators. The company he formed, Kentenia Corporation, moved into Harlan County, followed by Kentucky Coal and Iron, and later by other tycoons from the eastern states and Britain. They were cunning and aggressive, corrupt and greedy, and aided in their quest for profit by agents of the local and federal government. Before them the settlers— who had no idea of the value of the land they were living on, who could not read or write, let alone understand the meaning of contracts or taxes—were powerless.

So the mountain people sold their land to the city folk for twenty-five cents an acre, or one dollar per tree. They signed deeds forfeiting all claims, not only to the surface land, but also to the layers of coal that lay below it. They gave the buyers the right to use "any means" to remove the minerals and coal from the land, including the right to build roads through their fields—a practice that soon destroyed the farms off which the settlers had lived.

Those settlers who refused to sell their land had it taken from them for free: in cahoots with the coal companies, the government levied taxes on the land, waited a year or two, then confiscated the property as penalty for unpaid taxes. Or the settlers were simply starved off the land: mining stripped the hillsides that the families had used as pasture for their farm animals. Roads cut through the farms rendered them untillable. So the last of the mountaineers abandoned their lands and set off in search of a new way of life. City folk, educated men, the government, and the law had betrayed them. The only place left to go was into the coal camps.

CLARE'S FATHER, Cecil Watkins, was born in the coal camps of eastern Kentucky, and worked the mines from the time he was four years old. He had started with his mother, picking "bone"—refuse rock—from the bags of coal that his older brothers carried out of the mine before they were loaded onto the backs of mules and carted off to be sold. By age six he had moved into the mine, carrying water and shoveling coal, and later, working the seams. He worked fourteen-hour days, lying on his side with a potato sack as his cushion, water dripping from the mine roof onto his face and neck. He dug under the seam with a pick until the coal came loose, then knocked it out and shoveled it into the potato sack to carry it out. He went in when the sky was dark and came out long after sunset, never seeing daylight, except on Sunday when the work stopped and he went to church.

At nineteen he met his wife, Rose Cunningham, and married her. He had seen her first at the coal camp near Corbin Glow, in church one Sunday when she sat in the front pew of the women's section and sang louder and cried harder than anyone else. Her father had died a few years earlier, leaving Rose to take care of her mother and five younger siblings. The family had become itinerant workers, traveling from one coal camp to another in search of work, until Rose ended up working a mine alongside Cecil.

Women at the time were believed to bring bad luck in the mines—capable of causing explosions, collapse of the mine roof, or serious injury to the male workers. In some parts of the country, they were allowed to work on the surface as pit-brow lasses—hauling, unloading, and sorting coal outside the pit mouth—but in most places they couldn't go anywhere near the mine. Sometimes, especially in winter when families could not live off the land and when the need for heating fuel was critical, young girls dressed as men and sneaked into the mines, working there long enough to get their families through the season. Other times, as in Rose's case, greedy mine bosses hired girls over the men's objections: the girls would work longer for less pay, and they usually fit into holes too narrow for men to crawl through.

For four months that winter, Rose Watkins pulled a sledge across the mine floor next to Cecil. Dressed in denim overalls, she attached the sledge to her chest with a harness and chain, and she stayed stooped the entire day. Her face was lit by a pit lamp attached to her cap—a wick, afloat in lard oil, protruding from the top. She sat alone to eat her lunch, never spoke to any of the men, never paid attention as they growled and complained that she was going to bring death upon them all. Just as the weather began to thaw and her family packed up to move, Cecil approached her and proposed.

They had their first three children, all boys, in Corbin Glow. Rose worked through each pregnancy, breathing the coal dust and pulling the sledge until she felt the baby about to drop. Then she went home and drank a cup of boiling water mixed with black pepper—to open her womb. She stuck an ax, blade down, under her bed—to help ease labor pains—and she did not even bother sending for the midwife because the babies pushed right out without any prompting from mother or nurse. They were in God's hands, Rose told her husband, and they had no need for human intervention.

After their third son was born, the mine at Corbin Glow was stripped clean, and Cecil realized he must move to another camp. By then he had been in the mines for over twenty years, and he was coughing the dreadful miner's cough, suffering the depression and hopelessness that came from working in perpetual darkness, under constant danger, without the possibility of escape. He was making the pit with an auger now, sometimes even shooting the coal, and he spoke with bitterness of his memories of the mountains when they were green and lush— before mining had turned them into lopsided, hollow wastelands that threatened to cave in and bury everyone inside them.

Still, Rose Watkins claimed that it was not the hard work nor the harsh conditions of life that in time drove her husband to prison: it was the company scrip.

As in other states, the coal camps in Kentucky were run by the same company that mined the land. The company sent a camp operator to choose a site near the mines. He hired men to clear the area near a stream so that the waste from outdoor latrines and communal washhouses would be transported away. They cut enough hemlock, poplar, or oak trees to build a few rows of cabins, then imported workers from neighboring mountains.

The camps were overcrowded and filthy, their wells and water supplies polluted and teeming with disease. Most workers who lived there were separated from their families, as they abandoned one mine in search of a job at another. To keep them working for the company, and to prevent them from ever making enough to leave the mines, the mine bosses paid them in scrip.

Every company cut its own aluminum and brass coins, embossed with its logo and redeemable only at the company store. The stores, also situated on the campsite, sold everything from foodstuffs to clothing to magazines, but they offered substandard merchandise at grossly inflated prices, and they sold on credit at high interest rates. The coal company also deducted the cost of coal used for heating the miners' cabins from their paychecks, leaving the miners perpetually in debt, their pockets empty of real money, so they could not venture beyond the camp. If workers tried to buy anything outside the company store, they were fired from their jobs, beaten, and often killed by the mine bosses and their hired thugs.

Cecil Watkins had lived with the company scrip all his life, but in the years after his children were born, he started thinking about leaving the coal camps and getting out from under the company's debt. He told Rose he wanted a green patch of land, a sky where he could see birds fly, a stream of water that wasn't black from coal residue. To buy the land he needed real money, but he knew that the mines in Kentucky would never pay with anything but scrip. He had heard that in West Virginia a law had passed forbidding the use of scrip. When his wife became pregnant for the fourth time, Cecil left Rose and the children in Corbin Glow, and set off for West Virginia.

He got work at a camp belonging to U.S. Secretary of Treasury Andrew Mellon, in the southern part of the state. Cecil figured that a man at the top of the government hierarchy would have no choice but to the observe the law, and that he would therefore have to pay his workers with real money. He worked at Mellon's camp for four weeks. At the end of the month, the mine boss handed him company scrip.

Right then, with the brass coins burning holes in the palms of his hand, Cecil Watkins began to head for jail.

He returned to Corbin Glow in the dead of winter and found his children walking barefoot and half-naked on the frozen ground. With her husband away and her stomach too big to strap the harness around her chest, Rose had been laid off from her job at the mine. She had lived on credit, put her older boy to work at the mine, sent the younger ones looking for roadkill to eat and bits of coal that fell off the tops of sacks to use as heating fuel. She had also been going to church more often than ever.

The mine boss gave Cecil his old job back, but told him he could only work two days a week. He also said Cecil needed a new auger to cut the seam.

Cecil knew that any piece of equipment used at the mine had to bear the company logo, but he was too far in debt at the company store to be extended any credit. On Sunday, when Rose took the boys to church, Cecil hitched a ride out of the camps, stopped at the first family-owned store he came to, and traded two days' future pay for a new auger. The next morning he was hard at work when the mine boss stopped him and asked to see the company logo on the auger.

Cecil Watkins pulled the tip of the auger out of the coal seam, and drove it into the mine boss's larynx.

Rose Watkins never saw her husband after that morning when he left for work with his non-company auger in hand. For many nights before the murder she had dreamed of white objects and seen dead people parading through the dark. She had even heard the death rattle—that peculiar sound emitted only by dying men as they exhaled their last few breaths through channels already filled with mucus. Once she had woken up to see a crow flying through their cabin—a sure sign of imminent death—but as much as she wanted to, she was too afraid to see the future for what it was and so she had let it happen— she let Cecil leave that day knowing he was headed for disaster.

By midmorning Rose heard a commotion, and looked out her front door. She saw people running toward her cabin and she knew, without needing to be told, that her husband was in trouble. The mine boss was still alive when the workers carried his blood-soaked body out of the shaft and laid it on the black dirt. Before the blood had even gelled around his throat, he got the shakes and died. Locking her front door, Rose gathered her three young sons into the far corner of the cabin and knelt to pray.

People knocked on the door and screamed for her to come out, but she stayed put and kept praying. She heard Cecil's name, heard the company's thugs threaten the miners to stay back and return to work. And she heard the silence—the terrible silence of her husband as he walked bloodied and smeared with mud and coal dust, the auger still in his fist, and went off with the sheriff who would take him out of the camp, through the mountains, and into the city, where he had never been and which he would not survive.

Cecil's trial lasted less than a day. The judge sentenced him to death by hanging. The court-appointed lawyer told him about his right to an appeal, but Cecil believed that a man should take his punishment with the same courage he took his actions. Besides, he said, a mountain man like himself, who couldn't even write his own name, could never prove a judge wrong. He was shipped off to Kentucky's only maximum security prison—the Castle at Eddyville—to await execution.

THE DAY AFTER Cecil killed the mine boss, Rose and her children were evicted from the camp. Without a job or a husband to support her, about to give birth to her last child— Rose wandered outside the coal camp looking for the nearest shelter. Across the rickety old bridge at Corbin Glow, there by the side of a creek where the water ran black from soot, she found a rusted old train car. It was the kind used to haul coal away from the camp, but it had veered off the rails in an accident and split in half. When Rose found it, the ends of the car were stuck in the ground and the middle part of it was raised and open in the shape of a V, allowing rain and wind and any kind of element to hit the inside which was black from coal and filled with rust. Rose and her children had to struggle to climb into the car, then fight to keep from sliding toward the ends. She decided she would stay there long enough to have the baby, then move on.

She began to take in laundry—workers' soot-covered shirts and overalls, which she gathered in a large canvas bag and washed for twenty-five cents a load. She walked to the camp and back with her boys in tow, crossing the creek on foot, knee-deep in water and shoes barely hanging on, up the path along the train tracks, toward the mountain that was already lopsided and hollowed out from mining. Back at the train car she drew water from the creek, heated it on a coal stove she had built outside— a few rocks stacked together in a circle, the middle filled with coal that her sons picked off the ground along the tracks. She washed the clothes with her bare hands and Fels Naphta soap, dragged them wet and heavy into the side of the train car that served as her kitchen, and hung them on a line in front of a stack of wood that she lit for cooking and heating. As the clothes dried the sharp, sour scent of Fels Naphta filled the car and stuck to Rose's hair and skin.

Late at night Rose sat up in the train car, feeling the baby about to drop, and imagined Cecil standing before the judge in his work overalls—the mine boss's blood having dried and hardened and smelling sour—while Cecil tried to find the words, to explain to the judge the desperation he had felt the day of the killing, the sense that all was lost before the battle had begun.

If only he had had more faith, Rose thought.

She did not want Cecil to die in dirty clothes, certainly not in another man's blood, so she stayed up extra late and sewed him a new shirt and a pair of slacks, then walked with her new baby all the way to the company store which also served as the coal camp's post office. She asked the clerk if he knew where the law was keeping her husband.

"The Black Hole of Calcutta," the clerk replied without mischief. "I hear it's worse than hell. If the rats don't get you, scurvy will."

She asked if the clerk could take dictation.

"I can, but who's going to read the letter to your husband at the other end?"

Rose decided God would provide.

"The baby is a girl," she asked the clerk to write.

"I'm working again.

"Will try to bring the children for the hanging."

SHE WORKED HARDER than anyone she had ever known, cut corners everywhere she knew how, and yet she realized quickly she would not be able to feed all her children alone. So she went to church more often, and she always took the children because it was there, after the services when everyone brought food to share, that the kids got their only square meal of the week.

The rest of the time they lived on corn bread and pig lard: in late fall every year, some families in Corbin Glow butchered a hog and stored its meat for winter. They would trim the ham, then bury it in a salt box underground. A few days later they would dig up the hog, wash and trim it some more, then smoke it.

Rose went around with her children asking if the families would let her catch the small trimmings of fat that fell from the meat as it was being smoked. She gathered the fat into a kettle and dragged it home. Lighting a fire under the kettle, she boiled the fat until bits of meat previously stuck to the fat rose to the surface. She caught the meat and added it to her corn bread mix, saved some of the lard for cooking, and took the rest for making soap.

She made brown lye soap and used it instead of Fels Naphta to save money. She mixed lard with water and ashes from her cooking fire, then let the mixture cool until it coagulated into something smelly and unattractive but efficient enough for her purposes. She made all the children's clothes, their sheets and drapes and even underwear, out of feedbags. She created dye out of roots and barks and sea grass—walnut for brown, red sassafras for red, yellow root for yellow—then boiled a feed bag in the dye to give it the desired color before cutting and sewing it.

She planted her own corn and potatoes, did not consider buying shoes, never spent money on a doctor or a medicine man.

When the children were sick, she rubbed lard from the oil lamp on their chests to cure tonsillitis, gave them coal to eat or blackberry juice to drink for stomachaches. She stopped bleeding from cuts by rubbing soot from the coal stove on their open wounds, boiled yellow root and made the children drink the liquid for croup. If they ran a fever, she wrapped them in quilts and gave them ginger tea to help them sweat the fever out. If their bladders malfunctioned, she spread a cloth soaked in water and turpentine over their stomachs or forced them to drink sulfur and molasses to clear their blood. She chewed tobacco and spat out the juice, then smeared it over a bee sting to counteract the venom, made onion poultices to treat a cold, mixed kerosene with yellow root for strep throat.

Still, the money she took in from the wash was not enough to keep them fed.

She begged the new mine boss for a job, even offered her seven-year-old son as a laborer, but the company would not take the wife or son of a man who had killed one of its own.

One night during the social hour in church, Rose stuffed her pockets with all the corn bread and chicken that would fit, and told her boys to do the same. Back at home she wrapped the stolen food in a piece of cloth and gave it to her oldest son, Harvey. Then she sent him on the road with some workers who were going to a nearby camp to look for work.

"Don't tell them who your father is," she warned Harvey.

"Come back when you have money."

It broke her heart to see him go.

———

Harvey sent word that he had found a job at a camp two hours away, working as a canary in return for meals and a place to sleep.

In the first three decades of the twentieth century, the biggest danger in coal mining was the possibility of explosions that buried miners alive. Up until the time when the entire industry switched over to battery-powered electric cap lamps, the miners wore open-flame lamps on the front of their caps. The flame was usually powered by carbide, and produced by striking flint. But coal mines naturally accumulated methane—a flammable, colorless, odorless gas that ignited instantly and set off explosions. Sometimes, the gas formed an explosive mixture, known as firedamp, merely by mixing with certain proportions of air. Sometimes, too, it exploded the moment a miner lit a match.

To detect the gas before it killed them, miners used the Davy lamp. This was a regular open-flame lamp with a wire gauze screen that allowed the methane to reach the flame and burn, but that prevented the flame from exploding the gas outside the lamp. When dangerous levels of gas were present in a mine, the flame burned blue rather than yellow. But in more primitive mines, the Davy lamp was not available, or the mine's fire boss could not be trusted to detect the right color on the flame. So miners sent canaries, and sometimes other animals, into the mines as methane monitors: if the canaries died inside the shaft, the miners knew methane was present.

In some camps the mine boss hired people—often small children—known as "cannoneers" or "canaries," to do the birds' job.

Rose's son Harvey was sent in to crawl along the tunnel floor under a wet canvas before the start of each shift. He held an upraised candle near the roof of the mine, hoping to detect puffs of mine gas with the flame. He was told that methane did not have a color or a scent, but that it did make a hissing sound—like a swarm of bees in flight—and that if he heard the sound, he was to crawl out of the tunnel as fast as he could. What he wasn't told was that by the time the canary heard the hissing sound, the flame from his candle would have set off an explosion.

To ensure that her son did not perish in a mine fire, Rose Watkins felt she needed to have more faith. She began to travel farther from home, and she became a true Holiness woman—following preachers Sherman Sizemore and Lewis York and Garrett White to a brush arbor in Greasy Ridge, a barn in Poly Lot, a home or tent in Sand Gap or Hazel Green. She traveled sometimes for eight hours—all night in a fellow believer's truck, with her children asleep at her chest or on her knees. They arrived in time for a Sunday morning service in which the preacher wailed and sobbed and spoke in tongues, decried the world's ills—poverty and hardship and disease and deception—all the works of the devil and of his agents on earth.

Holiness people washed one another's feet to prove their humility, rubbed oil on one another's foreheads to give blessing or cure illness, but everywhere they went, they were confronted with nonbelievers who taunted and mocked them, threw eggs and stones at them, and sometimes even shot at them. The nonbelievers laughed at the mountaineers' appearance and at their language, set fire to tents and barns where meetings were held, or blew them up with dynamite. Believing that the attacks were a test of her faith, Rose kept her eyes locked on her Bible and her mind focused on the business of God. Still the winter remained as long and cold as ever, and the children were hungry.

The year after Harvey left, she sent her two younger sons on the road to find work as well. She made them jackets out of feed sacks, gave them whatever food she had in the house, walked them up the creek and across the bridge into Lynch.

"Stay together," she begged, knowing she would never see them again.

She went back inside the split-open train car then, knelt on the ground to pray, and did not get up for two days running. One of the women from the coal camp heard about the boys' departure and came over to check on Rose. Finding her despondent, the woman brewed a cup of elm bark and forced Rose to drink it to cure her sadness. Then she knelt next to Rose on the floor and started to pray along with her.

They prayed through the afternoon—the baby, Clare, asleep next to them on the floor. Rain fell through the opening in the top of the car, but they did not feel it and did not stop praying. Just when the sun was about to set, Rose looked up and saw God approach in the shape of a tiny man with rolled-up sleeves, faded overalls, and a rattlesnake wrapped around his neck.

LITTLE SAM JENKINS' ancestors had been settlers from Pennsylvania who had migrated down the Shenandoah Valley in the 1830s and eventually settled in Tennessee. His father, Jeremiah Jenkins, was a womanizer who continued philandering even after he was married and had children. Sam's mother, by contrast, was a religious woman so devoted to God and her church, she had once sent her last five dollars to the Church of God Tabernacle to help their building fund. She gave her husband ten children and a lifetime of obedience before he left her for another woman when he was seventy-nine years old and almost dying.

Growing up, Sam never had a birth certificate or any possessions of his own. Over time, he would claim different places of origin. Sometimes, he said he was born in Virginia, sometimes in Kentucky, sometimes in West Virginia. The date of his birth would also change depending on when he told the story so that later on, trying to put together the pieces of the man's life, Adam would come up with at best a likely date of the mid-1880s.

Little Sam never grew tall, but he was strong, and his eyes were a clear, light blue. He never learned to read or write; he went to school for three days, he once told his children, was expelled for misbehavior, and never went back. In his youth, he seemed to have inherited his father's knack for charming women—using them for his own purposes and leaving when they no longer suited him. He certainly showed no signs of having inherited his mother's religious fervor or the discipline involved in observing God's laws. Those qualities had gone to his sisters, Jane, a devout Christian, and Bertha, a Church of God preacher.

Little Sam grew up attending church with his mother and sisters three, sometimes four times a week. These were noisy, crowded events full of tears and sweat and the loud, rambling testimonies of church members. They gathered in the early morning and the late evening—coal miners on their Sundays off, wives carrying children and baskets of food they had brought for the postmeeting dinner. The men came in clean overalls, the women in long, simple dresses. They brought guitars and drums and tambourines, arriving early for what was, for most of them, the only social event of their lives. They listened to the preacher recite the Bible—or what he thought was the text of the Bible—from memory. They prayed for the spirit to enter their bodies, and when it did, they rose to their feet, trembling and crying, arms raised above their heads, knees buckling under until they fell sobbing on the ground and had to be revived by the preacher.

In church with his family, Little Sam watched the commotion and heard the sermons, but the Spirit did not move him when he was younger. That would happen years later, when he had a wife and six children he could not feed, two jobs he did not want to work, a home he did not want to live in.

In retrospect it was not surprising, not even unlikely that a moonshining, womanizing outlaw such as Sam Jenkins would become the founder of a branch of Christian worship in America. As with everything else in Appalachia, the mountaineers' religion had always been different from that of city people.

The first settlers who arrived from Europe had been so suspicious of authority that they had allowed no preachers among them, and would not have accepted any elements from within the established churches of the time. For years they had had no places of worship, no religious teaching of any kind, no education. Then the Methodist evangelists arrived.

The Methodists were circuit riders traveling through the mountains on foot or on horseback. Employed by the Methodist Church for a small stipend, they were illiterate and untrained, and had no prepared sermons. What they did have—because of the difficult circumstances of their own lives, or because they witnessed the settlers' conditions firsthand—was an ability to identify with the problems of mountain life, a willingness to talk about it as if it mattered to God or his representatives on earth, and a manner of speech that did not intimidate or humiliate their audience. They spoke for hours, preaching in barns and homes or in the open air, aware that they would be judged not by the content of their sermons or the extent of their education, but by the depth of the passion they managed to exhibit.

After the Methodists came the Baptist farmer-preachers. Also illiterate, they were not paid by their church for preaching. Nor did they dress in black garb and white collar like their counterparts in the East: they wore ill-fitting, homespun clothes, traveled in any kind of weather, swam the creeks and rivers, slept in the open air on the side of the road. When they came to a settlement of two or three families in a hollow, they stopped and preached for a meal or a place to sleep, and left again in the morning, only to return in a few weeks or months. Like the Methodists, the preachers saw their own church as too concerned with worldly success, and too ignorant of the suffering of the common man. They did not break away from the base of the Baptist belief as much as expound on its original philosophy, creating so-called "Holiness" churches which were rooted in the eighteenth-century Wesleyan emphasis on experiencing Christian perfection after redemption.

They spoke, therefore, of the importance of self-denial, the significance of dressing simply and foregoing amusements of the flesh. They allowed church members to speak when and where they felt the need. Forever entertainers, they preached with fire, performed miracles, healed the sick, and, of course, raised the dead.

Though officially a member of the Baptist Church, Little Sam was never active, and allowed his membership to expire around the time he was twenty years old. The following year, in Lenoir City, Tennessee, he married the first of his four wives.

Esther Parker was a wholesome-looking woman with a wide nose and an easy, confident smile. She moved with Sam from Lenoir City to a shack at the edge of his sister's farm in Ooltewah, near Chattanooga. Sam cut timber or worked at a local mine, digging ore for use in paint. The mine boss liked him because he was short and could crawl into tight spaces, but Sam quickly became bored with his job and quit the mine. For nearly ten years he drank and fought and mostly earned his living as a moonshiner. He disappeared from home for days at a time, came back repentant and promised to do better. Esther, in turn, remained faithful and patient, bearing six children in quick succession, raising them alone in hunger and poverty. Then Sam turned thirty and found God.

In the version of the story he would later recount to his

followers, he was traveling near Owl Holler, twelve miles south of Cleveland, Tennessee. The year was 1908, or 1911, or 1914—and all Sam had for worldly possessions was a patched-up white shirt and a pair of trousers Esther had sewn for him years earlier. He came upon a gathering of local people who had built a church and set a date to dedicate it. It was a Church of God belonging to the Pentecostal Holiness Church headquartered in Cleveland, Tennessee. Little Sam went in to rest his legs, and stayed, hoping to eat after the sermon.

The preacher that day spoke of the role of the Holy Ghost within Pentecostal Holiness. True believers, he said, experienced faith in three stages: Regeneration, Sanctification, and the Baptism of the Holy Ghost. During regeneration, believers experienced salvation from sin. During Sanctification, they set themselves on the course of a strictly moral, self-denying, ascetic lifestyle. Conducted properly and with true faith, this would prepare the believers for the final stage, when they would have an experience similar to that of the followers of Christ as recorded in Acts of the Apostles 2:4: "They were filled with the spirit of the Holy Ghost, and began to speak with other tongues, as the Spirit gave them utterance."

The preacher went on to claim that the Holy Ghost gave man the power to conquer evil. To prove this he quoted from the Gospel of Mark the words of Jesus to his disciples immediately prior to his ascension: "And these signs shall follow them that believe; in my name shall they cast out devils; they shall speak with new tongues; they shall take up serpents; and if they drink any deadly thing, it shall not hurt them; they shall lay hands on the sick, and they shall recover."

Little Sam left the church moved by the preacher's conviction and intrigued by the meaning of the words in Mark. Back at home in Ooltewah, he felt the urge to pray but decided he should be closer to God when he did so. One morning he climbed atop White Oak Mountain, to a spot called Rainbow Rock, and beckoned the Lord.

"Give me a sign," he asked. "Tell me what to do."

There, before him, straight out of the Pentecostal preacher's sermon, was a rattlesnake.

"They shall take up serpents..." the preacher had said, "it shall not hurt them."

Little Sam stared at the snake—the diamond-shaped blotches edged with yellow that covered its body, the tail already lifted in warning, the mouth open with fangs ready to strike. He realized that the snake resembled the devil himself—that its forked tongue, its seven feet of crawling, poisonous being instilled the same fear in man as did God's fallen angel. To conquer the devil—to conquer his own fears—he decided, he must conquer the snake.

He reached down and picked up the beast with both hands.

Fear coursed through his blood, into his heart and head, and down to his hands which turned ice-cold and began to shake. In his grip the snake bent and struggled, raised its head, and brought its mouth an inch away from Sam's face to show him its erect fangs. Its rattle sounded louder than before, and its weight seemed to increase with every passing moment, but Little Sam held fast and did not let go.

The snake fought harder. To overcome his own fear, and to drown out the sound of the rattle, Sam began to repeat the passage from Mark, then to hum any prayers he remembered from his childhood. Soon he found himself uttering sounds that were meaningless but powerful, and he realized he must be speaking in tongues. The terror in his throat gave way to a sense of empowerment. The snake began to tire of fighting, and Sam felt the cool rush of ecstasy in his veins.

He descended the mountain with the diamondback still in hand and went into Grasshopper Valley below. The Grasshopper Church of God was a ramshackle barn where a congregation of a dozen men and women sat praying out loud and singing hymns. Sam traversed the length of the church, still talking in tongues, and placed himself before the congregants to show them the snake.

"Look," he hollered. "This is the spirit of the devil, and it has no power over me."

He saw the stunned look on the church members' faces, felt their fear reverberate throughout the room. He realized they were bewildered and repelled, wondering if he were mad, if they should escape him or go closer for another look. More than anything, he saw that they were mesmerized, and felt a sense of complete and undivided control.

"Look!" he said. "I asked the Lord to give me a sign of his presence and he sent me this beast and said I must conquer it with my faith."

The congregation remained frozen.

Sam opened his fists and stretched his arms out to his sides—Jesus on the cross—then stood still as the snake crawled out of his hands, onto his right arm, and toward his head and face. Trembling, he remained before his audience as the snake curled around his arm, then advanced toward his shoulder. Sweat dripped from his scalp onto the back of his ears and down into his collar. His breath was short and choppy—little bursts of air sucked into his lungs at great intervals and made a dry, raspy sound. The snake climbed up the back of his neck, on top of his head, and coiled itself around his forehead like a crown. Sam felt his knees jerk back and forth and saw large patches of darkness all around him, but he did not move and did not stop staring down the church members.

If it bit him he would probably die.

"This snake is not going to bite me," he told the church.

"It won't bite me because I have the Holy Ghost within me and I am anointed with the Spirit, and I know the Lord meant it when he said that deadly things cannot hurt a man with real faith."

He looked into the eyes of each and every one of the congregants. He had them all, he knew, and he liked this, but not more than he liked the sense of being unafraid, for once feeling in control, protected by a greater hand, invulnerable.

"Sinners and nonbelievers, stand back!" he shouted.

He remembered a passage from John that his mother had been fond of.

"For God so loved the world, that he gave his only begotten son, that whosoever believeth in him should not perish, but have everlasting life."

A woman stood up, stretched her arms as if to embrace him, and yelled, "Amen!"

Encouraged, Sam took two steps closer to the row of seated congregants and continued to speak. He preached of the fear of the Devil and the love of the Lord, of his own sinful past, of his life of fighting and drinking and hard work. The snake crawled down the side of his face, over his neck and into his shirt collar, wrapping itself around his torso. Little Sam felt his heart race even faster, and kept talking.

He called on the congregants to come forward and take the snake, told them of the ecstasy of feeling the Holy Ghost inside one's body. He was reciting phrases from the Bible he did not know he knew—childhood memories of his mother screaming passages to her husband as she warned him about committing unholy acts.

"Behold!" he screamed, reciting a passage from Luke. "I give unto you power to tread on serpents and scorpions, and over all the power of the enemy: and nothing shall by any means hurt you."

He took the sides of his shirt and tore the front open, revealing the snake lying against his skin. In one swift move he grabbed the snake by the middle, wrenched it off his body, and slammed it to the ground. It hit the floor with a loud whack, contracted, and raised its head as if to attack. Sam pulled it up and slammed it again, and again and again until the beast lay limp and lifeless in his hands.

"That ye might believe that Jesus is the Christ," he called as he kicked the dead rattlesnake into the middle of the congregation, "the son of God; and that believing ye might have life through his name."

His moonshining days were over. He had found God, and he wasn't letting go.

HE WENT HOME and told Esther he was taking her on the road: he had been imbued by the Spirit of Christ, he said, and he wanted to preach the Word and spread the Gospel in the mountains and beyond. He was going to "follow the signs"—to pick up snakes and handle fire and "drink any deadly thing," all in the service of the Lord and through this he would prove his devotion to Christ and the force of his faith in God.

Esther packed up her children and followed her husband into his new life. Right from the start they were a sight to behold: Esther in her matronly clothes, overweight and heavy-footed, her face always flushed from the effort of walking while carrying one child or another, her breath short and choppy as she tried in vain to keep up with Sam. He walked ahead of her and the children, unconcerned with their state and often unaware of them altogether. He wore a patched white shirt and a pair of black pants that he kept rolled up at the cuffs because he had to cross streams and creeks so often. His shoes, having been soaked to the core so often when he stepped into rivers, were misshapen and discolored, and he wore no socks. He held his Bible in hand or tucked under his arm, and though he could not read a word of it, he often raised it over his head and waved and shook it to make a point.

They walked all day, eating berries or roadkill or anything they managed to beg from strangers they met on the road. They slept in abandoned barns or out in the open. They were dirty and ragged and malnourished, the children sick and scrawny and always crying for food.

Determined to live a life of abstinence and self-denial, Sam had stopped drinking, even promised Esther he would not chase women or fight anymore. If a man lived the good life, he had decided, God would not allow him to be harmed. If he allowed the Holy Ghost into his body, if he was innocent enough, he would not be bitten by snakes.

Esther knew all this, of course, because she had been a believer long before her husband discovered his calling, but she was so pleased with the apparent transformation in his character that she smiled and listened and acted truly interested in Sam's sermons. At night, after the children were asleep, she read to Sam passages from the Bible which he memorized and recited back, and helped him conceive and interpret the laws of poverty and simplicity. She did not disturb him with complaints about hunger or cold or aching limbs and burning fevers as they pressed ahead into the mountains.

They stopped every time they came to a settlement of a handful of people—a cabin or two, a coal camp, a half-crumbled church along a winding, forgotten road. Esther helped Sam gather an audience for his preaching, then settled down and listened as if for the first time. He was a powerful orator, to be sure, and he seemed truly moved by his own convictions and unafraid of the judgment of others. He spoke to an audience of one or a dozen, picked up snakes on his own or before a gathering, and invariably managed to stir up enough emotion in Esther and the others that they ended up speaking in tongues and gyrating to the rhythm of his words until they fell, exhausted and spent, to the ground.

Gradually, through that first year of travel, Little Sam Jenkins began to establish himself as a preacher to know and watch. He aroused enough curiosity for the believers to come see him with his snakes, enough skepticism for nonbelievers to go out of their way to harass him. Then he stepped up to the front of the group and put on a show no one could walk out of, charging at danger instead of backing away from it, making grand statements and impossible demands and challenging everyone else to step forth and test him, test him if they dared because here was a man who had heard the Lord call and who knew what was expected of him and was not afraid to respond.

Young people laughed at him and threw stones at his snakes. His old moonshining friends traveled great distances to catch up with him and heckle him during his sermons. Mine bosses sent their thugs to break up his church meetings and chase him away, and other preachers accused him of committing a sin by tempting fate, and yet, for every skeptic and hostile nonbeliever he left behind, Little Sam Jenkins managed to convert a handful of people to his cause.

One rainy day in Harlan County, Kentucky, he left Esther and the children holed up in an abandoned cabin where the family had camped for the night, and went outside on his own. Earlier that morning he had felt the Holy Ghost anoint him, and so he had hunted a snake and handled it alone. Now he held his Bible in his right hand, the snake wrapped around his neck like a scarf, and he was headed for a coal camp where he planned to conduct a service. Crossing a dirty creek where water ran the color of soot, he came upon a derailed freight car that was split in half. It was early afternoon, and Little Sam was soaked with creek water from the waist down—his shoes torn and wet and useless, his shirt offering little defense against the cold. So he looked through the opening in the side of the train car, saw Rose Watkins, and asked if she might build a fire to help him dry.

ROSE LET SAM inside the train car that day and lent him a pair of overalls and a work shirt she had just washed for a Slovenian worker at the mine. She fried the last of her biscuits in pig lard and gave them to Sam, knowing this meant she and Clare would have no dinner, and she did not even ask him what he was doing out on the road and why he had a snake wrapped around his neck.

He sat quietly by the fire, his bare feet pale and bony and scarred, his ears red and inflamed from exposure to cold and now the warmth of the fire. He ate without raising his eyes at Rose, but he did, of his own volition, take the snake from his neck and put it outside. The smell of the biscuits awakened Clare, and she went to him with her caramel-candy eyes and her cherry-red lips, wearing a knitted top but no pants—God's tiny angel seeking out his newest prophet. She saw the plate of biscuits in Sam's hand and reached into it to eat. Rose admonished the child but Sam interfered—letting Clare dip her tiny fingers into the lard grease and lick them dry—and then he picked her up and sat her on his lap with her bottom still bare and told her she could eat as much as she wanted.

He watched with a smile as she stuffed the biscuits into her mouth and chewed slowly, her eyes fixed on his face, her bare knees resting on his thighs. He told Rose that children were the Lord's gift to mankind, proof of his glory, extensions of his love. Clare tired of eating and reached out to touch Sam's ears, and he let her. She stood up on his lap, climbed on his shoulder and sat with her legs hanging over his chest, and he walked around with her until she laughed. The rain stopped, and night spread into the hollow. Little Sam Jenkins told Rose about his experience with the Holy Ghost and his purpose in handling snakes and the miracle of being anointed.

"When you are anointed," he said, "colors look different; people look different; you can see into the future; you can lay hands on the sick and heal them. You can even raise the dead."

Rose believed him.

He said anyone could handle a snake in a state of anointment. He recited I Peter 1:7: "That the trial of your faith, being much more precious than of gold that perisheth, though it be tried with fire, might be found unto praise and honor and glory at the appearing of Jesus Christ."

Rose let Sam spend the night at her home, then kept him for two more days. He ate her food and played with her child and did not mention the wife and children he had left in the cabin up the road, but it would not have mattered to Rose if he did because she had already brought faith in him and would not have judged him by rules that applied to ordinary men. On Sunday, she took him to the coal camp to preach.

Filthy and polluted and overrun by flies and the rancid smell of surface privies, the coal camp in Corbin Glow was no better or worse around 1912 than countless others in the southern Appalachians. A row of single-family cabins fronted a line of communal housing for single men—mostly imported labor from Russia and Eastern Europe. The cabins were finished on the outside with weatherboard nailed directly to the frame with no sheathing. They were old and unpainted, surrounded by mounds of garbage and streams of sewage decomposing in the open air. The outhouses were situated along a creek, leaving human and animal waste exposed, spreading dirt and disease into the wells and water supplies. The entire camp was covered with a layer of coal dust, which mixed with smoke from the burning "bone pile" and settled into every house, onto people's clothes and beds and dishes, into their hair and over their skin and under their nails.

The miners were overworked and malnourished and depressed. Their marriages often ended in divorce; their children died in infancy. To soothe their pain many of the men turned to the taverns that had recently sprung up in the camp—dancing and gambling and even cavorting with prostitutes brought in by mine bosses to entertain the unmarried foreigners but who obliged one and all, spreading venereal disease to nearly a third of the adult male population. Murder rates had jumped astronomically in Corbin Glow and in all of Harlan County, and moonshining was everyone's favorite pastime.

Little Sam Jenkins marched past the miners' cabins that day with a sure step, so small and insignificant-looking with his big head and cauliflower ears, that no one bothered to look at him twice or even notice his Bible or the lard can in which he carried his rattlesnake. Outside the foreign workers' dormitory, he found a tree stump and climbed on. The moment someone looked in his direction, he started to preach.

He spoke of a day when the belly of the earth would burst open, and fire and blood and smoke would pour out to claim sinners. He said the Lord was watching over the earth and keeping a roster on whom he would save on that day, and whom he would surrender to the burning flames. He said that unless they came into the Lord at that very moment, confessed to their sins and abandoned their unholy ways, everyone in the camp was going to burn in hell for eternity. Ten minutes into the sermon, he had attracted a crowd.

He said he had been a sinner man who was now anointed with the Holy Ghost, that he had worked hard to chase away doubt and fear and temptation from his soul and that, in return, he had been rewarded with the greatest of all gifts: the power to resist evil, to remain invulnerable before God's fallen angel. He spoke of Shadrach, Meshach, and Abednego, telling the story from Daniel, of how they had been cast into fire: "And the princes, governors, and captains, and the king's counselors, being gathered together, saw these men, upon whose bodies the fire had no power, nor was a hair of their head singed, neither were their coats changed, nor the smell of fire had passed on them."

Like them, Sam said, any believer man, woman, or child with enough faith would be immune to death and harm.

In response to his assertions, a few mine workers laughed and threw stones at him. The company boss came out of his cabin and ordered Sam to leave. Two prostitutes walked through the crowd flaunting their wares. Sam pointed them out as examples of sin and said they must recast their lives in the ways of Holiness—"not redeemed with corruptible things, as silver and gold."

One of the women laughed and asked if he was going to show her the way of Holiness.

"If the power be upon me," he said.

A mine worker asked if he needed help getting the power.

"Only from the Lord," Sam responded, then bent over and opened his snake box.

Noticing the snake for the first time, the crowd gasped, but Sam did not flinch. He reached into the box, let out a hellish scream, and yanked the snake out in a single move. It charged with lightning speed, bit him on the tongue while Sam was in midscream.

Rose felt as if she was going to faint, and the rest of the audience went into a mad frenzy but Little Sam Jenkins held on to the snake with trembling hands. He kept his tongue protruding from his mouth—the snake's fangs having broken in his flesh— and now blood was dripping from around the fangs and his tongue was becoming inflamed and turning black. He tried to swallow, but the tongue was too enlarged to fit back into his mouth, and he felt he was going to gag on the blood and saliva in his mouth. His knees were shaking from the effect of the poison and he saw black spots everywhere and he knew he would pass out at any moment.

He looked at the miners' pale faces, their incredulous eyes, and with his tongue barely moving and hardly able to articulate words, he muttered: "That ye might believe that Jesus is the Christ, the son of God; and that believing ye might have life through his name."

THE ENCOUNTER WITH Sam changed Rose's life.

It wasn't as if she had not known God before, but in Jenkins she found a conviction she had never thought possible—to bet one's life on the strength of one's faith and be willing to lose—and after that none of her earthly suffering mattered anymore. She stayed in Corbin Glow and never bothered to think of moving again, lived in the train car and covered the opening in the roof with a piece of canvas dipped in tar to provide protection against the rain. Sometimes the wind would blow the canvas off the roof, or rain and snow would pile on it enough to bring it down with their weight, but none of this bothered Rose anymore because she had her eyes set on a warmer, more comfortable place. One night a week and three times on the weekend—Saturday night, Sunday morning and evening—she took Clare and went off to pray with Little Sam.

She became much stricter in her ways, careful not to allow any corrupting influence on her own or her daughter's life. She spoke with fervor of miracles she witnessed at every church gathering, recited the Bible every chance she got, handled snakes as often as Jenkins introduced them into his sermon. She grew Clare's hair and never cut it, dressed herself and her daughter in feed sacks that she no longer painted or bleached, so as to avoid even a trace of vanity. For punishment, she made Clare kneel on corn kernels until she bled. For entertainment, she took her to visit other Holy Rollers in their homes and cabins up and down the mountain.

And so she was there, in Wallins Creek, one sweltering summer day, when John Sherman, the evangelist from Path Fork, Kentucky, walked in from the wild and raised little Jean Stanton from the dead.

Little Jean Stanton was three years old and had died in her sleep early the previous night. Taking advantage of the cooler morning hours, her parents had washed and dressed her corpse, then laid her out on a flat board across a sewing table in their home. Fearing that the heat would spoil the corpse and force a quick burial, they had gone next door, to a church meeting where Rose and others had been handling snakes, and asked the congregation to come and pray for their child's soul.

Inside the Stanton house the windows and mirrors were covered with black fabric, and clocks had been stopped at the hour of the child's passing. Little Jean lay in the middle of the room, dressed in a long white gown, her hair long to the floor, her skin pale and dry and already starting to flake. Copper pennies had been placed on her eyelids to hold them shut, her hands had been folded on her chest as if in prayer, and she was every bit as dead, Rose would later remark, as the sewing table she lay on.

Forming a circle around the child, the Holy Rollers had knelt in prayer and had not stopped, in spite of the heat and the humidity which made breathing difficult and induced no less than eleven fainting spells among the congregants, until late at night when John Sherman walked in.

He had been awakened that morning by the heat, he said, and immediately felt the Spirit move on him. Falling to his knees in prayer, he had asked the Lord what he must do, and the Lord had told him he had a mission to fulfill in Wallins Creek. So he had walked there, fourteen miles in the direction the spirit had urged him, and the moment he had seen the Stanton house with the front door open and the smell of a rotting corpse wafting from it, he knew he must go in and pray for the child.

By then, of course, twenty-five hours had passed since Jean's death, and her body was ice-cold. John Sherman asked Mr. Stanton if he might pray for his daughter. Then he got on his knees, took the girl's hand in his own, and fell into prayer so deep that nothing and no one could distract him. By the first light of morning, at the hour when the night creatures fall silent and ghosts turn pale again, little Jean Stanton opened her eyes and sat up on the board. Then she descended onto the floor like an angel come to life by the will of God, and started to walk.

For all of her belief in the cause of Holiness, however, Rose never managed to instill the faith in her own offspring.

Away from her, in the coal camps, her sons became drinkers and fighters and followers of the devil and his agents on earth. Harvey died in a mine explosion in 1920. The other two boys joined the United Mine Workers of America and helped Mary "Mother" Jones organize 1200 workers in a strike against the coal companies of southern Colorado. It was a brave and valiant effort, uniting workers who, among them, spoke twenty-four different languages—all of whom were imported from abroad to help supplement the American labor force. They drove their wagons through snow and sleet, down treacherous canyons, and into tent colonies set up by UMWA where they hoped to press their demands for safer working conditions and better facilities at the coal camps. The largest tent colony was in Ludlow. When the strike dragged on, the coal companies sent in a militia that opened gunfire on the strikers. They did not stop shooting for twelve hours.

One of Rose's sons burned to death in his tent. The other was smothered in a hand-dug cellar where he was hiding with his wife and daughter.

Yet, looking back on her life, Rose Watkins would insist that it was not her sons' deaths, but her daughter's life, that had caused her the greatest sorrow.

CLARE WATKINS GREW up in the train car, surrounded by the blackness of the coal camps and her mother's fire-and-brimstone mentality, but neither the poverty of her days, nor the isolation of the mountains, nor even the shadow of the Lord hanging over her like a blade could dim her lust for life and for all things unholy. Early on, she went with Rose to all the holiness meetings and listened to her recite the Bible at every chance. She let her hair grow as Rose wished, listened to stories of Hell and damnation, and even helped her mother clean and sweep the church after services, but none of what she witnessed made an impression or bore the fruit it was intended to.

From the moment she could walk, Clare liked nothing more than to go around half-naked, to pick up things shiny and glittering and colorful, and to look at men—preachers among them—in ways that made them blush. It was as if she made a point of being noticed and not forgotten, as if she wanted to be remembered at any cost, as if she enjoyed watching her own reflection in the men's eyes, enjoyed raising their women's ire.

When she grew older, she walked with Rose to the mines and back, helping her mother carry the heavy loads of clothes from the miners for washing. Too poor to own shoes, she went around barefoot, her legs blue from the cold in the winter, wet and dirty from creek water in the summer. But she had a way of finding men the moment her mother looked away, climbing onto their laps and pulling at their clothes and their skin until they laughed uncomfortably or squeezed her too hard. When she turned six, she discovered the company school at the coal camp.

She begged Rose to let her go to school, ran off every time they were at the camp and sneaked into the classroom before her mother could stop her. Rose needed the girl to help her with chores, and she did not believe the coal-company school had anything of value to teach her child, but Clare begged and the school's spinster of a teacher encouraged her, and in the end Rose gave in and let her go.

The teacher said that Clare was the brightest of her students, her best reader, her most clever thinker. She told Rose that being at school kept children out of trouble but still gave them enough time to do their chores, that children who knew how to read might someday get jobs outside of coal camps, bring in real money, help ease the family's poverty. But Little Sam Jenkins said teachers were not to be trusted and should not be believed, and he said that Claire's teacher in particular must be a Jezebel because she cut her hair and wore tight clothes and told the children that the earth was round.

"The Bible says there are four angels standing at the four corners of the world," Jenkins slammed his fist down during a church meeting in Harlan, shortly after Rose had disclosed to him the details of her daughter's education. "Can someone tell me how the earth could have four corners if it's round? Those people who claim the earth is round are Satan's messengers. The devil has put them on this earth to corrupt our children and teach them lies."

Clare lasted at the school for a season and a half before her mother put her foot down and took her out, but by then the damage had been done because Clare had learned to read, and she was not going to stop.

She read the writing on the flour sacks that made up her clothes, and the words on the lard cans where Rose stored her belongings. She read the inscriptions on the pages torn from old catalogs that miners used to wallpaper their cabins, and the faded words on the sides of the train cars that carried the coal out of the mountains. Most of all, she liked to linger around the company store reading the headlines on the magazines and newspapers, even if she did not understand their meaning. And then, of course, she discovered *True Confessions* magazine.

In 1917 a camp had been built in Lynch, the largest of its time in Kentucky, and the company store was stacked up with novelties that would send shivers up a Holiness woman's spine. The worst of these was a magazine full of stories of love and loss—tales of young women tortured by longing for men they could not have, or by dreams of lives they would not live. They were sharecropper girls who married "gentlemen of means" and left their cabins to live in forty-room mansions, spoiled heiresses who fell in love with servant boys and became sick, lay in bed feverish and delirious and died young. Those who did manage to marry their lovers often died at childbirth, or woke up to find their husbands sick and dying of consumption. In between their trials and suffering, however, they managed to curl their hair and wear red lipstick, spend entire afternoons getting fitted for a dress they would wear to a ball, and walk around their homes in silk pajamas and hand-painted slippers.

When she first discovered the magazine, Clare could barely read enough to make sense of a single sentence, much less understand the entire contents of a story. Yet she stood in the store with the pages before her, mesmerized by the lines, aware that they represented a link to another world, a possibility of access to something brighter and more dazzling than she knew. So she taught herself to read, bit by bit and day after day, right there in front of the clerk's counter where miners and their families came and went and where she took refuge as soon as her mother had turned her head or gotten busy with work. She learned quickly that she could get free bits of candy and bottles of soda if she charmed the store clerk, that miners would buy her ice cream if she smiled at them the right way, that they would stop and play with her hair if she curled it with her fingers and tied it with little bits of rope and ribbon.

By the time she was ten years old, she was defying Rose in every aspect of life and refusing to abide by Holiness rules. She sat outside the train car all day, her bare feet caked in mud, her long hair matted and dirty and wild, and did little more to help her mother than bake the pan of corn bread she and Rose ate in the morning with molasses, or fry potatoes in lard and serve them for dinner. The rest of the time she daydreamed about things and places Rose had never heard of and could not imagine wanting to see, or looked for an excuse to walk to the company store.

"This child is heading straight for the devil," Little Sam Jenkins warned Rose every time he saw Clare. He said this with a spark in his eyes, barely able to look away from Clare as he spoke to her mother, blushing all the way to his ears every time the child walked past him. "You'd better bring her to church and pray that the Spirit takes a hold of her."

When Clare did show up at church, however, Sam found himself anxious and distracted and so desperate to be near the child, he got bitten by every snake he picked up.

Still married to Esther Parker, he had stayed on the road and spread his reputation farther into the mountains. He held a revival in Indiana that lasted thirteen days and created hundreds of converts, conducted a service at the Tabernacle in Tennessee that drew in local law enforcement officials and even the press. Encouraged, basking in the attention and the notoriety, he became more careless with the snakes, bolder with his promises of faith healing and miracles. Not content with handling a single snake at a time, he brought them into the church by the dozen, threw them on the ground and walked on them barefoot as he preached, or grabbed two or three in each hand and waved them about until they either died or bit him.

He was bitten often, but he always refused medical attention, always carried on with the service in spite of the pain and the swelling in his face and limbs. In Owl Hollow he promised a group of reporters from local and state newspapers that he would walk the waters of the Tennessee River the next morning "so that unbelievers may believe." The press reported this, as they reported most of his other actions by now, and the next day reporters gathered at the spot where Sam had said he would perform his miracle. He showed up late, and said he was not going to oblige: "I said I would walk the river if the Spirit be upon me," he explained, "and today, the Spirit is not."

He moved to Soddy, Tennessee, and preached with N. P. Mulkey, then to Harrison, and later to Dividing Ridge. In 1917 he applied to the Church of God for an evangelist's certificate. On the application which someone filled out for him, he said he had no education, and that his worldly belongings amounted to a shirt with fifty patches and a debt totaling twenty-five dollars.

All this time Esther stayed with him and kept having his children. Sam liked fathering them well enough, but he did not enjoy having them around and kept pushing Esther to leave them in an orphanage so she and he could travel together more freely. She refused, and Sam became angry and started to drink, accusing Esther of standing between him and God, ignoring her and the children, and vanishing for long spells only to return repentant and tell his wife to pack up, and get back on the road.

They lived in the woods, in a parsonage, in the churches where Sam preached and where his whole family camped in a corner separated from the worship area by a quilt draped over a rope. Sam was holding revivals all the way up and down the Tennessee River Valley, homeless and ragged and malnourished but gaining momentum and notoriety, and Esther would have stayed with him, would even have traveled with him for the rest of her life except that Sam started to sell liquor again and decided he wanted a divorce.

One wife and eight children, he told Esther, was too much weight for a man destined to do God's work.

She took the children to Chattanooga where she found a job at a hosiery mill. For years they would not hear from him. Then, one day, Sam would appear unannounced: he had managed to borrow a car, he said, and he wanted to take his children for a ride.

He drove the kids around for a few hours, left immediately after, and did not return for twenty years.

He told anyone who asked about his family that he had left his wife and children in good hands—with his son, Charles, who, Sam insisted, was old enough to earn a substantial amount of money and responsible enough to care for his mother and younger siblings. Charles was nine years old.

Little Sam began moonshining with a black man, and in March of 1923 was caught by the sheriff. He was fined one hundred dollars plus court costs and sentenced to four months in jail. He was sent to work detail in Silverdale, Tennessee, but the confines of prison did not appeal to him, and so he escaped.

For a while, he hid out in the mountains above his sister's farm in Ooltewah. Law officers combed the area looking for him, but Sam stayed one step ahead of the sheriff, and soon ended up in Corbin Glow. Twelve years after he had first walked into her train car, he called on Rose Watkins again and asked for shelter against the oppressive forces of the law.

She took him in immediately because she believed wholeheartedly in Sam's good intentions, and because she would do anything to spite the men and institutions that had taken away her first husband. She washed Sam's clothes and made him food and let him sleep in the warmest, driest part of the train car, and she prayed, too, that he would stay for good, that he would take her on the road to preach as he had done with Esther. Three days later, Sam proposed.

Then, of course, all the trouble started.

THE MOMENT HER mother married Sam, Clare determined she was going to seduce him. Twelve years old and aware of her own beauty, she cut her hemline first to her ankles, then to midcalf, and finally up to her knees. She went to the company store at Lynch and convinced the clerk to give her nail polish and lipstick, smuggled them home, and put them on when she knew Sam would be around. It didn't matter that Sam pretended to look away, or that Rose beat her and made her wipe her face and nails with lye: Clare could still see the tremor in the old man's hands and the desire in his eyes, and she knew she would succeed. An old Kentucky mine boss gave her a pair of silk stockings, and she put them on even though they were too big and sagged around her ankles. A Russian mineworker bought her a pair of high-heeled shoes with an entire month's salary—money he had planned to send home to his wife and children—and Clare showed them to Sam, asked him if he would help her put them on, if he wanted to see what she looked like walking in them with her short skirt. She even went for a ride with a man she didn't know, sat in the new Ford he said he had bought for $299 that year, and made him drive to the site of a Holiness meeting where she knew she would find her mother and Sam. Less than a year into the marriage, Rose Watkins realized she was about to lose both her daughter and her new husband to the devil and asked Sam to leave.

He took off in 1925, came back twice more, and finally divorced Rose in 1926. By then the die had been cast, and Clare's fate had been sealed: she had learned that she could corrupt God's most devoted servant, tempt a body that had withstood the attack of venomous snakes and the force of raw poison, and she knew it was only a matter of time before she conquered Little Sam Jenkins.

HE WENT TO Ohio and began preaching at the Salvation Army around the time of the Scopes trial. Twenty-four-year-old schoolteacher John Scopes had been arrested in Tennessee for violating a law that forbade the teaching of evolution. A hundred reporters covered the trial, and the attention of the entire country focused on the goings on between defense attorney Clarence Darrow and prosecutor William Jennings Bryan. Scopes was convicted by a jury that had read the Bible but not *On the Origin of Species.*

Little Sam Jenkins followed news of the trial and realized he was no longer the focus of attention in the South. Having lain low following his escape from prison, he became bold and started to hold revivals again.

In Ohio he met a young girl from a German Lutheran family. Her name was Helen Kiessling. She was twenty-two years old, and Sam was in his mid-forties. She had fair skin, curly brown hair that she parted on the side so that it covered half of her face and gave her the look of a silent-film star. She wore satin dresses that left her arms and ankles bare, sat with her legs folded to one side and showed off her high heels. She told Sam that her family owned a hundred-acre, well-managed farm in Cleveland, that they believed in working hard and worshiping even harder. She said she suffered from a mysterious illness that made her faint every once in a while without warning or apparent reason. She said the illness was the result of a curse placed on her by a Gypsy woman while Helen was still in her mother's womb, that the curse had made her vulnerable to fainting spells and other kinds of witchcraft, that her parents had tried everything to find a cure but had failed.

Little Sam Jenkins took Helen for a walk and told her he had cured many a young woman with witchcraft illness. He put his hand on her forehead and recited a prayer, told her she must allow the Holy Spirit into her body and feel it dislodge the curse. Then he laid her down and put his hand under her skirt, ran his fingers the length of her thighs and imagined her white flesh, told her that, in order for her to receive the miracle cure, she and her family would have to abandon all their Lutheran beliefs and become Pentecostals.

They were married in March 1927, in Alliance, Ohio. They moved to Washingtonville, where Sam found a job in a coal mine and continued to preach. He drank, too, had two more children, and kept looking out the corners of his eyes at young girls and middle-aged women.

At the height of the Great Depression, in 1932, Little Sam Jenkins moved his new family to Malvern, decided he was tired of feeding them, and went on the road to preach alone. Helen turned to her parents for money. She wrote to her mother that Sam was an evil man with secret perversions, that away from church members and other believers he neither prayed nor spoke the name of God nor showed any interest in the fate of his fellow man. She said he enjoyed the notoriety and attention that his preaching brought—that he handled snakes, touched live wires, drank battery fluid and strychnine only to get himself into the papers. His adventures, she said, had gotten his name into every local and regional paper and even the *New York Times*. He had been invited to speak on the radio, forced local legislators to pass laws governing the conduct of adult members of the community in pursuit of their religious beliefs. Laws were passed against snake handling but hardly enforced. Sheriff's deputies were sent to meetings to restrain Jenkins, and came back either entertained by him or converted to his cause. The moment a service was over and the audience had gone home, Helen said, Little Sam shed his faith like a bad fever.

"Yet you cannot deny, my dear," Helen's mother wrote back, "that the man is immune to the forces of nature and to the harm he inflicts upon his body."

They moved to Toledo, Pineville, Pennington Gap, Saint Charles. All through the Great Depression Little Sam Jenkins preached to the hungry and the unemployed, and he gathered a flock larger than that of any other preacher in the mountains. With his small stature and large ears, his passion and his knack for words, he sought God's most forgotten subjects and gave them a message of hope and redemption that no other man or prophet dared deliver.

"I am willing to bank my life on this gambit of Faith," he screamed and they saw that he meant what he said. He was in his late forties already and had lived longer than the average person expected to live in the mountains, and yet he had as much strength as the young children he had abandoned along the way. Time and again he was bitten and refused to stop preaching. His head and face were scarred and disfigured from the effects of snakebite, his body swelled to three times its normal size and turned black as shoe polish, but Little Sam Jenkins kept preaching and traveling for four more years until the day in Lynch when he saw his former stepdaughter coming toward him at the end of a revival, and already he could read the sin gleaming in her eyes.

CLARE HAD LEFT home at sixteen, no longer willing to stand the force of her mother's anger or be restricted to the tight and narrow roads of Rose's faith. She was headed north, she said, to Ohio and Pennsylvania and New York. She would find a man who would buy her nice clothes and take her to one of those places she had heard about—where one could sit in a car and watch a movie and even hear the sound. It did not occur to her that she would need money or a job to get her there, and so two weeks after she had left Rose's train car, Clare ran out of food and the means to travel, and her journey North ran aground.

She moved in with the first man who would keep her, found a host of other friends and admirers willing to spend their week's salary just to see the promise of a smile dangling off the corners of her red-painted lips, and the more she made the men spend and the more she saw them suffer, the more she became convinced of the power of her looks, and she grew bolder and more reckless, reveling in the attention she received and savoring the passions she aroused, moving through lovers and across coal camps with the confidence and the shortsightedness of one who, true to her youth, is unable to believe in failure, and it was with this same poise and self-assurance that she pursued every preacher and Holiness man she came across, intent on proving to herself and the world that she was not one to be ignored or passed up—that she had powers that transcended faith and fear and that drove men to indulge in the very sin for which they knew they would burn til eternity. Most of all, she pursued Little Sam Jenkins.

———

She followed him across state lines and into brush arbors and tents, places where he held church meetings and where, often, her mother would be in the congregation. Rose had divorced Little Sam but not his church, and as she grew older and more imbued with the Holy Ghost, she brought ever greater faith in his powers and took on the task of fighting the devil with increasing zeal. She watched Sam marry Helen and abandon her, watched him let his own children starve or run ragged through the mountains, and she even watched him tremble every time Clare walked into his church in her harlot's clothes and her high heels, the locks of golden brown hair falling in jagged lines across her neck and shoulders. Rose watched all this, but it was not Little Sam Jenkins she blamed for the way his face flushed when he saw Clare: the real culprit, Rose thought, was the woman who tempted him.

In church Rose always led the attack on her own daughter, screaming at her from a distance and raising her voice as she got closer, demanding that she leave the premises and find a creek or a river where she could wash the devil's paint off her face and that she come back ready to receive the Spirit, but all her efforts were in vain and all her prayers were left unheard, and in the end Clare managed to seduce the old man. She even had the child to prove it.

THE MOMENT CLARE began to show, her boyfriend kicked her out.

She was twenty-four years old then and already restless in the coal camps, and so she took off eagerly, northbound once again hitching a ride in the cab of a truck, and she even made it as far as Richmond, even worked for a week at a diner wiping floors and tables before her back started to ache and her feet swelled from the weight of the pregnancy and she quit her job, certain there must be a better way to live. Only the way did not make itself evident, and the men who in the past had stepped forth to offer their home and their help every time she was on her own, now stayed away from the sight of her bloated stomach, and Clare found herself alone and stranded.

Six months pregnant, she went back to the derailed train car with the tar-paper roof and the rusted insides, and submitted to her mother's conditions and lived by Holiness rules, until Adam was born. She had the baby on June 10, 1936, the day of the last public hanging in the state of Kentucky, when twenty thousand people gathered in Owensboro to watch a black man being put to death. A week later she bounded out of the train car, baby in her arms, and announced she was going to find Little Sam Jenkins.

She didn't know what she wanted from him, but when Sam ignored her the first time and then continued to refuse to own up to having been with her, she became increasingly resolved to assert herself in his church. For three years she kept up with him as he traveled and preached and handled snakes, always moonshining on the side. But as Adam grew bigger and the roads Sam traveled became longer, Clare began to feel more desperate and less certain of her own mission, and she kept going home to Rose for two- and-three-month spells and letting her care for Adam.

Rose bathed the child in the freezing creek water, which was dirty and polluted and smelling of disease. She dressed him in Holiness clothes, took him to church, and asked the congregants to pray over him to cleanse his soul. She made him sleep with snake boxes under his bed and forced him to watch as she drank strychnine in mid-prayer and vomited blood and poison, and he endured it all in a state of terror and expectation, not knowing truth from fantasy or right from wrong in those years, and aware only that he wanted his mother to stay with him.

So he clung to Clare with all the might in his weak and undernourished body and felt as if she would vanish the moment he turned around. He tried to draw solace from his grandmother Rose's prayers, and sensed relief every time Clare mentioned Little Sam Jenkins and told Adam that was his father—that one of these days they were going to establish this as undeniable truth. But Clare's promises never came true, and Rose's prayers always ended in shocking acts of violence against her own body, and the preacher who was supposed to one day start loving his son, made a point of ignoring him instead.

Clare found a job at a coal mine, moved in with another man, turned up at church meetings in Florida and Alabama and all the way north in Ohio. Finally one day Little Sam Jenkins stopped and patted Adam on the head.

"Take him to an orphanage," he advised Clare.

He even recommended a home.

THE TENNESSEE STATE Home for Children sat on the edge of Highway 63, barely an hour outside Knoxville, at the end of a long stretch of farmland dotted by wooden silos and hand-carved crosses planted in the ground. A narrow, unpaved road led from the highway to a giant metal fence surrounding a gravel yard. Beyond it was a tall brick building with small tinted windows and a heavy wooden door reinforced by strips of black metal. On the other side of the building were a green lawn, a vegetable patch, and an orchard. A second structure, lower and more recent, contained a mess hall, four classrooms, and additional housing.

The main building was dark and quiet, inhabited by seventy young boys who went around in ragged uniforms—denim overalls and patched-up white shirts—barefoot in the summer, wearing only socks in the winter. They walked noiselessly and spoke in whispers, read with their heads lowered over the pages of books by the dimmest of lights, worked the fields surrounding the orphanage, and harvested sugarcane and corn, wheat and tobacco. Three hours a day they attended classes taught by the widowed ladies who belonged to the nearby Methodist church, and who had taken on the moral and ethical burden of saving the souls of children abandoned by their parents. The rest of the time, they lived under the tyranny of the home's superintendent, a retired sheriff's deputy named Mr. Harris.

Tall and thin and always dressed in military colors, Mr. Harris had made it his mission in life to "make honest citizens" of the offspring of "God's lowliest subjects"—the mountaineers and coal miners who occupied, he was convinced, a rank not above that of animals on God's good earth. To that end he ran the orphanage like a prison camp, imposing absolute discipline and exacting harsh punishment on those who did not obey his rule, or on those he simply did not happen to like. He disliked the weak and the ignorant, the arrogant and the ungodly. More than anything, he despised the ungrateful.

"The smartest thing your parents have done," he routinely told the children in his care, "probably the only smart thing they will ever do, was to leave you here and spare you a life like their own. Recognize it and give thanks."

He looked with equal disdain upon foreigners and city folk—people who believed themselves above God's laws and who tried to rewrite his commandments to fit their own purposes—but he reserved his greatest scorn for the Holy Rollers who inhabited the lands immediately surrounding the home and who often traveled past it in convoys of trucks and cars heading to one church meeting or another.

He made no exception for Little Sam Jenkins, had even gone so far as to send some of the older boys in his care to break up Sam's revivals in nearby counties, and so there was no reason to think he would feel pity for any offspring of Sam's, but he did run a tight home, and he did feed the children without demanding that their parents contribute, and this alone managed to impress Sam enough that he insisted to his first and third wives, and later to Clare, that they leave their children in Harris's care and free themselves, and Sam, of the burden of raising them.

Sam had had no luck with the wives, and at first, it looked like he would have no luck with Clare. The mountaineers were nothing if not doting parents, and Holiness people especially believed in the sanctity of family ties and kinship. But five years after she had given birth to Adam, Clare was exhausted and disheartened and feeling as if she had run out of options for keeping him, and so Little Sam's urging—gentle and well-intentioned as it seemed—lodged itself in the corner of her mind and began to take on greater weight with every passing month until, in the end, it managed to convince her.

She would leave Adam in the home for only a short while, she thought—long enough for her to get some rest, gather her courage, and move to a real town with paved sidewalks and green trees, where people bought their coal instead of digging it out of the ground or off the sides of railroad tracks. She would live in a place where women bought their clothes instead of making them out of feed sacks, where a girl could wear pants without being denounced by the preacher for "imitating men and before you know it, she has become a lesbian." Then she would come back for Adam—she was sure of this—and when she did, even her own mother would not recognize her in her big-city clothes and her fancy salon hairdo.

She said this to Adam, one day as they rode in the cab of a farmer's truck, the driver too old to demand any favors in return. She sat Adam on her lap and smoked and cried and told him about the orphanage as if it were good news, as if she were taking him to a real home and real safety.

"They have clean beds and a sturdy roof that doesn't leak," she said. "No coal dust under your nails and no blood in the grown-ups' cough and you can eat three meals a day and even learn to read and write."

What she didn't mention, Adam later remembered, was that he was going to have to stay there alone.

MR. HARRIS HAD liked Adam at first, or rather, he had liked Clare—the way her mouth was red and round and pouting like a spring apple, the way her face was young but drawn, pretty in a way that broke the heart. She had worn high heels right off the highway, dragging Adam by the hand as he clung to her a little too stubbornly, obviously suspicious of the new surroundings and of Clare's purpose in bringing him here.

Mr. Harris made Clare wait half a day before allowing her into his office, and he noted that she remained standing the entire time she waited—though she was clearly exhausted and hungry and aching from the heels she stood on. Once inside the office she sat up straight and crossed her legs as if to impress Harris with her manners, and she did not lose her poise even after Adam had refused to follow her inside.

"Leave him." Harris smiled indulgently. "We'll teach him discipline in no time."

He closed the door in Adam's face and sat down to lecture Clare about the importance of what she was about to do.

He told her that having a child was a decision made by the Lord and carried out by his servants, that leaving a child to an orphanage was a commitment before the law and the Lord himself. It was not a step to be taken lightly, not reversible, not negotiable. That's why, he said, he made mothers wait outside his office when they brought the children—so they could change their mind if they were so inclined, because once they had given the children to Mr. Harris, they were not welcome to take them back.

In the hallway directly outside the office, Adam had fallen asleep on the bare floor. Mr. Harris opened the door and stepped over the boy, then held out a gallant hand and helped Clare do the same. The dinner bell had just rung, bringing out the children who marched in single file through the house and into the mess hall in the next building.

"Leave him while he's asleep," Harris told Clare. "I'll break the news to him when he wakes up."

Years later, an adult already, Adam would still awake from restless sleep as if to discover for the first time that Clare was gone.

THAT FIRST EVENING he had cried until his throat shut down, and then he had cried some more, convinced, he later realized, that Clare would hear him and come back, that she would turn around, far away in the void she had stumbled into while Adam slept, understand his fear, his need to be with her, and come back and get him. Around him the other boys stood in ragged clothes and bare feet; one of them even tried to approach and soothe him, but that only made Adam cry harder and then Mr. Harris stepped in.

"You can sleep in a bed or in the boiler room," he told Adam, "but you can't stay in this hallway, and you can't interrupt the order of things by crying."

When Adam cried harder Harris sent one of the boys to fetch his whip, and he beat Adam—twelve strikes on the back of his pants while the other boys watched—then ordered him into the boiler room. It was a tight, dust-filled space lit by a lamp that hung from the ceiling, packed with pipes and machines that roared and hummed and looked like monsters.

Terrified, Adam struggled and tried to escape, but he was thin and small and weak from malnutrition, and maybe he didn't quite understand the proportions of what he was up against because in one instant he had been picked up off the floor and thrown into the room, and then he heard the key turn in the lock.

All night long he screamed and kicked at the door. In the morning, when one of the church ladies let him out in time for prayers, he bolted past her and tried to run away.

He made it as far as the highway directly outside the home, and he even ran a few yards in the direction he had come from before he stopped and realized he had nowhere to go and no one to run to, and then the other boys and the church widows caught up and brought him back for twelve more strikes of Harris's belt and three more nights in the boiler room.

He became Harris's toughest charge, the one boy Harris could not quite break in, the exception that challenged his rules. For months in the winter of 1941 and the spring of 1942, Adam fought Harris as if to defend his life, as if the superintendent was all that stood before him and his lost mother. He was smart but stubborn, scared but unwilling to surrender. He waited until he was near starvation before he ate the food in the mess hall. He slept on the cold ground rather than lie in the bed assigned to him by Harris. He spent many nights in the boiler room, received more beatings than even the oldest, most rebellious boys. And he kept running away.

Mr. Harris decided that Adam was "a special case—one of those who need to be tamed or they will end up in jail or committing murder." To that end he assigned Adam to field duty—carrying buckets of water to older boys who did the planting and the harvest—and he put Adam on a reduced diet of only one meal a day, two servings of potatoes fried in pig lard, and one glass of watered-down milk. For every infraction he beat Adam till he drew blood, or locked him outdoors on freezing nights till Adam had learned to appreciate the comfort of a bed.

"Your mother is not coming back for you and your father won't even acknowledge you as his own, and you'd better realize this is all you've got and this is where you're going to live or die—it's up to you but don't even think about defying my rules," he screamed at Adam, but in vain. He found himself staying up nights trying to contain his own rage at the boy and worrying about Adam's disruptive influence on the other children. Then one of the church ladies put her nose where it didn't belong, and made a suggestion that saved everyone: she proposed that Adam be allowed to attend school.

In class Adam sat still and paid attention as if mesmerized by the signs and numbers drawn before him on the board. He was soothed by the voices of the widowed ladies, comforted by the distraction of new thoughts, the mental challenges that forced him to look outside of himself and the home, to see beyond his pain, focus on a place that was neither hostile nor frightening— the North of Clare's imagination, the cities and states she had talked about incessantly but which Adam had never been able to visualize. True to Harris's standards the widows were strict disciplinarians and harsh judges, showing neither love nor indulgence, or even pity, for the boys. They did not accept failure and did not praise achievement, but even they were impressed with Adam's quickness and concentration, the hardheadedness with which he came to class straight from a beating by Mr. Harris—his skin often cut, the welts from the whip still swollen and angry on his face and hands.

He advanced two years in one. Reading reminded him of his mother, made him feel as if she weren't so far away, as if the two of them could engage in the same act at once: look at the letters on the sides of the trucks that passed on the highway, read the hand-painted signs on the fronts of churches, together again. His grandmother Rose, he remembered, had said that reading had ruined Clare, that any woman who went to school became a whore or a lunatic. But the widows of the church were neither whores nor lunatics, Adam observed, and neither was his mother, and he thought she would be proud to learn that he could read just like she could.

Slowly he settled into the home. He received fewer beatings the second year he was there, and he almost never got locked in the boiler room, but he did not allow himself to make a friend, to confide in another boy, or feel as if he were there to stay—as if Clare would forget to come back for him, lose her way in the city with the paved sidewalks, and let Adam stay in the home forever.

CLARE HAD GONE to Akron, Ohio, found a job in a rubber factory, moved in with a Ukrainian worker who had lost three fingers in a plant accident. She lived with him in a single room on 7th Avenue in East Akron. Rubber ruled the city at that time, and jobs at the Goodyear and Firestone factories had drawn tens of thousands of immigrants from Europe. The city was divided into four sections: Italians in North Hill; educated whites in West Hill; Firestone workers in South Akron; Slovaks, Ukrainians, Russians, and blacks in East Akron.

The Polish women in the building where Clare lived sold bootleg whiskey out of their apartments and breast-fed one another's children when one of them was too dry to nurse. The Russians celebrated Christmas on January 7 and drank more than anyone Clare had ever known. Her Ukrainian lover hardly spoke a word of English and did not seem to notice her except when the lights were off. The rest of the time, he spoke in his own language to the other men, and he took his meals alone, following a tradition whereby the woman of the house ate the leftovers after the main bread winner had had his fill. Both with him and the others, Clare felt uneasy and awkward and forever the outsider, talked about without being spoken to, looked down upon as a mountain person, which she would always be, regardless of how much she wanted to transcend her past.

So she left the Ukrainian and moved in with a man she had met in the outskirts of North Hill—an Italian with a gold tooth and a first model year Dodge. He gave her money to have her hair done at the beauty shop and bought her clothes she never could have made for herself, but he beat her every time he drank, and so she ran away, on December 8, 1941, as he sat in his

Dodge listening to the radio broadcast the voice of President Roosevelt announcing news of the Japanese bombing of Pearl Harbor.

She hitchhiked from Akron all the way into Richmond, Kentucky, found a job in a sewing factory, promised herself she would not return to Adam until she had saved enough money to support them both. She worked through '42 and early '43, but everything she made was spent on rent and food and the little caprices that were essential for a girl who was trying to keep from merging into the sea of other women, all of them poor and exhausted-looking, walking the downtown streets of every city she had crossed. Two boyfriends and three jobs later, she left Richmond with a suitcase full of pretty clothes and went back to the orphanage to see her son.

She arrived on a Sunday morning in late autumn, two years and nine months after she had left Adam asleep on Harris's office doorstep. She looked thin and drawn but determined, her clothes more faded than she would have liked, her hair cut in jagged lines that fell around her face without a trace of a salon do. Mr. Harris saw her walk in from the gravel yard and went out to greet her immediately. He was glad to see her, he said, took her into the darkened office where he had received her the first time. He sat behind his desk and picked up a sharp letter opener, watched the light reflect off the tip of the blade as he turned it in his hands.

He was glad to see her, he said again, but he did not approve of parents coming back for their children once he had taken the time to teach them the ways of civilized living, and he would not allow Clare to violate the laws she had agreed to honor only two years earlier.

Across from him Clare stood with her arms crossed and her eyes avoiding his, and Harris could tell, by the way she did not answer him or even sit down, that she was as stubborn and defiant as her son. He got up from behind his desk and went closer, took her hand that was chapped and rough, turned it over and examined the nails that were dirty with factory grease.

"I can let you see the boy if you want," he whispered.

He placed two fingers under her chin and raised her head slightly so their eyes met.

"You can watch him from a window, without letting him know you're here."

Her eyes avoided his. She shifted her weight, pulled her hand out of his. He put his other hand, the one under her chin, around her neck and began rubbing the back of her head, his fingers dipping into her hair and over her scalp. He felt her relax for a moment, thought she was about to give in.

"I can let you rest here awhile, bring you something to eat."

His thumb reached across the side of her face. She opened her mouth just a bit, let his thumb move onto the fleshy part of her lower lip, smudging her lipstick, reaching in. He put his other hand around her waist and pulled her closer. Just as he was about to kiss her, she stiffened, broke free, and ran for the door.

She ran through the hallway calling Adam's name, Mr. Harris and a herd of boys behind her. Adam was outside on the lawn picking up trash and raking leaves, and he heard the commotion without realizing at first what had caused it. Then he saw the other boys looking at him as if he had caused trouble, and suddenly he heard his own name, a voice that was distant but familiar. He was too afraid to respond, or even move, so he stood with the rake in hand, trembling as the noises got louder and then he felt his own tears sting his eyes and face, and he thought he would never be able to move again but already, Clare had burst through the door and was sweeping him up into her arms.

SHE TOOK HIM on a train to Virginia, then begged a ride with a family to Norton and spent three nights in an abandoned gas station directly outside of town. With America at war in Europe and gasoline rationed in the eastern states since May 1942, travel by car had become more difficult than before. In December gas was rationed nationally, and two months later, in February 1943, shoes and canned food had also become rationed, and it was understood that any wise person without a pressing need to travel would stay at home and aid the war effort by holding down a factory job instead of running aimlessly through the country looking for luck—but Clare was homeless and out of work and determined once again to break out of the life she had been born to, and so she stayed on the road with Adam, begged for food or a place to sleep, worked odd jobs and all the while, kept looking for a man who would save her. Two months into the adventure, she gave up and took Adam home to her mother.

Rose's hair was long and silver and rough as corn leaves, and her back was stooped from too many years of leaning over a tub to wash miners' clothes, but she recognized Adam immediately and greeted him with open arms and a blessing. He stood against her and breathed in the smell of lye and starch on her skin, felt the roughness of her fingers poking at him through his shirt. Then he looked up and saw that Rose's eyes were misty and tear filled, and this made him want to cry as well—put his face on her belly and tell her about the nights in the boiler room and the beatings with the whip. Instead, he felt anger rise in his chest and into his throat, and he had to pull away to gasp for air.

They ate potatoes and corn bread fried in lard. Rose showed them her box of cottonmouth moccasins, her bottles of Red

Devil's lye. She spoke of washing her children in the Blood of the Lamb and immersing them in the Word, told Adam she was certain her sons had died knowing the Lord. The tarpaper that had once served as a roof had come undone in places and was letting in a cold March wind. Every night Adam wrapped his arms around his mother's neck and fell asleep by the coal fire.

He awoke every morning terrified that Clare had left him. She would be gone all day looking for a job, or just escaping her mother's rules and prayers. Often she came home with whiskey on her breath and makeup smudged all over her face.

"That girl is going to have herself killed any day now," Rose told Adam every night before Clare returned from her day's adventures. They knelt together on the ground and prayed for Clare's soul, went to the neighbor's and prayed some more.

"I've been seeing visions of my dead husband," Rose told Adam, "and I saw a crow flying through the train car. These are omens of death, so I know something's going to happen to your mother unless she finds the Lord."

One Sunday they went to a Holy Rollers' meeting where Rose drank an entire glass of strychnine diluted with water. The weather had begun to thaw and the melting snow on the mountains had made the water rise in the creek, and so it took longer than usual to get home but even then Clare was nowhere to be seen.

Rose dreamed she was walking through a room with white drapes hanging from the walls and windows.

"That's the second sign of pending death," she told Adam.

He knelt by his bed that night and prayed to God that He return his mother to him alive.

"I'm seeing visions," he heard Rose speak in the dark. "I'm being warned of your mother's death, and I can't do anything to stop it."

Two days later, when Clare did come home she had bruises all over her face and arms, a broken tooth, blood inside her mouth.

"The same man who's been beating you is going to kill you," Rose warned.

All week long she saw dead people walking around the train car. On Monday morning, they took her away.

Adam found her sitting with her eyes open and her hands folded on her lap, and for a moment, he didn't realize that anything was wrong except that she had a weird look in her eye—a stunned expression, he thought, as if she had seen something at once pleasant and bewildering. Then he noticed that she had not moved for a long time, and he went closer and touched her hands that were ice-cold and he understood what had happened.

It had never occurred to Rose that the death she was being forewarned about might be her own.

Clare was gone again, so Adam ran to the neighbors' house and called for help. The husband came over and picked Rose up in his arms, carried her into his own home where he helped his wife lay out the corpse. Taking the entry door off its hinges, they laid each end on the back of a chair, and put the body over it to wash. By then Rose's limbs had hardened a bit, and the neighbor's wife had to use hot water to help stretch out her legs. They tied the body down to the board to keep it from jerking, folded Rose's arms across her chest, and kept her mouth closed by wrapping a handkerchief around her head. Instead of copper pennies, which might be stolen, they placed stones over her eyelids.

All day long they prayed over the corpse and waited for Clare to come back. They sent Adam to look for her in nearby homes and stores, asked him if she had said where she was going, if she had mentioned whom she intended to visit, how long she normally stayed away. By evening the body was getting discolored and emitting sucking sounds—a result of gastric juices. Cats roamed the house waiting to eat the corpse's eyes to steal its soul, and the neighbors began worrying that bugs would attack Rose's corpse and that the smell of death would set in because of the warm weather. By the next morning, when Clare was still missing, they told Adam it was up to them to bury Rose.

They sent him home to find the black shroud that Rose had woven for herself years earlier, and which she had hung out to air every spring so moths wouldn't eat it. Back in their house again, he helped the husband nail together some boards and create a box. They wrapped Rose's body in the shroud and placed it in the box, dug a grave directly outside the train car, and planted a hand-made cross in the earth.

They waited for Clare.

She had been gone twenty-four hours when Rose died, forty-eight when she was buried, and after that the sun kept rising and setting and the days kept rolling away, but there was no sign of Clare and no word of her whereabouts. Adam looked for her alone and with the help of the neighbor's wife, sat up waiting for her until his eyes burned with exhaustion and his hands went numb. He kept looking at the clothes she had left on the ground outside the train car, telling himself she would come back for the clothes, if not for him, that she would not leave him again, would never leave him after she had returned from the North to take him from the orphanage. The neighbors looked at him sideways and talked about him in whispers and smiled when he told them his mother would not be long now, not long at all, she must have been held up at a job and would soon come back for him. They gave him food and took him along to church on Saturday afternoons and Sunday mornings, and when they became tired of feeding him they put him in a car and drove him up Highway 63 to the orphanage.

They let him out of the car on the side of the road and said it was up to him to go in and beg Mr. Harris for a place to live, or to walk away.

He didn't walk.

He wanted to, but didn't have the nerve.

As much as he hated the orphanage, it had given him the only stable home he had ever known, the only real bed he had ever slept in. Nine years old and already twice abandoned by his mother, having recently buried his grandmother, Adam could not conceive of a life without any attachments at all, but he could not imagine going back to the home either, could not bear the thought of what Harris would do to him knowing that Clare had left him again and that Adam had come back willingly.

So he stood on the side of the road and prayed that he would vanish into the dirt without a trace, watched dusk set in and fought the tears that welled up in his eyes and forced their way onto his cheeks. Without daring to turn around and look, he felt that Harris was watching him from his office window, that he was waiting, because he knew Adam would give in to his fear and stumble back to him. Darkness fell and the stars came out and Adam was still standing there. Cars drove by and slowed down to look at him, then sped away. Truckers, who routinely drove past the home, knew better than to stop.

Keep walking, he told himself, but his legs would not obey and his hands were frozen into fists, and then he heard the sound of the final bell ringing in the home and realized that if he did not go in right away, he would have to spend the night outside. He dashed up the dirt road and through the fence.

Mr. Harris looked at him in the doorway. His very proximity frightened Adam. The man's body, though perfectly still, seemed charged, as if about to attack, as if certain it had its prey. He had known Adam would come back, he seemed to say without speaking. Some children didn't, but Adam was different, and now he was here and it was up to Harris to give him shelter or deny it.

HE NEVER DID forgive himself for going back, never did recover from the anger he felt for not having had the courage to keep walking. That's why he would keep moving as an adult, why, he imagined, his mother had kept running all her life: to cover the distance between the place she had been left by God or destiny, and that other place—the one she knew existed without having seen it, where she knew she was meant to, that she deserved to, be. It wasn't about accepting one's place in this world and longing for a better one in the next. It was about setting right what had been wrong in the first place—even if that meant having no home, no life, at all.

Ironically, it was the orphanage that, in the long run, gave him the means to walk.

It took twelve years of his life, but it gave him an education as good as any available in the state, enough food and shelter to keep his body growing into adulthood, the skills to make a living once he was out on his own. He went to class in the morning and worked the fields in the afternoon. He plowed the earth and planted it, filled silos in the summer, fed cows in the winter. He learned to drive a truck and a tractor, to kill hogs. Mostly, he learned to work tobacco.

In his mind tobacco would forever be linked with the possibility of relief—colors that were soothing to the eye, fields that were long and wide and isolated, a loneliness that gave him time to grieve—out there away from Harris and his whip; away, too, from the other boys at the home, boys whose very existence reminded Adam of his own loneliness.

Every tobacco crop required thirteen months of work, and

near-constant care. In December Adam and a group of boys were sent out to pick a site near the river, clear it of trees and brush and debris, and light a fire to disinfect the soil. After that they tilled the burnt soil, sowed it with tiny tobacco seeds, and stretched a cloth over the land to protect the sprouts from frost damage. They planted burley tobacco for cigars, dark-fired tobacco for cigarettes.

Through the winter Adam watched the blackened earth and tended the seedlings that emerged from the ground and would grow taller in the spring. In the summer, when the shoots were around eight inches tall, he pulled them from the bed, plowed the field, and reset the shoots in the patch. As the plants grew in their new beds, he watched for weeds, pulled the suckers that popped out on the stalk above each leaf, snapped the top off each plant when the tobacco flowered. All along he watched for worms: they were plump, three inches long, the same color green as the leaves they fed on. He had to search for them on each leaf, pick them off by hand, and crush them.

At harvest time he split the tobacco stem from the top down with a curve-blade knife, then cut it just above the ground. He let the plants wilt in the sun, then hauled them into the barn to hang on six-foot-long sticks. Burley tobacco leaves turned from green to light tan as they air-dried, but the dark-fired tobacco was heavier and needed heat to dry.

Inside the barn he lit a bonfire on the floor to dry the leaves. The heat made the worms that had escaped his scrutiny fall from the plants like rain. Through November he guarded the tobacco as it hung in the barn. In December he stripped the leaves from the stalks, sorted them into piles according to the darkness of their shade, and sent them off in trucks or took them on a train to places where they would be auctioned. Then it was time to find a new patch of land and prepare the earth for another crop.

He worked tobacco every year he was in the orphanage, and after a while he realized that Harris counted on him for this, that he needed someone who was hardworking and smart and able to concentrate on a job long enough to see it through. He realized, too, that Harris resented Adam's progress at school, that he became angry and found a reason to punish Adam every time one of the widows mentioned how well Adam could read, or how quick he was at grasping new ideas. By age twelve Adam had exhausted the widows' knowledge and was helping them teach boys younger than himself. One of the teachers, Mrs. Kelsey with the enormous breasts and the husband who had died in the war, took it upon herself to suggest that Adam should be allowed to attend the local high school. She was a fleshy young creature with bright eyes and a delightful smile, childless because she had been married only a week when her husband had left for the war, unable to remarry because the preacher in her church said that marrying more than once, even with a dead husband, was like being "double-married," which the Bible said was a sin.

Mrs. Kelsey liked Adam's quick wit, and she was naïve enough to think that Mr. Harris might be proud to hear of the boy's talents, so she suggested that Harris let Adam attend the public school outside the home.

"He can continue to learn." She beamed before Harris, unaware of the damage she was causing. "And he can serve as an example for the other boys."

Mr. Harris told Mrs. Kelsey that women were well-advised to keep their mouths shut, for fear of exposing their stupidity. Then he sent for Adam.

INSIDE THE OFFICE, Harris had laid his whip down at the edge of the desk, and was pacing the room with his hands clasped behind his back. He had left the blinds open to invite anyone brave enough to look in—something he did only when he intended to administer a beating.

Adam stood at attention and kept his eyes on the ground. He listened to Harris pace the floor, saw the tips of his shoes that were polished military-style, the edge of his anklebone pushing out against his frayed dark socks, the starched-and-pressed cuffs of his khaki-green pants. It was these moments—the silence before Harris began to speak, the calm before he started a beating—that were most frightening, most painful, to the children. But Adam was not afraid.

For a while now, whenever he found himself alone with Harris, he had felt a rage he had to fight hard to contain. He would suffer the beatings and the demeaning remarks, the hunger and isolation Harris imposed on him for every infraction, but instead of feeling defeated as he had done in the past, Adam increasingly became emboldened by his anger: he found himself engaging Harris' glare, refusing to answer his questions or feeling pain at his beatings. He imagined attacking Harris back, dreamt of killing him with a sharp knife the way his grandfather had killed the mine boss in Kentucky—and it was the lack of emotions, the complete absence of fear or remorse at what he would do to Harris, that satisfied Adam most.

"Mrs. Kelsey has asked if I might give you permission to go to the city school," Harris said in a cool voice.

Adam raised his eyes from the floor and stared at him.

He crossed the length of the room once, and then back.

His heels squeaked against the bare floor. He stopped in front of his desk, turned to face Adam, waited for an answer.

"She tells me this is her own idea," he said when Adam did not respond.

Adam was looking at him with glass eyes.

"She tells me she thinks it's in your interest."

If Harris hit him, Adam decided, he would hit back.

Harris must have felt this—Adam's anger—or at the very least he must have felt unsafe because he started to pace again, putting the desk between himself and the boy. The distance he put between them made Adam feel relieved. Then suddenly he grabbed the whip off the desk and struck Adam across the face.

Adam heard the sound of leather tearing his skin. He felt the whip sink into his muscles till it had found the bone. For an instant, the whip remained embedded in his face. Blood gushed out around it and blinded him in the eye. When Harris pulled back his arm, the whip took away a bloody strip of flesh and left a gash half-an-inch wide in Adam's face.

It ran from the corner of his right eye, down over the side of his mouth onto his chin. Adam felt the burn but not the pain. Blood spilled off the front of the whip and onto the floor and the desk. It poured down Adam's face, onto his shirt and his hands, then his feet. Harris was looking at him triumphantly.

"This is for thinking you can go around me to get what you want," he hissed.

Adam was looking at the whip on the desk.

He did not move or make a sound, did not raise his hand to touch the place where the whip had landed.

Harris sat in his chair, put the tips of his fingers against the edge of the desk, leaned back till the front legs of the chair had come off the ground.

"You can go now," he said, but his voice wavered in mid-sentence and his eyes grew wide and he saw Adam rushing him from across the room, climbing onto his desk like an animal in the wild, and landing on his chest with all the weight of his twelve-year-old body.

The chair gave out. Harris fell on his back—Adam's knees digging into his ribs—and before he could fight back Adam had grabbed his temples in his hands, raised his head, slammed it on the floor, raised it and slammed it again. He would have killed Harris—would have killed him with a few more strikes except that the door burst open and some of the boys who had been watching through the opening in the blinds rushed in and pulled Adam off.

Harris spent two days in a city hospital recovering from the attack. He came home with a bruised face, swollen eyes, three broken ribs. He gave Adam a beating in the mess hall before all the children and their teachers, ten days in the boiler room around the clock, only one meal a day for thirty days. Then, inexplicably, he gave him permission to attend the city school.

Maybe, Adam would reason later, Harris had come to fear the boy as much as Adam had once feared him. Maybe the old army man in him respected a show of force and responded better to the twelve-year-old's violence than he had to the five-year-old's tears.

Maybe, too, Mr. Harris really did believe that salvation came through learning, that educating the orphans was the only way to give them a chance. That's what haunted Adam in all the years after he had left the home and escaped Harris: that the very man who had poisoned his childhood with his vengeance had also given him the only chance he could have at life beyond the mountains.

THIS IS WHAT he learned early in life, what he was convinced had saved him throughout: that the longing for safety was man's greatest weakness, the need to connect his biggest downfall.

He had learned this from Clare's attempts to be recognized by Jenkins, from the nights, too, he had spent waiting for his mother to come home. He had learned it from Rose who had put her faith neither in men nor in earthly things and who, therefore, could not be betrayed by them, learned it from his own experience fighting Harris at the school: the true victors, the ones who prevailed most often, went into the fight feeling they had nothing to lose.

When he started the city school in the fall, he kept to himself and refused any attempts at friendship. He went to class four hours a day, reported back at the home for lunch, then left for the fields. He said nothing to his teachers or the other children about the home or Mr. Harris, nothing about his wayward mother or preacher father. If he heard people speak about Jenkins, he never acted as if he recognized the name or knew its owner. He wasn't lying, he told himself. He had never belonged with Jenkins, and now, he didn't belong with Clare either.

He made a conscious effort to remove himself from the people and memories that had clouded his past. He saw himself become taller, saw his hands grow larger and his body become more confident in its strength and he liked this, but not as much as he liked feeling disconnected from everything that had hurt and frightened him for so long. Mr. Harris never beat him again after the day he left the scar on Adam's face, and Mrs. Kelsey with the enormous breasts and the dead husband in the war waved at him from across her desk every time Adam walked past her classroom, but he felt neither grateful for the former's neglect nor moved by the latter's affection because to do so, would be to put himself at their mercy once again. He learned to survive on his own—without his father's recognition or his grandmother's blessing, without faith and without prayer and, in the long run, even without his mother's love.

That's why, when Clare finally did come back for him, Adam would have no part of her.

IT WAS MIDDAY in June, a week before the end of the school year. He was sixteen years old. He saw a woman on the side of Highway 63. She had on a faded taffeta dress and torn black stockings, a cigarette in one hand and a bunch of wilted rhododendrons in the other. She was smiling at Adam politely as if at a stranger. She asked him if he might direct her to her son whom she believed might still be at the orphanage.

Seeing Clare then, smelling the odor of rancid dreams and sunken hopes and all the lost battles that had taken her from him, Adam thought she was a remnant of the Biblical tribe of wandering souls his grandmother Rose had warned would walk the Earth till eternity, and quickly looked away. Then he remembered the caramel candy eyes, the pink, upturned lips, the blonde wisps of hair that fell onto Clare's forehead and cheeks and gave her the look of a young child even in middle age, and he looked again. She had lost most of her front teeth, and she was standing as if her feet ached. She was accompanied by an old man in city clothes, who limped behind her on a wooden leg and who might have owned the car that was parked on the side of the highway across from the home.

She asked Adam if he lived in the home. When he didn't answer she became irritated and started to ask again. Then she looked at him harder, and her hand began to shake. The rhododendrons fell out of her fist, and tears gathered in her eyes, and he could tell from the way she said his name, the way she sighed and remained in place without daring to come any closer—he could tell she knew she was too late.

He would never believe her again and would never trust her and she had come here in vain, seeking forgiveness, perhaps, or even love, but he could tell she knew they were both out of her reach and long wasted.

Some months after that meeting the man with the wooden leg returned to tell Adam that Clare had died—drowned in the foamy white waters of the Cumberland River where it poured into the Ohio, he said, and washed ashore, as if to prove she could not escape the mountains even in death.

HE SPENT HIS senior year in high school trying to prepare for departure. He knew Harris would turn him loose as soon as he had turned eighteen, and he welcomed this, it was true, but he had no idea where he would go or what he must do once on his own. Mrs. Kelsey with the enormous breasts kept asking him if he had a job outside of the orphanage and if he knew where he was going to live once he had "come of age," but her questions only increased the anxiety Adam felt about his future. A boy he knew from the farm had found a job driving a coal truck for a buck and a half a load, and offered to help Adam do the same. The principal at the public high school asked if Adam might like to stay on and teach first grade. One of his teachers that year told him about her nephew, who worked for a big Chicago newspaper and who might, if approached, help Adam get a job as a copy boy.

The day Adam turned eighteen, Mr. Harris called him into the office.

He had gotten old over the years, and thinner, too, and he did not speak as much or lecture the boys as often. He seemed tired, jaded, not as eager to confront or prevail. He still carried his whip everywhere he went, held it whenever he called Adam into his office.

With the whip he pointed to a piece of paper on his desk.

"Your birth certificate," he said quietly.

Adam took the paper but did not examine it. He felt Harris' gaze on himself but did not return it. They stood face-to-face, both of them quiet. Between them was the chair where Clare had sat the first time she had come to drop Adam off.

"You can keep the clothes you're wearing," Harris finally said. "Everything else belongs to the State."

It was still morning when Adam left the home. He took away only his high school diploma and his birth certificate, walked out without saying goodbye even to Mrs. Kelsey. The older children were in class, and he did not stop to see them. Two young boys stared at him from their work stations in the yard, and he did not wave at them as he left.

On the gravel pathway outside the home, he turned around and looked at the building one last time. He wanted to remember that moment exactly, to remember the orphanage precisely. He had no idea where he would go next. He knew only that he would never come back.

HE HITCHED A RIDE to Kentucky, pumped gas for a dollar a day and a place to sleep, ate leftovers at the local diner where he cleaned the floor and picked up heavy loads after work. After a few weeks, he called his teacher at the school and asked for the nephew's name and number in Chicago, said he might look the man up and see if he could get started in the paper. Before that, however, he said he was going to see his father one last time.

Sam's marriage to Helen Kiessling had lasted long enough to produce four children and a mountain of debt Sam could not repay. Having failed to cure Helen of the Gypsy's curse, or convince her of the sincerity of his faith in God, he had sent her and the children back to her family farm, where the grandparents could feed and clothe them and where Helen could find work in a nearby stocking factory. She lasted at the factory only a few months, then returned to the farm and abandoned herself to the increasingly frequent seizures which soon took her life.

Little Sam Jenkins received notice of Helen's death while en route to a revival meeting in Georgia. He sent word that her children should be sent to an orphanage if possible, or released to the care of their grandparents until they were old enough to leave home. Then he went on to marry again.

Throughout the 1950s he was interviewed and written about regularly in the press, and he even went on the radio to preach his version of Christian worship to those unfamiliar with his movement. He offered conflicting stories about his own background, avoided mention of former wives or the number of children he had fathered, but he never did waver in his view of the Bible and the manner in which the Lord operated.

Adam found him in Jamesboro, Kentucky, at a meeting attended by five hundred people. The day of the revival, traffic leading to the site was so heavy that sheriff's deputies had been dispatched to the area to direct cars onto and off the highway. All around the tent where Sam was going to preach, believers had gathered since the early morning, playing their cymbals and guitars and singing hymns. Gangs of hecklers loitered around. Women with hair long to their knees rushed about setting tables full of food.

Inside the tent the sheriff had roped off the front section and reserved it for those worshipers who planned to handle. He stopped a twelve-year-old boy who had tried to pass into the front.

"Children can't handle," he told the boy. "It's the law, and it better be obeyed."

Reluctantly the boy sat next to Adam, in the row directly behind the rope. He kept muttering to himself as he looked at the makeshift pulpit and the snake boxes around it. Then he turned to Adam and said he was going to handle one of those snakes regardless of the sheriff's orders.

"God's law is above man's law," he said.

Increasingly excited, he rubbed the palms of his hands together and moved his torso back and forth as he spoke. "Man's got to beat the devil if he's gonna live in the Spirit."

He wore a yellowed dress shirt closed in the front with a single button—the others having fallen off and never been

133

replaced—and he kept his pants around his waist with the aid of a rope. His shoes were clearly too big for him, and he had a scar across the top of his right hand and over his wrist and arm. He said he had been burned a year ago at a service in Jolo when he had tried to handle fire.

"I was anointed all right," he explained, "but just when I put my hand in the furnace I got scared, and fear lets the devil into your soul, and that's why I burned."

Two itinerant farmhands, brothers, each with a family to support, had died of snakebite at the same service in Jolo. At their burial the next day, their father had handled snakes over his sons' coffins.

The boy stopped rubbing his hands together and sat up straight.

"Here he comes," he said, motioning with his head toward the pulpit.

Adam felt his heart drop but did not look up. He waited till he had overcome the initial excitement he felt at the prospect of seeing Sam again, till he had reined in his emotions and could see the preacher with a cool eye.

Little Sam Jenkins wore the same patched white shirt he had worn when Adam was a boy. Unusually short, he had rolled up his pant bottoms, and he walked with a clear limp. His face was red and swollen from a recent snakebite, and his fingers were twisted and scarred from poison, but he was every bit as wired and charged and full of danger as he had been the last time Adam saw him. Now he was famous, too, Adam remarked—famous and obviously enjoying it.

He paced the length of the tent, holding his arms out to the believers who had gone into a frenzy at the very sight of him, shaking hands and kissing friends and beckoning the hecklers to kneel down and pray to the Lord. The twelve-year-old with the urge to handle sprang to his feet.

"Brother Sam!"

Jenkins came up and patted the boy on the head, then took his hands in his own. He looked directly into the boy's eyes and said a prayer, then walked away.

The music inside the tent was so loud, Adam wanted to cover his ears and run.

Two doctors had come all the way from Charleston to examine Sam's body in search of clues to his apparent immunity to poison. He showed the men the glass of lye he was going to drink that day, invited them to check it for authenticity, to join along in drinking if they felt the Spirit move upon them.

"I am an Apostle Paul," he said, "I plant seeds that others will water."

The sheriff warned he would arrest anyone who broke the law or became rowdy, and Sam invited him to do so in the name of the Lord. Then he preached.

He spoke for seven hours that day. He recited from the Bible, spoke of his past experiences with the Lord. He walked through the congregation and interrupted his sermon to ask individual members about the health and well-being of their children and spouses, sat down a few times and caught his breath before springing up into a frenzy and continuing to preach. Twice he stopped in front of Adam.

The first time, he patted the twelve-year-old on the head and spoke directly to Adam:

"Jimmy Ray here was born in the Word and has walked in the Spirit as long as I've known him," he said. "He's walked in the Spirit and he'll die in it, I know, all to serve the Lord."

The second time, he defied the sheriff's orders and handed Jimmy Ray a snake.

But at no time during the service did Little Sam Jenkins treat Adam to more than a friendly glance, or act as if he had recognized his own son.

BLUE WAS WAITING FOR ADAM OUTSIDE HER HOUSE, EX-pecting him with as much certainty as if his visit had been planned by them both. Her hair was pulled back from her face, and she wore a stark white dress that covered her arms and legs and rose to the edge of her neck. She looked as if she had not felt the heat at all, as if she had just emerged from a block of ice that had been left melting in the heat to expose the radiant perfection of the prize it held.

He parked the car directly in front of the house, got out and circled it until he had his back to the passenger-side window. He had the uneasy feeling that he was playing into her hands by pursuing her the way he was, that what he had believed was a conscious decision on his part to set the facts straight about Sam's death was nothing more than a response to Blue's silent calls. For a long time he watched her—his eyes following their own desire to travel along the curve of her neck, the arch in her back, the soft dip in the crook of her arm. He imagined her turning in the dark, smiling the way she had to the hotel owner from Michigan when he brought her sweets. She spoke first.

"What if I told you about the snakes?" she asked.

Her question shocked him. He took a moment to understand it, weighed the words in his mind, and tried to read the message behind them. She was pulling him in, he thought, pulling him close.

"What *about* the snakes?" He shrugged.

With her hair pulled back from her face, he could see the edge of her lower jaw, the soft, transparent skin directly below her ear. "White porcelain," an Arab cab driver in Beirut had said to him once, paying the highest compliment he knew to Western women. "As fair and delicate as white porcelain."

"What if I told you why I handle?"

His hands were stuffed into the pockets of his jeans, his body leaning carelessly against the car, but his heart was already racing with anger and the effort to contain it.

"Doesn't matter *why*," he said, knowing full well that it did—matter—to him, that he despised all handlers and distrusted every one of them and that, whether he liked to admit this to himself or not, the very fact of her religious practices made her a suspect in Adam's eyes.

She knew it, too.

"It's not about what you do to *yourself* with the snakes," he insisted. "It's about what you do to *others*."

"What I did to *Sam*," she corrected. "It's about what I did to *Sam*."

He shrugged again. "To anyone."

Blue smiled indulgently. Her eyes were amused, her body devoid of the tension he had seen the previous night when she had followed him in the rain. She descended the steps leading from the front yard to the sidewalk, came close enough to observe the tiny lines around his eyes, the shape of the scar on his face. Without touching her he could feel the coolness of her skin, the lulling comfort of her breath as it poured, balmlike, into the air around him.

"My friend Anne Pelton thinks she knows you," she whispered.

Suddenly he felt the color drain from his face.

"She's been handling for almost forty years," she said. "She knew Little Sam in the very beginning."

She spoke without malice, didn't intend to frighten or embarrass him. She was putting together the clues to a mystery, he thought, looking through him to understand a bigger puzzle.

"She says you went out to her twice to ask questions. She thought you looked familiar the first time. The second time she realized why."

Anne Pelton was a seventy-year-old widow who lived in Pineville and boasted of knowing everything there was to know about God. Her husband had died of snakebite in Alabama. Her daughter had moved to Nashville and sworn to become a country-western star or to die trying. She was the subject of most of Anne Pelton's prayers.

"She says your mother was so pretty, it would be hard to forget her face. She says you have the same face, the same color eyes."

Adam offered Blue his most sarcastic glare.

"I didn't realize that woman could still see," he said.

It wasn't his nature to be cruel. He was trying to buy time, to decide how to react to the news that he had been recognized, remembered, talked about by the very men and women he had assumed knew nothing about him.

"At any rate, I wouldn't put much stock in what she has to say if I were you."

He could almost feel the sharpness of his own words, taste the blood they drew as they rose through his throat and onto his lips.

Blue didn't flinch.

"Anne thinks you may be Little Sam's child," she said.

Mrs. Roscoe across the street was watching them from her doorstep. Blue was aware of the woman's presence, Adam could tell, but she refused to grant the woman so much as a glance, refused to let her movements be inhibited by her neighbor's presence.

"Come to church with me," she told him quietly.

When he didn't answer she went around the car and sat in the driver's seat.

THEY DROVE WEST on Interstate 40, then south on 75 toward Chattanooga. In the passenger seat Adam smoked two cigarettes back-to-back, threw the butts out the open window, and kept his eyes on the road.

The highway cut across miles of open field. Around it the earth was flat and wide and emerald green, the road running through it like a smooth, shiny ribbon—quiet and still and slow as a dream. Watching it, Adam thought about the irony of what had happened—what he had done—only moments ago: confronted with Anne Pelton's knowledge of his background, Adam had tried to deny his past, to hide his link to Clare and Rose Watkins and certainly to Little Sam. He had been blinded by shame, rendered mute by the anger that had coursed in his veins and settled on the tip of his tongue, and he had done what he had always blamed Sam for doing.

In Sweetwater Blue stopped at the first house they came to and knocked on the door. A young boy in cutoff pants emerged from the field behind the house and stared at the car, then at Blue. She asked if he knew where the Holy Rollers were meeting that day.

The boy kept looking at her. He was barefoot and shirtless, dirty from field work, clearly malnourished.

"You're that *woman*," he said after a moment.

She nodded.

He looked briefly at the car, then down at his hands.

"He's not from around here," he muttered, referring to Adam.

Blue turned to Adam and smiled.

"He used to be," she said indulgently. "He still may be."

A moment later the boy pointed to the east and told Blue to look for a barn with no roof and a sign that read PREPARE TO MEET THE LORD.

It was four-thirty in the afternoon when they drove up to the barn, and a group of believers had already congregated in the clearing outside the makeshift church. The men had brought their guitars and tambourines and were already playing music and singing "In Heaven We'll Never Grow Old." The women had brought food and were laying it out on tables erected in the back of the barn. The very sight of them, the realization that he was back after almost two decades, close again to people he had sworn he would never see—the very sight of those women made his stomach turn.

John Dewey was there with his wife, who had been mute and found speech through Little Sam's healing, and Liston Cunningham, whose young daughter had died drinking lye in church. There was John Sherman, who had raised two people from the dead with his own faith, and Bob Reynolds who must be in his eighties, Adam calculated, and who had just married the fourteen-year-old granddaughter of a childhood friend. Bob had taken the girl to a McDonald's in Pineville on their first and only date. She had married him because he was kind, and because he had bought her two milkshakes the night of their date.

The girl was the first to notice Blue's car and point it out to the others. Suddenly heads began to turn, conversations came to a halt. Less than two months after Jenkins' death, having signed a pledge to the DA and the sheriff that she would never handle again, Blue was back. And she had brought an outsider—a man—with her.

She sat behind the wheel with the engine running and looked at the believers staring at her.

"I won't go in there with you," Adam told her.

She turned to him then, as if to understand. He saw her teeth dig into her lower lip, saw her hands tremble ever so slightly. For a moment he let go of his anger and let the hardness out of his eyes. Then he realized what was about to happen and pulled back: she had brought him here to make him understand, brought him into her world so he could see it from within—so he would lose perspective, objectivity, the willingness, ultimately, to decipher right and wrong.

"I won't do it," he said again.

I left this church eighteen years ago and swore never to set foot in it again and I won't do it now, he wanted to say—not for you and not for Little Sam's legacy and not even for the sake of a story.

The words, unspoken, fell like leaves into the silence.

She went alone.

SHE DIDN'T LOOK like the others, he thought, didn't talk or move or act as if she belonged with them. He saw her walk across the green field toward the church, and he thought that this was a creature who was used to being different. She knew she did not belong, he thought, knew that she never *would* belong.

She was like the fairy-tale wings on a small child who dreams of flying away—startling, exquisite, out of place no matter where she went.

She approached the crowd without a pause in her step, without showing the slightest sign of fear or adopting the defensive posture of one who expects to be attacked. Adam knew she was afraid. He had sensed it before she left the car, seen it in her hands as she had grabbed the handle to open the door. Yet, watching her, he thought she looked aloof and strong and willing to face any challenge thrown at her.

He slipped into the driver's seat and told himself he should drive away, leave her there with her snakes and her believer friends and all the lies and illusions they lived and died by. He thought of her moving inside the barn, enduring the hostile and judging glares of other believers, sitting in the women's section and feeling their suspicion burn holes into the back of her neck. He imagined her standing up at the right time during the service, singing in the right tune. She would not look away from those who despised her, he knew, would not bend under pressure from those who wanted her to vanish.

He watched the sun set over the fields, watched the darkness seep into the car. With the window down he could hear the sound of music and words, the talking in tongues and the screams and hollers of men and women in the throes of ecstasy. Sometime after that, he saw shadows—some still singing, others quiet and spent from the emotions they had experienced during the service—begin to drift out of the church. These were the hardest times, he thought—when he watched groups of people who belonged together, who felt a bond of family or friendship or common beliefs, and whose very existence reminded Adam of how disconnected he was and would always be.

His eyes searched for Blue.

She walked out alone—a bright white flame in the night—and stopped only to hug Anne Pelton and say a word. She did not look toward the car, did not search for Adam through the windshield, but he could tell that she was conscious of him, that she had been thinking of him all the time she had been in church, inviting him to stay, to wait for her, to see her again before he left. Something about her was both worlds removed and impossibly close—a longing, once urgent, that has turned into memory and seeped under the skin.

She came up to the car and slid into the passenger seat. Adam felt his heart race at her proximity and held his breath to contain his relief. Her skin glowed in the dark and her hands looked small and cold on her dress. He felt like holding them, so he looked away.

She watched him for a moment.

"Thank you," she said.

She knew why he had waited for her—understood that he had wanted to stand by her, stand *with* her in the face of the doubt and the blame she would receive.

145

Without looking at her he turned the car on and put it into gear. She put her hand on his arm, waited until he had found the courage to turn to her.

Then she put her lips against his cheek, touched the edge of his mouth with her tongue, and kissed him.

MAKING LOVE TO HER, he thought, was like driving blind across narrow mountain passes—the road hanging halfway between ecstasy and annihilation, traversed by faith more than reason, by madness more than faith. Adam had traveled that way a few times before. It was how outlaws and gun traffickers smuggled people and goods into and out of countries at war with one another in the Middle East, how convicted criminals and political prisoners escaped the borders of their native countries: a moonless night, a car with the headlights turned off, a passenger hiding in the back while the man behind the wheel floored the gas pedal and prayed to stay one step ahead of his pursuers. They stayed quiet—passenger and driver both, strangers bound together by the threat of detection, the certainty of death if captured. They braced the road and prayed it would not give out from under them, moved by instinct, by memory, rather than by sight. Minutes stretched to unimaginable lengths, and the passengers could hear each other's heartbeat. Every time the car turned a corner there would be silence, then a gasp, then—as they realized they were still alive—joy beyond what they had known possible.

They were in the cave directly across from the church, in the underground chambers that led to the Lost Sea. He had driven here after the service, taken Blue into the cave and made love to her standing up, his hands grasping her as she leaned against the cold stone wall, tearing off her dress and holding on to her as if he would never let go, as if she had been his from the start and he had come to claim her at last.

One wrong turn and he would be lost in the curves of this woman's body, buried in the folds of her hair. He would be blinded by the hands that had touched his face as if to preserve the memory of his skin, by the way she gave in to him, bore her face into the crook his neck, and whispered his name.

"Adam."

Like a wish that won't come true if spoken out loud, the name hung between them, opening a floodgate of questions he did not know to answer. He pulled away from her, looked at her white frame against the black stone wall.

A woman, naked as hope, exposed and unprotected and strangely, strangely unafraid.

They drove home in silence—their eyes cast on the road that took them across the open fields surrounding the city and into the labyrinth of narrow alleys and dead-end streets of Fort Sanders. Nineteenth Street was empty. Clinch Avenue lay under the spell of an evil witch and a thousand years of silence. In Blue's house a single yellow light burned behind the lace curtains of the living room which overlooked the street.

It was the Professor, Adam thought, waiting for his wife.

THE BOARDINGHOUSE owner was sitting on the balcony of Adam's room, sipping brandy and smoking a cigar. He had left the door open a crack to warn of his presence, and he displayed the same ironic smile and feigned indifference with which he always greeted Adam.

"What is it?" Adam asked in the doorway.

The owner raised an eyebrow and acted surprised.

"Brandy!" he said, and took a sip of his drink.

He wore a white linen shirt and khaki pants, soft leather shoes, a musky cologne. He was acting friendly without daring to admit it, trying to engage Adam without having to ask for attention.

"Would you like some?" he asked, still with sarcasm in his voice.

Adam was exhausted and confused and feeling overwhelmed by his encounter with Blue. Part of him longed for a quiet place in which to reflect. Part of him, too, was glad for a diversion that might save him from his own thoughts.

He moved inside the room and sat on the bed.

"What can I do for you?" he asked with a sigh.

The owner smiled mischievously.

"Hmm," he mused. "We could start by making love."

Adam leaned against the headboard and crossed his legs.

"What else?" he asked without looking at the man. He had a bottle of Jack Daniel's on the nightstand. He lit a cigarette and looked on the table for a glass.

The man from Michigan was looking at him quietly.

"I liked you the first day you came in," he said when Adam met his eyes. Quickly he caught the softness in his voice and switched to a more sarcastic tone. "That's until you spoke, of course."

Adam had come into the boardinghouse with his backpack and his three-day stubble, looking exhausted and smelling of airports and cigarette smoke. He had asked for a room without looking at the owner, paid for a week without counting his change. He was a gorgeous specimen, the owner had thought as he showed Adam up to the room—a fairy-tale prince arriving in a land of poisoned apples and insomnia. It wasn't until later, when he started asking questions about Blue, that the owner had begun to distrust the man.

There were no glasses in the room. Adam took a swig from the bottle of Jack Daniel's and left the top open.

"Isiah Frank," the owner introduced himself. "I thought you might be curious."

Adam nodded once, did not bother to say a word, took another sip from the bottle.

The owner was disdainful.

"At least no one can accuse her of softening your edges," he sighed.

He saw the tension, like lightning, strike through Adam's eyes. Frightened, he recrossed his legs and looked down at the burning tip of his cigar. He had gotten too close, he realized, touched a vein that might erupt any moment and drown him in blood.

"I've known her for years," he said, extending an olive branch.

He couldn't resist poking further.

"Known her *husband,* too."

Adam was fixing the man with his gaze—aggressive and hostile and unrelenting. Suddenly Isiah Frank did not know why he was here, what he had hoped to get from this man who clearly did not return his interest.

It's a dark and humid night, and I'm far from being loved and all I want is to fall asleep in this world of glass animals and cursed princes—fall asleep alone and know that when I die, I will be missed.

Painfully, he forced his eyes to meet Adam's.

"She's a splendid creature," he said, his voice suddenly devoid of irony.

"If you break her, she'll cut you to the bone."

ADAM STAYED UP all night in his room, drinking Jack Daniel's and making a mental map of the story he had come back to write. He had not called the paper since speaking to the night editor from Frankfurt. The newspaper staff had no way of getting hold of him, no way of knowing where he was or if they would hear from him again. He should have been worried about his job, but he wasn't.

He would write the story about Little Sam and the thousands of men and women who had followed his faith when he was alive and who would continue to do so after his death. He would speak of the snakes that did not kill, the oil that was used to anoint, the hands that healed the believers. But he would not make a single mention of Blue, he knew, or of the manner of Sam's death.

She would be there, of course, reflected in every line, laced into every word, conspicuous by her absence. She would be there, and yet, Adam knew he could not mention her.

He wanted to protect her, he realized. This, more than anything, scared him.

He told himself he should leave—tomorrow, when his eyes had cleared and he could muster the will to drive away and find an airport and go anywhere at all. He thought he should walk away while he still could, while he still wanted to.

Yet something about the city, about the mountains surrounding it and the life that brewed within it was fine and hypnotic and seductive in a way he had not been prepared for—a way he had not experienced in his childhood—and so he stayed, day after day with Blue's image everywhere he looked, and it was all he could do to stop himself from going to see her.

She had turned to him that night, in the moment before she stepped out of the car and vanished into the house she shared with her husband—turned to him and looked at his hands as if to wonder if they would save her.

He stayed away for three days. Then he went to see her.

He stood outside Mrs. Roscoe's house at night, tucked his hands into the pockets of his jeans as if to hide his need, stared up at the walls with the cracked and faded blue paint, the moth-eaten lace moldings, the overgrown front yard. He imagined Blue moving quietly through that house, eating dinner with her husband in a dining room full of starched linen and old china. He saw her as she waited for the Professor to finish reading his books, as she sat in bed and watched him put his clothes away. They lay next to each other with their eyes open and talked in slow whispers about things no one else must know.

He sat in his car smoking cigarettes and watching the house. He felt haunted, charmed, connected to Blue as much by his anger as by her will, unable for once to walk away, unwilling to leave.

Did he see in her his own destiny, only reversed?

He saw her loneliness, her desire. He saw the reflection of the road in her eyes. It was the same road he had traveled to save himself from his past, the same one he had traversed again to come back. He saw her body reaching for the one path that led away, that cut through the land and led to the open seas of imagination. He *wanted* to stay.

In the first-floor window, a light went off the moment Adam appeared. A shadow—the Professor's—moved behind the curtains and closed the blinds, walked around the house and made sure the doors were locked, that the windows were shut and the phone was off the hook, and that they were safe—the Professor and his wife and everything Adam might intrude upon.

Mrs. Roscoe across the street came out of her house and frowned when she saw Adam.

"Better go away now," she warned. "The Devil's in that house and he might get into you if you don't watch."

He drove home through the empty city with the broken streetlights. He did not look behind him, did not stop, but all the while he could feel Blue moving toward him in the dark.

Isiah Frank let her in with a smile.

"You are more beautiful in love," he told Blue, then stepped away and watched her go to Adam.

EFORE MY DAUGHTER DIED I USED TO WONDER WHAT I would tell her when she was old enough to ask where I came from, or why it is I cannot go back there or even point to the place on a map.

Blue was standing by the French doors that separated Adam's room from the balcony overlooking the courtyard, facing Adam without looking him directly in the eyes. He lay in bed with his back against the headboard, the dress he had peeled off her still next to him. He studied the way the curls in her golden-red hair fell against her white skin, the lines of her body as if drawn with a sure hand on paper—lean, spare, certain. Across from the window a wall mirror with a black wood frame reflected her image.

You did not know this—that I had a child and that she died. The newspapers have written much about my snake handling, but they never mentioned my daughter or her passing. It doesn't make good copy: a little girl catching fire in the middle of the afternoon, running across the yard without a sound or a whimper as the flames rise around her body and over her face and head, running toward her mother with her arms open as if to embrace her, and me standing there, too stunned to utter a sound or make a move.

Would she have been saved if I had acted a moment sooner?

The newspapers didn't write about this, and the townspeople hardly seemed to notice at all. They have always thought of me as an outsider—because I came from abroad, and later, because of the church and its practices. They looked at me and talked about me, but they never saw me as anything but an oddity and so it was easy for them to ignore both my daughter's birth and later, her passing.

She fell to the ground half a foot away from me, flames rising from the tips of her tiny white fingers, and by the time I threw myself on her to choke the fire, I knew I had lost her.

So the townspeople do not mention my daughter, and the church members, who know what happened, rarely spoke of her afterward: they could not explain it, you see—how such a thing could happen to a five-year-old. They could not explain it and could not accord it any greater importance than all the sorrow and misfortune that has tainted their own lives, and so they responded the only way they knew how: accepted it as the will of God and moved on.

This is the essence of faith, the Professor always says: not asking questions, not daring to disagree. He says that is why the church members brought faith in me even though I am not from among them, even though I have never spoken or acted or lived like them. They see how I can fight a snake, and they close their eyes on the rest of my story and that is why, to this day, most of them do not know that I wasn't born with Jesus.

I might have told them the truth if they had asked. I might have told them that my mother was a Jew and the Professor is too. I might have told them but they did not want to know, and so the truth remained unseen—untouched and unwanted and gathering weight, until it became a lie I had to hide.

My daughter, though, would have asked. I know this because that is the way daughters create a bond with their mothers—instinctively, by asking the most trivial questions, by wanting to know the most obscure facts. They ask all through their childhoods without knowing what they will do with this knowledge— without knowing that every word, every memory they take from their mothers will become a link in a bridge they have started to build unconsciously. Through years of separation and hardship, through adulthood and beyond, the bridge stands invisible, stretching longer the farther the child travels, until the day she stops, counts the years and realizes she, too, is a woman, and all she has to do to return to her mother is to cross the bridge of words and memories she built in childhood.

I had a story to tell my child. I prepared it and saved it and then watched it spread itself around me like an interminable wasteland that serves only to remind me of her absence.

WHEN I WAS *a child, my mother would take a thin brush, made from the hair of blue horses, and dip the tip in henna. In the early morning hours when the light was thin she would sit outside, in the foothills of the rocky Zagross Mountains of Asia, and with the brush draw figures onto the palms of her own hands.*

My mother was a good artist when she was sane, an even better one after she went mad. The old people in the village where I grew up used to say that it was her Jewish blood that had caused her madness. They said that all Jews were inhabited by the devil and that he compelled them to do and say strange things. Years later, in America, I would hear that story again.

My mother's father, she once told me, was a Jewish Tar player in the court of the Persian prince Zil-el-Sultan, in the city of Esfahan where there was a palace built entirely of glass. He was a handsome man with a hypnotic voice and a fortune that evoked many a legend. His name was Solomon, my mother said, though she had no direct memory of him at all. He was generous with his money, even more generous with his heart. He fell in love and conquered women as if they were ships on a calm sea, anchored and moored and ready to fall into his pirate hands. Even after he was married he continued to set off on wild and adventurous trips to the heart of Egypt and India, looking for fabled beauties whose stories he had heard at home, and that is how he found my grandmother, in a Kurdish village in the year 1893, in the part of the world they now call Iraq, near the city of Mosul, where many Kurds live.

Most people around here have never heard of the Kurds or the place we called Kurdistan, so it would be difficult to explain that it's a country within many others, a state with too many leaders, a nation without a name on any map. If I had to describe it to my daughter, I would have said that it's a ghost country the color of God, a land of silver rocks and lavender plains, of black winds and amber roads and saffron sunsets so glorious, no man has been able to claim them as his own.

I would have sat my daughter on my knees, in that room where for years the Professor taught me, on that chair where I first learned to read and later came to discover the history of my people. I would have spread before my daughter a map of the East, let her eyes swallow the rust-brown sheet where entire countries lie the size of a child's hand—silent and constant, their mysteries unspoken, their secrets unrevealed.

"Look," I would have said, "here are the Torus Mountains. This is the Black Sea."

I would have taken her hand, guided her tiny fingers over the edge of the mountain, into the depths of the sea.

"These are the Rivers Aras and Euphrates," I would have said. "These are the Hamrin Mountains. This is Mesopotamia, the Armenian Anatolia, the legendary Mount Ararat.

"In between these lines," I would have told her, "in an area divided among five countries, live twenty-five million people who call themselves Kurds."

They are a strange breed, these Kurds—the children of fairy-tale Jinns and their real-life lovers: five thousand years ago King Solomon ordered the Jinns in his service to search the four corners of the earth and bring to him the most beautiful virgins alive. The Jinns searched far and wide, but by the time they brought the maidens back, King Solomon had died and the Jinns themselves had fallen in love with the girls. So they

159

married the mortals and had children who belonged neither to this world nor to the planet of the fairies, destined to live in the neverland of exile, in perpetual movement, forever restless.

Kurds lived in caves at first, and later in villages and towns. Many of them were nomads, traveling great distances every year in search of grazing land for their cattle. They spoke different dialects of the same language, observed different customs, prayed to different gods even, but the one trait they all had in common was their ferocity and their strength: they were all good fighters, these Kurds, their women as well as their men. This is why they lasted the ages, why, also, they never knew peace.

Themselves of Indo-European stock, they were dominated over time by Parthians and Arabs, Mongols and Turks and Persians. After the First World War they were conquered by Western men who took a pen, one day when their souls were filled with the pride of the conqueror, and drew lines upon the map of Asia, creating countries where previously there had been none and, in the process, dividing Kurdistan for all time.

My grandmother's village was called Sandor, and it was populated by Kurdish Jews. Into this village rode the man called Solomon and stole my grandmother's heart. By then he had slept with a thousand virgins and fathered many a bastard child, but my mother's mother could not believe he would ever leave her.

Leave her he did.

To make the pain of his sudden departure easier to bear, or to repay my grandmother for the life she had wasted on him,

Solomon the Man sent her a hundred gold coins and a bracelet in the shape of a snake.

He had bought the bracelet in Egypt, where he had once lived with a black woman versed in the arts of the occult: it was a gold contraption that twisted three times and ended in the shape of a snake's head, complete with rubies for eyes. He had intended the bracelet for my grandmother—believing the Egyptian lover's claim that it represented good fortune—but she could not accept the message it bore—that Solomon had left her and did not intend to return—and so she wrapped the snake around her daughter's ankle instead. Then she braided my mother's hair into a hundred strands and tied each one with one of the coins Solomon had sent, told her she could open the braids only when her father returned to them to stay.

My mother was twenty years old, her hair still braided into a hundred strands when she tired of waiting for her father to return. Then her own lover came to call.

He was a Sunni Muslim Kurd, a nomad with a restless heart and a fast horse who had spent his life fighting in one volunteer army or another, supporting revolts by Kurds wherever they took place, being beaten every time but not accepting defeat, because to do so would mean giving up the only life he had ever known. Between the two World Wars, he had fought in three major Kurdish revolts in Turkey alone, every one of them lost. He had watched 250,000 of his people die in battle or get killed in their sleep at the hands of government soldiers, and he had seen the Turks burn hundreds of Kurdish villages and ban the Kurdish language from being spoken. One morning in the spring of 1937, he rode away from yet another futile war and happened upon a dusty village tucked away in the heart of the Zagross Mountains. He rode through narrow walkways crowded with children and sheep, past houses built of yellow and red clay and tucked into the side of the mountain in terraced rows—so that the roof of one house was a yard for another. Tiny windows, their frames painted a stark blue, opened inward to reveal white grouted walls decorated with painted flowers. Inside the houses young girls sat on the floor weaving thread out of cotton or tying knots onto a loom to create a rug.

At the end of the alley, my father came to a house and stopped. A wooden door, painted dark green, opened into a large room with a beamed ceiling made of tree trunks. One side of the room was reserved for sheep. The other side, where people lived, was crowded with bedding and pottery and an underground oven dug into the clay floor. Rows of fruits and vegetables hung from the roof where they had been left to dry for winter. A smaller door, directly opposite the entryway, led onto an enclosed terrace drenched in sunlight.

My mother stood on the terrace speaking to a girl in a neighboring house. Her back was turned to the door, so she did not feel my father come in and did not turn around. Standing behind her, my father watched her body covered by layers of brightly colored fabric, her hair dark and smooth, braided in three layers, every strand tied with a single gold coin. When she moved her head, the braids swayed back and forth, catching the light and the reflection of the gold.

He fell in love with her, he later said, without seeing her face. Then she turned around.

She was light skinned, with dark eyes and black lashes and the easiest smile he had ever seen. He liked this about her— that she smiled so readily, that she wasn't shy or reticent or afraid of a stranger. Unlike other women in the Middle East, the Kurds did not have to wear veils to hide their faces from men, and they did not have to keep their voices from being heard. He asked her if she could direct him to a tea house, a place where he could rest his horse and get some food. She told him he could stay with her, offered him honey, freshly-made yogurt, hundred-year-old wine that had been buried in the earth.

My father went back to see the girl many times that year. His intentions were clear, but his hopes were misplaced: Jews and Muslims were not allowed to intermarry. A girl raised in a village would not be able to cope with the harshness of life in the wild. But my mother was fearless and obstinate and driven by her heart's desires. She met my father at night, in the mountains outside the village, and she let him take off her sheer red scarf and kiss her on the mouth. She told my father he had two choices: he could wait for her until they were both old and heartbroken, or he could follow the spurned lovers' traditional recourse of kidnapping the girls they desired.

He took her away at midnight, when the moon cast their shadows against the mountain, and by the time the village awoke to see the girl's bed empty and her honor violated, my mother was far away and already sleeping in the nomads' tent.

THE WOMEN IN *my father's tribe wove black goats' hair into strips of cloth on a horizontal loom, then sewed the strips together to create a giant canopy. Every summer, in the grasslands near the Turkish-Iranian border, they erected the black top on posts three meters high, then closed off the sides by a straw fence that stretched from the ground up to the edges of the canopy. The inside of the fence was painted in vivid, geometric lines of red and blue and yellow. The floor was covered with colorful rugs woven by the tribe's young girls. Within each tent lived extended families and their sheep—dozens of people bound together by blood and circumstance, their campground consisting of no more than a few tents dotting the plains.*

Within the tribe women worked and traveled and interacted freely with the men. Girls learned to ride a horse and to shoot a rifle as well as the boys. Parents named their sons after brave, war-like mothers. But their connection to the land lasted only as long as the season, and then they were gone, packing their homes in the space of one morning and tying their tents onto their saddlebags, leaving the mountains of Iran for the valleys of Iraq, where they would spend the long winter months in stone houses erected on harsh, infertile ground.

You see, I have no memories of my mother's childhood places, or of the lands of her ancestors. In my mind they are fairy-tale kingdoms populated by men with luminous voices who went riding in search of beautiful women. I only knew that other world—my father's country, where I was born and where I grew up. I remember a tent, a tribe, a house in the mountains of Iraq. Even now, with my life so different from the past I hardly recognize myself in it, even now I can see the light of those early mornings in the grasslands where I camped as a child. I see the color of the hills in the spring, when a million wildflowers bloomed as far as the horizon, and a thousand stars fell in a single shower deep in the night. I hear, still after all these years, the silence of those mountains, the sound of our tribe living in the midst of a world unpenetrated by strangers, the freedom of crossing any border at any time and belonging nowhere. Snow would pile knee-deep across mountain passes, and I would bend from my mother's waist as she sat on the back of her horse, and touch the ice. Heat would rise off naked rocks, and I would find a stream made of melted snow from the winter and run into the water with my clothes on. I remember a world of beauty and peace and freedom, and yet I know that this same world, that same unsoiled country I loved so much, destroyed my mother.

She knew, almost as soon as she arrived, that she had made a mistake. She was a village girl, bound to her home, born and raised in a place where her ancestors were buried, and for her, the life of constant motion was impossible to bear. She felt unsafe and unprotected in my father's tent, a stranger to his tribe who would never accept a Jew as one of their own and who had their doubts about her origins and her intentions in marrying my father. She must have contemplated leaving, of course, yet she knew that her own people would not allow her back now that she had been kidnapped by, or had escaped with a Muslim, and she knew she would never survive the journey home on her own—or even find her way through the mountains without my father guiding her. So she stayed in the tribe and wove rugs, sheared sheep and baked bread and roamed the hillsides in

search of medicinal herbs to soothe her sorrows. When she realized she was pregnant, she decided to settle into her life and create a home for herself and her child. She made a new straw
fence to surround her part of the tent, painted it from seam to
seam with the flowers and birds of her own village, the fairies
of her childhood in Sandor, the protective eyes and amulets of
her own heritage. She wove a crib of soft cotton, a stretch of
brocaded silk in which to wrap me when I arrived, a soft new
rug on which to lay me at night.

Then she began to dream of snakes.

She dreamed of them every night, and in the beginning
they did not scare her: golden snakes lying in her bed, crawling
up her thighs, staring at her with their ruby eyes. She recounted
the dreams to the tribe's midwife and was told that she was
going to have a girl: in a man's dream snakes meant great
riches; in a woman's they meant the arrival of a female child.

My mother was delighted with the midwife's interpretation:
a girl, she thought, would be her mother's best friend, her constant companion, the one person in the world who understood her
best. But every night the snakes in her dreams grew darker and
more threatening. They each had more than one head, lurked in
the dark and bit her when she wasn't watching. They reminded
her of the story she had heard as a child—of the bad king
Zahak who had killed his own father in order to inherit his ten
thousand horses. Presiding over the seven countries of the earth
and the land of giants and fairies, Zahak was visited by the
devil who kissed the king on his shoulders. In each place where
the devil's lips had touched, a snake appeared and grew—testa-
ments to the man's evil thoughts and his selfish deeds.

Night after night the snakes of the devil's kisses came into my mother's dreams and terrified her until she woke up screaming and exhausted and too afraid to go back to sleep. Then they came into her awake hours.

She saw them in broad daylight and in shadows, ran from them when no one else could see a threat, pleaded for help. Once, trying to throw off a snake that had dug its teeth into her, she threw herself into an open fire and burned her right leg. Another time she took a knife and cut her arm down to the bone, extracting, she said, the snake's poison.

Trying to cure his wife of the dreams, my father took her on a pilgrimage to the tomb of a holy man, near the city of Saqqez. My mother planted a wooden pole in the earth near the tomb, hung her scarf like a banner from the post, and prayed to the holy man's spirit. The minute she turned around, the pole turned into a two-headed snake and attacked her.

They made a second pilgrimage, this time to the home of a holy man in Iraq. A blessed soup was made, ceremonial drums were beaten to scare away the demons that inhabited my mother's soul. By then my mother was nearly eight months pregnant, and the tribe had moved from their winter dwellings back into the tents on the Turkish-Iranian border. For a while the snakes disappeared.

I was born in the tent. My mother held me in her arms and sang me to sleep, walked around with me strapped to her back and talked to me as if I could understand. Then one morning she looked up at the sun and saw the sky break into a thousand pieces, sending down on her a shower of black snakes.

ALL THROUGH MY *childhood I watched my mother for signs of madness setting in. I grew up weaving rugs and herding cattle, washing clothes in the ravine and planting food. I was strong at an early age, stronger than the other girls in our tribe and even stronger than the boys, because with my father gone and my mother sick so much of the time, I was left to do most of their work. I did not learn to read and write, but I knew the uses of medicinal herbs and how to deliver a mare of its foal, and I knew how to fight.*

I fought with the other children who thought me odd because of my mother's condition, fought with their parents who treated my mother as if she were less than human. I fought with my father when he returned heartbroken from his lost wars and acted as if my mother were the enemy—grabbing her when she went mad and tying her to the poles that kept our tent erect, letting her struggle and scream and beg to be freed, until she exhausted herself or chewed through the ropes that bound her and escaped.

We lived in a state of constant change, dependent for our safety on the will of God, the kindness of the elements, the benevolence of faraway kings and conquerors who distrusted the Kurds' independence and who tried to tame and settle us on their own terms. When the Second World War started, my father joined another rebel army and was gone for months. He came back with his lung punctured by a bullet from the Syrian police, and after that he could not breathe well or ride long distances.

My mother would go through months of calm, then suddenly become possessed. She was the most stable of hands, the surest refuge, only to leave home without warning one day and run into the mountains where she would stay for days, without concern for me or my safety, hiding from the snakes until my father found her and brought her home. She sat me on her lap and talked to me before I could understand language, lay me in her bed and held me until I fell asleep, and then suddenly she would pick me up and throw me across the tent to protect me from a snake.

"Her soul has been taken over by a Jinn," the tribe's elders declared, and set out to cure her with age-old remedies. Prayers were said and written into talismans that she was forced to wear around her neck. Animals were slaughtered, and their blood was smeared on her hands and feet. Fires were built, and the names of all my mother's enemies were fed to the flames. The Jinns left for a while, then came back.

In between her bouts of madness, my mother drew on her hands.

Every few weeks she woke in the dark and took her brush. I felt her rise, because I slept next to her, and so I watched as she mixed the dry brown henna powder with a bit of water, then went outside to sit on the bare ground. Oblivious to the bitter cold of winter or the morning fog, she drew patiently, with great precision, never moving from her place or looking up from her hands or reacting to anything that went on around her. I followed her out of the tent and climbed into her lap, but she did not see me. My father called her, but she would not respond. The tribe's women rose to do the day's chores, asked her to help, chastised her for her indifference to the needs of the group, but she did not hear them. The sun would rise and set, night would fall and she would still be sitting, her hands glowing in the moonlight, still drawing.

The next day, the henna had dried, and my mother would open her palms and hold them before me to see: she had beautiful hands—white and fine and uncalloused. I said this to my husband once and he corrected me, told me it was impossible for a woman who led my mother's life to have soft hands, that weaving rugs and herding sheep and erecting tents were bound to scar the palms and toughen the skin.

My husband is welcome to his logic. I know what I remember. What I choose to remember.

The lines she had drawn were so fine and pale, so intricately woven, I had to look awhile before I recognized the images she had created. She started at the tips of her fingers and worked her way into the center of her palm, then drew from the wrist up toward the fingers, so that the entire painting on each hand revolved around a central figure. She drew a different image every time—a village with goats and horses, a chain of mountains with snow melting off their caps and pouring into ravines, a house with many chambers and a courtyard full of people. Every shape was small but precise, complete with minute details. At the center of each world, surrounded by walls and barriers she could not climb, was a lone woman with bewildered eyes and a crown of gold coins.

As I got older I realized that the entire painting was a maze, that the woman at the center was searching for a path that led away from the center and off my mother's palms. Wanting to help her, I would take my finger and trace the lines, edge my way backward and forward, around and then back again across the rivers and the pathways of my mother's imagination, but every road led back to the center and every outlet was a dead end, and even the surest of escapes proved to be only a false hope.

It became essential for me to find a way out. I felt as if my mother wanted this from me; as if, by painting her hands and showing them to me, she was asking me to help her find a way out of the labyrinth. Breathless, I searched until tears of frustration poured from my eyes and my mother, knowing my disappointment, closed her fists and told me to stop looking.

I loved her hands and loved those drawings in spite of their hopelessness, loved them in spite of the fact that the tribe's women said they were the works of the Jinns who inhabited her soul, in spite of the fact that my father, believing this perhaps, or desperate to save her from her madness at any cost, broke her brushes one day and threw her henna in the river. None of the tribe's women knew my mother the way I did. Even my father, who may have loved her, I think, but who at any rate had thought that her love would save him from his own despair—even he did not know my mother well.

It wasn't the paintings that drove her mad. It was the fact that she could not find her way out of the life she had ridden into one night on the back of a horse.

Like the woman at the center of her palm, surrounded by roads that led nowhere, dwarfed by the enormity of obstacles so small, they fit onto the tip of a miniature brush—like the woman she drew over and over, my mother was looking for a way out.

It's strange how hope dies: we hold on all our lives, in spite of the evidence to the contrary, until one day, a single incident, a single loss, marks the end of our faith. One morning when I was eight years old, I woke up and found her staring at me with hollow eyes. She had cut off all her hair.

It was true, I thought, what the tribe's elders said: that the snakes were a result of my mother's Jewish blood, that it was I, the infant she had borne, who had brought the evil spirits into my mother's body. The madness was in both of us, and it would be in my children, too.

My husband, of course, would in time provide a different explanation for what ailed my mother: "Schizophrenia," he would read out of his thousand-page book of medicine. "A severe mental disorder characterized by unpredictable disturbances in thinking. The onset of the illness usually occurs around the age of twenty. Patient characteristically withdraws from reality and thinks in illogical, confused patterns."

The Professor is always looking into books to explain life, always seeking comfort in the distance, the impersonality of scientific theories. "Science is what separates man from beast," he used to say when we were first married. He spoke in that haughty way that made me feel small, the tip of his tongue resting for a split second between his teeth, producing a tiny lisp, his upper eyelids descending slowly over his pupils, as if to feign modesty. For years I resented him for his aloofness, the way he dismissed the human heart as "animal instinct, an obstacle to be overcome in the interest of civilization," the way he labeled emotions as "unscientific, and, therefore, unjustified." Now I know he did this to save himself from his own torment.

He had seen my mother at her worst, you see—chained to the poles where the tribe's people kept the horses, unrecognizable to anyone who had known her only a few years earlier, allowing no one but me to approach or touch her. The Professor knows this: that I was the only person my mother trusted in that state of alienation, the only human contact she could bear, and so he knows how hard it was for me to leave her and come here with him, how I have blamed myself for abandoning her. That's why he wants me to buy into his medical explanation: "The woman was ill," he says. "She needed a doctor, not a nurse."

Have I made her, my mother who once chased me with a butcher knife, trying to cut off the arm she thought was a two-headed snake—have I made her into someone she never was?

She would sit behind me on the back of our horse, my father riding ahead of us with his rifle drawn against bandit attacks. The sun would be warm on our faces and her hands would cradle me against her chest and I would close my eyes, my ear to her heart, the sound of her breath pulling at me like strings, bringing me down an inch at a time, surrounding me until I was afloat and weightless and I could sleep without fear.

She loved me, I know. She loved me and wanted to protect me if she could, and in return, she trusted me to save her from the snakes.

I WAS THIRTEEN *years old the summer my husband first appeared at our campsite with his fountain pen and his notebooks, speaking a dialect of southern Kurmanji that few people in our tribe understood, and using elevated words and phrases that instantly set him apart from us. He was bone-pale and thin, and he wore a black suit—the kind morticians wear here in America, that they keep pressed under a mattress or hang on the back of a chair at night, the fabric so worn it shines even in the dark, the creases so accustomed to a human form, they give at the knees and elbows even without a body pushing at them from within. But the Professor also wore a vest, and a watch chain, and leather shoes with laces. He was well-shaven and well-combed, and he carried white handkerchiefs with his initials embroidered on them, a gold cigarette holder, and a walking stick. He was an aberration, I thought—a creature so unlike any I had ever known and so unsuited to the world I lived in, I wanted to strike out with my fists and shatter him like the frail image of the man I thought he was. He had come to study the language of the Kurds, he said through an interpreter who walked with him everywhere and acted as his guide and food taster and personal valet. He was an important man who taught at a famous university in America, the interpreter claimed, and before that he had lived in France, and what he liked most in the world was to study dead or dying languages and trace their origins and their roots and the culture of the people who spoke them.*

To me he was a girl dressed in men's clothes, so afraid of the mountains, he could not travel through them alone, so revolted by the earth, he stood with his toes always raised slightly off the ground. He even brought his own chair everywhere he went—a hand-carved wooden stool that the interpreter carried and set down for him. Before the Professor sat down, the interpreter wiped the stool with a rag, and even after that the Professor ran the tip of his finger over the surface to make sure all the dust was gone. Chairs, he told me later, were invented to separate men from beasts.

I looked at him once and realized I never wanted to see him again. But he had already noticed me and was not about to be ignored.

For a while he studied me. He showed up in our tent pretending to interview my father's relatives, to transcribe the words and phrases they used and to determine the roots of our dialect. The language of Kurdistan is called Kurmanji, but it has two major and two minor dialects, and each one of those is spoken in half a dozen subdialects. Kurdish Jews, what's more, speak Aramaic—an ancient language that was already dying when I was a child. The Professor asked questions and recorded the responses on a log he kept, which he handled with as much care as if it were holy.

I was old enough to understand the source of his interest in me, old enough also to realize that my prospects for marriage within the tribe were at best grim: I was a half-Jew and a madwoman's daughter, a wild child even my father could not control. Ever since I was very young, the elders in the tribe had warned my father that I might be kidnapped by a Kurdish Khan and taken away, because the Khans sent riders to look through the country for pretty girls who would grow into pretty women.

The elders had told my father that this might be a good thing, that if it should happen my father would be wise not to fight or try to stop it. Later, as I grew up, I could see boys looking at me, could hear their mothers admiring my looks, but I also knew that the blood that runs under the skin counts for so much more than any outward attribute, and so part of me was aware that I should have been thankful for the attention the Professor extended me—but I wasn't.

I was repelled by his smallness, by the way he never touched his own clothes or any part of his body except with the tip of a finger, the way he acted as if we Kurds were nothing more than the drops of ink he painted onto the pages of his log: touch them with your hands and they become a big smear on the page. After I married him I realized that he was shy and that he covered it up with arrogance, that he was uneasy and compensated for it by making others feel inept. He was afraid of his own emotions, of the torment of rage and lust and sorrow that brewed beneath the surface of his affected manners, and so he approached everything with a scientific mind, putting out the fire before it burned him. But even after I had learned to understand him, I could not overcome the sensation that underneath it all—underneath the black suit and the gold watch and the years of education—underneath all that was a man who had already missed his luck.

TWO MONTHS INTO *his first visit to our campsite, the Professor went to see my father.*

Speaking now in our tribe's dialect, he said he had a few words to say about himself, that he wanted me to hear them as well, that, even though I was young, he believed I should not be excluded from any discussion involving my fate. By then my mother was chained to a pole outside the tent all the time, and my father and I hardly spoke. When he commanded me to come in and listen to the Professor, I refused, but I lingered close enough to hear what was said.

The Professor said he had come to Kurdistan for two reasons: to study the language of the Kurds, to be sure, but also to find a wife he could take with him when he left. He said he had considered his options carefully before deciding on a Kurdish girl, and he had narrowed his wishes down to what was practicable as well as desirable. He said he had a big house in America and the best job a man could hold, that although he was born in Iraq, he considered himself a Western man because he had spent his adult life in Europe and then America. For a wife, he had decided on a Kurd because we were of the Aryan race, because we were a physically and mentally strong and adaptable people, because he felt that our light features would fit in easily with Americans. He wanted a young girl so he could train her himself, was willing to marry an illiterate because he would educate her himself. He said a great deal about civilization, speaking in his slow and methodical way, without making eye contact with my father or any one of the others in the tent, punctuating his sentences with long silences as if to impress upon them that they were in the presence of greatness. He said man's purpose in this world was to achieve civilization, that the history of mankind was that of a battle between the rule of law and chaos. Then he offered to take me out of the wilderness and to America.

Before my father had had a chance to wet his lips or even consider a response, I stormed at the Professor. I told him to go away, that I would sooner cut his throat than leave with him, that I wanted nothing better than to see him vanish from our campsite and go back to the land of civilization he was so proud of. Enraged that I had answered for him, my father charged and grabbed me, and we began to fight—I kicking and biting and he trying to subdue me, until the others stepped in and separated us. I looked at the Professor then and saw he was paler than ever, so I charged at him one last time and shoved him with the flats of my hands:

"Go to hell," I said, but of course, he didn't.

HE KNEW THE ART of waiting, you see. He had learned it from his years of study, from also the years of waiting to metamorphose into the person he wanted to be. Growing up in Iraq, he had known he wasn't meant to live the life of his ancestors, that he had a destiny unlike any of his peers'. But to get there he had had to wait, to keep his desires in check, to maintain a calm surface as he slowly reinvented himself, first in his own mind, and then in the eyes of others. So he knew how to wait and knew how to use logic to overcome simple desire and in the end, I think, he knew how to buy a heart that he could not win with love.

He stayed away from me a few weeks, went back to the town of Mosul and sat in a rented room recording his findings and conclusions. In his absence the tribe's elders had a chance to admonish my father for not having controlled me, to remind him of my age and my predicament and how the Professor, in spite of his looks and his affected manners, was probably the best chance I had at marriage. Those were the years of Kurdish despair— the years after the Second World War when every independence movement had failed and hundreds of thousands of Kurds from Turkey alone had abandoned home and country and headed for the West. In West Germany their numbers would become staggering, but they also went to other parts of Europe, some even to America. My father, who had lost his youth and his health in defense of his homeland, had less hope for the future than anyone else, and so he wasn't altogether averse to the idea of sending me to America except that he disliked the Professor as much as I did, and so he was relieved to see him go.

Just when we were about to break camp for the summer, the Professor appeared again with his notebooks and his interpreter in tow.

He had brought me gifts from the city—a set of gold bangles, a Western-style dress, a box of marzipan candy in pastel colors that he had bought from an Armenian bakery in Mosul. He came to our tent one early morning and offered the gifts to my father as if the two of them were old friends, as if he were performing the traditional duty of bringing souvenirs for friends and family after an extended journey. He took the gifts out one at a time and laid them on the rug my father was sitting on, explaining their value and their use, taking care to avoid even a glimpse in my direction. He did not, as is the custom in the East, proclaim modesty, did not insist that the offerings were of little value, that nothing he could bring my father would do justice to his rank or character. This was a Western trait, I would learn in time, but to my father and myself that day, and to all the tribespeople who saw the Professor interacting with us, he appeared arrogant. Then he took out his grandmother's ring.

He put his hand in his vest pocket and introduced an emerald the size of a gold coin. It was oval, set in diamonds, so clear and luminous, it could bring tears to a jeweler's eyes. It had been his grandmother's wedding ring, the Professor said, willed to him and collected upon her death. It had a tiny crack on the left side that was not readily noticeable and that affected the value of the stone, to be sure, but that made the ring even more of an heirloom to be treasured.

He set the ring before my father, on top of the dress that lay on the rug like a happy corpse, and then he stood up and announced that he would give my father and me a chance to think his proposal over and decide for ourselves what was best.

HE CAME BACK *twice more that winter, brought my father gifts, sat with my mother and spoke to her in the Aramaic of her childhood until he managed to get her attention. He told my father that human beings should not be tied to posts like animals, that in the absence of other means to control my mother's madness and save her from her snakes, he should use opium to calm her nerves and put her in sedation. He even convinced my father to give her back the brushes and the henna he had taken away long ago.*

Slowly, as the snow began to melt and the earth thawed, I felt my resolve weaken.

It wasn't that I stopped resenting the Professor, or that I wanted to leave the nomad's life I loved so much. It wasn't the ring he offered me, nor the life in America. It was the possibility, however faint, that through it all I could change the course of my own life, lessen the weight of my parents' sorrows.

I believed this, I think, and so did my mother. One early morning in the spring of 1951, she came into the tent where I was sleeping and took my hand. I was startled to find her so calm, shocked that she was able to get so close to me, to touch me without fear. I sat up and realized she wanted something, so I followed her out of the tent and saw the brush and the henna she had already set up.

Only this time it was my *hands she wanted to paint.*

She took my right hand in her left, knelt on the ground, and started to work. I bristled when the brush first touched my skin, but my mother smiled and continued. She painted with her head down and her shoulders haunched, her hair—long again but matted and dirty and in knots—falling onto her eyes and all around her face. I watched her hand move slowly above mine, tracing faint brown lines onto my skin. The images she drew became more vivid as the henna dried and settled, and after a while I began to detect the old picture and wondered what this meant—if my mother, in painting my hand instead of hers, was giving me her own legacy.

There she was—the woman at the center of the maze, surrounded and trapped and unable to leave. I gasped at the sight of her, closed my fist and tried to leave, but my mother held me by the wrist and forced my hand open again.

"Look," she said. "Look harder."

Through my tears I saw the line that ran from the middle of the painting down toward my wrist—a narrow river that led out to a sea and, beyond it, to places my mother had left unpainted.

"Look again," she said. "For you there is a way out."

WE WERE MARRIED *in 1951, in a Sunni Kurdish wedding at our campsite in the mountains of Iran. I wore a cherry-pink skirt long to my feet, a lavender top with silver embroideries, the traditional red veil over my face. The Professor came dressed in a white suit—the kind, he said, that men wore to the races in England.*

He had paid a traveling mullah to perform the ceremony. The mullah recited prayers in Arabic, which the Professor repeated easily because he was fluent in the language, and afterward he signed a marriage contract that stated our religion as Muslim. He did this with a sure hand—the Professor—using a fountain pen with a gold tip, but even as he put his name to the paper I knew he was hiding more than he revealed.

He never lied to us, you see. He never told my father or me that he was a Muslim, but he did not say he was a Jew either. He had the light skin and fine features of many Arab Jews, as my father had once remarked, and he came from Basra, where many of the merchants had historically been Jewish, so it wasn't inconceivable that he would be one himself, but he never admitted this and we never asked. He spoke of religion in abstract terms, never stating his origins except to say that, in leaving the East, he had left all its trappings behind.

In the tent he sat next to me on the rug, facing a mirror and a lamp, and he tried to be cordial and kind to the tribe's members who had crowded around to witness the marriage and who were singing and talking loudly and touching us to show affection. Afterwards he walked with me through the campgrounds as everyone sang prayers and carried the lamp and the mirror—symbols of light and good fortune—past every tent. His face was covered with a thin coat of perspiration, and his body shook with a slight tremor every time the crowd thickened or the singing became too loud, and he was careful not to stand too close to me, so that our bodies would not touch and our eyes would not lock.

I looked at him then and thought that he harbored a deep and bleeding secret; that I had bought into this secret by marrying him; that he would take me now into his house of silence and lock the door for good.

WE DROVE IN *a car to the Caspian shore, then took a train to Tehran. It was the first time I had been out of the mountains in my life, the first time I had ridden anything but a horse. It was also the first time I saw the sea.*

I was so terrified of my new surroundings, I stayed awake every night and wondered if I would survive this new world, if I would ever learn to sleep under brick and plaster, if those streets we crossed, those buildings we saw, would ever feel like home to me. I thought about my parents back home and wondered if my mother realized I was gone, if the other girls in the tribe still spoke of me, if my father was angry with me.

In Tehran we stayed in adjoining rooms in a hotel. By then we had been married two weeks already, and the Professor had not tried to touch me. He said I had nothing to worry about by being alone with him, that his purpose in marrying me was to raise a wife and not to obtain a lover. He talked to me without looking me in the eye, his gaze always fixed on an object directly behind me or next to my face. He went out and bought me Western-style clothes, two pairs of shoes, makeup, sent it all to my room with a woman he had hired to teach me how to dress and paint myself.

I told the woman at my door to go away and take the clothes with her. The Professor did not admonish me for this, but he came in later and hung the dresses in the closet next to my bed, arranged the shoes in their boxes on the floor. My wedding ring sat on the dresser. He touched it gently but did not ask why I would not wear it.

He called on me twice a day—mid-morning and at 8 p.m. He came in his suit and hat, sat in the only chair in the room,

185

asked if I was well, if I had slept enough, if I had enjoyed the meals he had sent to my room. I never complained to him, but I think he saw my sadness, and he did his best to respect it.

"In America," he said, "everything will be better. We will start your education, and I will teach you how to function in society."

On our last morning in Tehran, he came in with a small briefcase and said he needed to prepare me for the journey. He showed me a tube of lipstick, opened a shiny powder case, and a case of eyeliner he had bought. He wanted to paint my face, he said, so I would look older than my age as we passed customs in New York.

I sat on the edge of the bed and let him dab the lipstick on my lips, draw dark lines on the edges of my eyelids, darken my eyebrows with a pencil. He worked with the fascination of a child who is allowed into forbidden places for the first time, smiling faintly as he appraised his own creation, sighing with pleasure every time he opened one of those shiny silver cases that reminded him, he said, of the house of his own childhood—he had grown up among women, he said, all of them bored and nostalgic and always wishing they looked better.

When he was done he asked if I wanted to see myself in a mirror. He smiled when I refused.

"In time," he said, "you will grow to appreciate the value of illusion."

He opened his briefcase then and showed me his own passport, pointed to a page with my picture and a line of Latin letters.

"It says here you are nineteen years old," he said, then paused to make sure I understood.

"It's very important that you remember this, that you repeat it if anyone asks you the question."

He said that in the West marriage to a girl younger than eighteen was frowned upon and considered uncivilized. He said he had lied to the passport officer for the sake of convenience, but that he wanted me to think of myself as nineteen from that moment on.

"I have also stated that you are Christian by religion," he said. "In America no one trusts a person who does not belong to a church."

Then he said he had changed my name.

"Your given name," he said, "will not resonate with the people among whom you are going to live. It will make them think of you as foreign and therefore strange, and they will punish you for this in subtle ways you will not be able to overcome," he explained.

"So I picked a direct translation of your name," he said. "Blue. Like the waters of the Sea of Marmara, the most beautiful site in the world."

WE FLEW EIGHT HOURS *from Tehran to Germany, waited a day, took another flight for New York. I wore a long gray skirt I could hardly walk in, a beige silk shirt that felt slippery against my skin, black leather shoes that pinched my feet and made me feel as if I were about to topple over with every step. The moment the plane landed in New York, I told the Professor I wanted to go back. He smiled and took my hand, guided me gently through the aisles of seats, off the plane into the customs hall.*

The customs agent stared at the Professor's passport far too long. Then he raised his eyes and examined each of us as if trying to divine our relationship.

"Step aside," he said.

The Professor forced a smile and grabbed the rim of his hat tighter in his hands.

"He's going to ask questions," he whispered, clearly mortified.

We stood with our backs against the wall and waited. An hour later, having cleared everyone else, the agent leaned back in his chair and motioned for us to step forward.

He asked me something in English, and the Professor stepped in to explain that I did not understand the language. The agent turned his lips up and leaned farther back in his chair. It was clear he had not bought the Professor's story, that he was mocking us with his questions, enjoying the level of anxiety he caused in my husband. He asked the Professor a second, then a third question. He paused for a while, then, without turning around, called someone's name.

I watched as the Professor's eyelids fluttered and sweat beaded on the back of his neck. Another agent walked up. The first one showed him our passport and said what I assumed was our story. Rushing to convince him, the Professor pulled a notebook from the briefcase he had carried on the plane, pointed to various pages and explained things the agents did not seem to want to hear.

"University of Tennessee," the Professor said over and over, bristling with rage at the way he was being ignored. "Doctor of Linguistics."

The two men on the other side of the booth would not acknowledge the Professor any more. They were looking at me now, talking about me as if my husband did not exist. He must have found me in a slaves' bazaar somewhere in Arabia, the Professor later translated their words. He must have paid a good penny, must have blown a year's salary to get such a young girl.

The first agent closed our passport and threw it on the table in front of him. For a minute, no one moved. When he realized what the agent had done, the Professor reached with a tentative hand, touched the passport without daring to pick it up. His fingers rested on the little booklet and his eyes probed the agent's face. The second man let out a loud laugh and walked away. Afraid they would change their mind, the Professor snatched the passport off the table and stuffed it in his breast pocket.

"Very well," he mumbled, his voice barely audible.

The agent was still staring at us. The Professor put his hat back on, took me by the arm, and picked up his briefcase in his other hand. He had managed to take a few steps before his pride got the better of him and he stopped.

He let go of my hand, put his briefcase down on the ground, and walked back toward the agent.

He extended a proud hand at the man behind the desk.

"I thank you, sir," he said.

His hand remained extended before the agent.

"And I wish you a delightful day."

I remember marching with my husband through the customs hall, under the still-mocking gaze of the two agents, toward tinted-glass doors that led to the area where our bags had been left. A woman came toward us. She had long hair and white skin, and she wore strange clothes, and I would never have recognized her, I thought, would never have imagined I might know her except for the little man in the sad black suit who walked next to her still holding her arm.

IN KNOXVILLE, THE Professor *had reserved two rooms at the Andrew Johnson Hotel. He wanted us to spend the night there, he said, because it was already late when we arrived, and he did not wish for me to enter his house in darkness. It was an old superstition from the days of his childhood in the East—that one should not enter a home for the first time in fading light; that opening the door onto dusk would let in evil Jinns and jealous spirits.*

He called the hotel by its original name—The Tennessee Terrace—told me it was the tallest building in the city. He took me onto the roof and pointed to the Gay Street Bridge, the Tennessee Theater, the university campus which he said had grown from one building into dozens. We went to dinner at the S & W. We were the only customers that night. I remember we sat at a table amid dozens of empty others, spread across a checkered terrazzo floor with inlaid wood and marble, beneath a giant staircase with ornate bronze railings. We ate quietly, under the gaze of a row of waiters who stood, white napkins in hand, watching us. By the time we finished most of the waiters had gone home.

I loved this town from the very start.

I loved its quiet sidewalks, its neglected parks, the spartan gravesites of foolhardy soldiers who had died for the losing cause. I loved its dust-smeared windows, its ghost-ridden hotels, its kudzu-filled backyards. I felt as if I had stepped into a fairy-tale world where all the women were asleep in beds of feathers, and the prince who was destined to awaken them had lost his way in a maze of brown lines drawn upon a snow-white hand.

———

In the morning, we walked from Hill Street down to Fort Sanders, then onto Clinch. There was a house with blue paint and white wooden railings, a Victorian frame with a rounded porch and a turret. The paint, then, was not chipped, the railings not broken. The porch was lined with flower pots that the Professor paid a student of his to water twice a week. The yard was well kept and green.

It was the house of the Professor's dreams before he lost the will to sleep.

He went in ahead of me to open windows that had been shut for months.

"Come inside," he invited. "Feel at home."

I walked into a place of velvet drapes and Tiffany lamps, down-filled armchairs and silk-upholstered daybeds. I saw cabinets full of china, drawers filled with starched linen, a dining table set with silver candlesticks.

The kitchen counter displayed a hundred different spices, each measured and labeled and arranged by color. The powder-room downstairs had wallpaper made of fabric. There was a grand piano in the living room, a hand-carved wooden desk in the Professor's study.

Upstairs in the bedroom, a four-poster bed with a dark mahogany frame sat under a sheet of mosquito netting that rose around it like a pyramid. The ceiling fan was painted in soft pink. A wind chime on the balcony hung perfectly still.

"This is where you'll dress in the morning," the Professor showed me around the bedroom. "This is where you'll bathe."

In the bathroom was a porcelain tub with enamel faucets, a

white-and-yellow-tiled floor, a set of towels stacked on a brass stool. I sat on the edge of the tub and turned on the water. I watched it pour out, imagined standing naked in the tub, water filling the space around my ankles, rising to cover my legs.

Back in the bedroom I opened the window, pushed back the mosquito netting around the bed, and lay down with my clothes on. I listened to the water still pouring in the tub.

I dreamed that the water filled the tub as I slept, that it spilled onto the tile floor, seeped under the door and into the bedroom. It flowed slowly, consistently, until it had covered the entire bedroom floor, and then it began to drip through the wood and into the rooms below. I dreamt that it poured down the stairs and through windows, filling the house from the bottom up, rising around the dining room table, across the hand-carved desk, over the grand piano. When it reached my bed, I remained asleep till it had covered my body and risen to the ceiling. Then slowly I opened my arms and started to swim.

I swam through the flood I had created—the white mosquito netting gathered around me like a veil—toward the front door. I went past the Professor who stood terrified in his black suit, his features distorted by the weight of the water, his mouth moving in a plea for help. On the other side of the door was a dry, quiet town with wide streets and empty buildings. I swam past my husband and into the town, leaving him to drown in the waters of the Sea of Marmara.

FOR YEARS AFTER *I arrived here, my husband spent each morning educating me.*

He taught me how to sit in a chair and use utensils at the table, how to make a bed and hang my clothes in a closet, how to do my hair the Western woman's way, and how to iron my clothes. We sat in the downstairs study—the Professor in a high-backed chair that made him look even smaller than he was, across from a desk on which he spread books and papers meant to teach me to read and write English, to speak properly, to carry myself as the wife of a distinguished gentleman of letters. The lessons were long and tedious, but he was always patient, and he never scolded me for my mistakes. At the end of the morning, he packed his notebooks and put away the pens, told me he was impressed with my progress, and left for the university.

In his absence I roamed the house alone and wondered at the unforgiving order of the objects that filled every room, the silence that ruled not just the house but the entire town, the people who strode past our windows, walking slowly, as if without a destination or hope of ever arriving. I paused before the mirrors and looked at my own, now unfamiliar, image, repeated out loud the words I had learned that day and let their echo—so foreign it made my heart ache—rest in my ears. I touched the hard surfaces of wood and glass and marble in the house and imagined the soft earth, the emerald grasslands I had recently left behind. I imagined my father drinking in a corner of our tent, wondered if he thought of me, if he wished, as I did, that we could undo the past, reach for each other, make peace. I wondered if my mother still painted her hands, looked at my own palms and tried to imagine the lines she had drawn there and that had long since faded. I wondered about the snakes in her mind.

The Professor returned home at exactly ten minutes to seven, having walked the fifty-minute distance from the university, and put his hat on the chair directly next to the front door. In the kitchen he asked that I watch and learn as he prepared our meal—French cuisine, he said, the finest in the world. After dinner he retreated into his study to work, and I went to bed alone.

He came in late at night, changed in the next room, slipped quietly into bed. Then he lay with his eyes open and stared at the ceiling. Even when he fell asleep he looked half awake, charged to the point of paralysis, afraid of his own thoughts. And he never touched me.

He kept me in a state of suspended doubt, never declaring his intentions or explaining his acts. He spent hours taking care of the smallest details—the edge of the crease in his trousers, the sharpness of the blade he used to shave his face, the curve in the letters he taught me to write. But he did not address the larger, more important questions—why he had married me, what he expected our life together should be, why, having managed to shape me into the image he preferred, he did not show the slightest intention of claiming a spouse's rights from me.

He is a quiet man, my husband. He carries his silence like a box of treasures—secrets resting in the dark, gleaming and radiant and yet full of danger. He used to say that man was created to contemplate and to learn, that too much speech, unnecessary speech, spoils one's chance for understanding. That's *why he studies dead and dying languages, he claims: to dis-cover the mystery of words no longer spoken.*

That's why, too, he once took an interest in the phenomenon of "talking in tongues," why he started attending church ser-vices in areas where he knew Holy Rollers gathered. It wasn't religion that he pursued or believed in. In all the years I have known him, first, when he denied his Jewishness even to him-self, and later, when he secretly embraced it while still hiding it from the world—in all these years the Professor has insisted that God does not exist and that faith belongs to the stupid masses. But he was fascinated by the Church of God and by the principle that one sign of receiving the Holy Spirit was the ability to talk in tongues. Outside the church, people dismissed the practice as the act of lunatics uttering incomprehensible sounds. A language, they said, was defined by its capacity to convey meaning. Anything else was noise.

The Professor, though, thought differently. As a man who spoke many languages, he knew the mind's capacity to store words and tongues, then to draw on them at the appropriate oc-casion. What if, he wondered, the Holy Rollers' "tongues" were not meaningless sounds, but actual languages—ancient ones no longer comprehensible to ordinary men? What if our subconscious minds were capable of storing language as our genes store physical and emotional traits? What if, in a state of heightened sensitivity, the believers were able to tap into that repository, recapture the memory of tongues spoken by their ancestors?

What if, the Professor asked, the Holy Rollers held the key to understanding man's capacity for language?

His colleagues at the University heard him pose these questions, and smiled as if to imply that the Professor was strange, that one could not expect much more of a creature who had come from Egypt, or Iraq, or another one of those places that never truly exist for the West. Feeling their condescension, the Professor became more determined to prove the validity of his questions, and so he set out to find Little Sam Jenkins and test his own theories.

Little Sam, of course, disliked him immediately.

He disliked all outsiders, it is true, but he tolerated most of them well enough, because he felt he could impress them with his powers of oration and his unwavering faith. Even the hecklers who raided his services often went back convinced they had been in the presence of a holy power. He catered to the reporters because he wanted the fame they could bring him, and accepted the doctors because he enjoyed seeing their baffled faces once they were through examining his snakes and declared that the animals had not been defanged and that their poison was indeed potent. But the Professor was unlike anyone who had ever attended Sam's services, and this alone made him a target and so he was asked to leave, by the church's deacons at first and later by Sam himself. When he went back again, Sam told him he wasn't welcome. The Professor offered to leave his tape recorder and his notebooks in the car, but Sam wouldn't let him in.

Returning from that visit, my husband lay on our bed with his clothes on and his eyes open. For a long time, he was silent. Then he said he was going to take me to Sam's next meeting.

He was going to use me to make his way into the church, hold me before Jenkins like a winning card in a high-stakes game of wills, but it never dawned on him that he was taking me to a place from which he would not be able to take me back.

He did not believe in putting passion above reason, you see, and it did not occur to him that his wife might do so now that she had been educated and trained and exposed to the ways of civilized society.

THAT FIRST DAY *in church, I understood nothing of what Sam said, could not comprehend his mountaineer's accent or the culture and way of thinking that led to the pronouncements he made. But I did recognize the snakes. To everyone else they were the personification of evil, symbols of their poverty, their helplessness, their sense of impotence against the world. To me, they were my mother's madness come to life, her fears captured and placed in a box.*

I remember walking into church that day and seeing the preacher turn red and flushed the moment the Professor walked up to the front of the men's section with tape recorder in hand. Sam raised his Bible in the air and was ready to attack the Professor with his words when he saw me. Slowly, the Bible came down again. Sam looked from me to the Professor and back. He must have known everyone in the church was watching him. He put his Bible on the pulpit, cleared his throat, and began to preach.

I sat through the service and all of Sam's testimony thinking only of the snakes. I remember Sam opened a box and let the first snake wrap itself around his arm like a bracelet, then took it off and wound it around his head like a crown. He looked at me—glassy eyed but alert, his lips drained of color, his ears a bright, angry red. He wanted to see my reaction, I thought, to see if I was frightened, or excited, if I looked away in weakness. When I didn't flinch he reached down into the box and took out a fistful of smaller snakes, held his right hand out with the serpents trapped between his fingers and waved them at the church as he talked. The Professor was frozen in his seat, at once terrified and thrilled, wanting to save himself but also to record every observation he made about the worshipers' behavior and language. All around us people were making loud clacking sounds, and someone in the back had started playing an accordion, but Little Sam was neither talking in tongues nor singing with the rest of the congregation.

He dropped the snakes from his hand and let them slither toward the church members. Then he unwound the rattler from his head and came toward me. He was walking slowly, holding the snake in both hands with his arms outstretched—an offering, I thought, an invitation. The noise around us died down.

Adam, I know about seduction.

I have heard its silent music, walked its empty, echoing chambers.

I knew that Sam was tempting me, that he wanted to seduce me with the mystery of his faith, the danger of his actions. I knew this would be a fight to the finish—against the snakes, against him, against my husband who had brought me here for reasons that had nothing to do with faith.

I reached out and took the snake from Sam.

I WENT BACK *with the Professor every week, and for a while the believers resisted us. But Little Sam wanted me there and his will prevailed over the suspicions of others, and so I was allowed to stay. I was given snakes to handle, and soon enough I managed to make everyone forget my husband and his tape recorder and all the science he had tried to bring to the church. The harder I fought the snakes, the stronger I felt and the more the believers brought faith in me.*

Little Sam was pleased with this in the beginning. He took me under his wing, spoke about me in his sermons, pointed to me as an example of how even city souls could be saved. In church, his eyes were always seeking me and his hands were grasping for me, and I could tell he wanted me—that his lust for the flesh had not been subdued by his love of the Spirit— but I stayed away from him and braced for the fight I knew was imminent. The more I resisted, the harder he tried.

My husband saw this, of course, as did all the others, and after a while he decided he had had enough of the Holiness Church and its practitioners. The "tongues" the believers spoke, he concluded, were nothing but noise. The faith they professed was only the poor man's opium. My handling the snakes was an invitation for death, one that he could not in good conscience allow. He told me we were not going back.

For the first time since I had married the Professor, I disobeyed him.

I told him I liked handling snakes, liked the kindness and friendship that the believers offered one another and that a few of them had begun to offer me. I said I would follow my conscience, whether the Professor approved of my choices or not. I was nineteen years old, I said, and ready to take charge of my own life.

The Professor sat in his chair and examined me with the same expression he used to read his manuscripts. He was not angry, not perplexed, not even jolted by my rebellion.

"You're trying to test your strength," he explained, "and you want to punish yourself for leaving your mother with the snakes."

The next time I heard Little Sam was preaching near Knoxville, I asked Anne Pelton to take me.

Little Sam did not miss the meaning of my act, of course—that I had come to church without my husband or his blessing—and to him this meant only that I should give my body to him as I had given my soul to his church. For a year, he pursued me. When I refused him, he fought. When it became clear that I would fight back, he went to war.

He began to tell the believers that I was an unholy woman who had no real faith in the Lord, that I had been sent to church by the devil. He said that I wasn't a woman at all, that real women would have children in a marriage. He said I was the devil himself, that no one but the devil could tempt men with her looks as I did. Anne Pelton and a few others tried to speak in my defense, but Little Sam was stronger and more determined than the rest of them and so the battle went on.

I don't know why I stayed in church those early years. I didn't deny Sam's accusations, you see. They were true enough, and I had no interest in portraying myself as anything other than what I was. I don't believe in Jesus and never did; don't believe in Holiness either. I was there only to fight the snakes. But before I knew it—before I could understand what had happened—I found myself surrounded by loving people whose friendship brought me comfort.

Sam must have known this. It must have scared him to see me settle among his people so well. One day, in Harlan, he stood up and pointed to me in church, told me I was a temptress and a devil. I had been in his church for three years already. He said I could never come back.

I WENT HOME *dejected, and began to wonder if I had come to the end of my hope—the place from which my mother could not escape and that had driven her mad with anguish. I had given myself to the Professor thinking that the road that led out of the East might lead away from regret, given myself to the church thinking that the signs the believers followed might lead to wider, more open passages. All those years traveling along the streets of my mother's dreams, alone but for the memory of her need, I had told myself that the price I paid for the journey was worth the prospect of arrival. But my marriage to the Professor had only brought me to a house full of silence, and my battle with Sam Jenkins had ended in defeat, and so I thought that I must start again—a new page with new lines, and this time, I would draw them all myself.*

I told the Professor I wanted a child.

It was an outlandish notion, because he and I had never made love in all the time we were married, and because he was already old—fifty-five in 1959—with no desire to act young. The very suggestion of a child made him shudder in disbelief, then stare at me as if to try and fathom my motivation.

He told me that my desire for a child was unreasonable and incorrect. He said I was trying to absolve myself of a misplaced sense of guilt toward my mother, that I wanted to compensate with a child for the loss of the church.

He said this with a tinge of anger, as if trying to contain his alarm at my request, and then he looked away, slightly past my face and into a void where I knew I was not allowed.

I waited a few months, then asked again.

He said that this was a request he would never be able to grant, that he expected me to defer to him without question. He acted as if I had crossed a line drawn in blood—a wide, red border across which I was not allowed.

I told him I was adamant, that I had lived by his rules for six years and wanted to create some of my own.

He said it was in my best interest not to perpetuate an argument I was not going to win, that he had given the matter deep and analytical thought and did not need to explain further.

He said that having children was a choice and not an obligation, that at any rate, a woman with madness in her genes was best advised not to procreate.

"Any child of ours," he said, "any creature made of our blood, will be doomed from the start."

I knew he was talking about more than my mother's illness, that he feared a greater demon, was hiding from a bigger foe. Suddenly I wanted to know what it was that he had kept from me all these years—what deep and driving secret he was guarding with this silence. I asked him why he had never married before, why he had not wanted children even in his youth. I asked why he had spent twenty-five years in Europe only to abandon his life and start again in America, why he had never kept in contact with anyone from his past, why he had come to the East, a place so far from his new home, to search for a wife. The more I asked, the more he refused to answer.

So I crawled into bed, naked to the waist, and asked again.

WHEN HE FOUND out I was pregnant, the Professor pleaded with me to abort. He took me to a doctor in town, showed me the office which was clean and sanitary and private, and asked the doctor to explain to me how the procedure would be done quickly and with little danger, how no one but a nurse would know what had happened in that room, how afterward I would have years to conceive again if I wished. Coming back from the doctor's office, the Professor stopped at the McClung department store across from the library, and told me I could buy anything I wished, anything at all as long as I agreed not to have the child.

My daughter had blue-black hair, purple eyes, Arab skin. She looked like those pictures you see of exotic children in foreign places with names you can't pronounce, those girls with the piercing eyes and striking features who capture a photojournalist's imagination and end up on the cover of magazines that write about countries you never knew existed.

When she was born the Professor came into my room at the hospital and brought a bouquet of violets, a jug of water, a silver mirror, and a gold coin. In another world—the one he thought he had left behind—the water symbolized a clear conscience, the mirror stood for luck, the coin represented wealth. He stood by my bed and stared at the baby far too long, then caressed her tiny face with the side of his finger. He was sad but not angry, resigned but not resentful. He had done his best to keep her from being born, done his best, once he realized I was not going to lose her, to keep himself from being drawn into our world. Now that she was here, he accepted her without bringing faith in her presence.

"Give her a name," he said, "that you can easily forget."

I did not buy into his prophecy, did not think for a moment I was going to lose that child.

I nursed her until she was a year old, let her sleep in my bed even after she stopped looking for me at night. I let her follow me into every corner of the house, let her talk to me until her voice filled every silence the Professor had so carefully created. He was back in his own universe by then, reading ancient manuscripts and learning new tongues, trying his best to remain oblivious to his child. I saw him only during our morning lessons and then at night, when he sat alone to eat in the dining room while my daughter and I played upstairs.

I would take her hands into my own and place them on my eyes.

"Make a wish," I would say, "and I will imagine it to life."

She died when she was five years old.

IT WAS FALL. *We were burning leaves in the yard. My daughter wore a long dress and no shoes. I was watching her from the kitchen, saw her go up to look at the flames.*

I remember thinking I should stop her.

"Come back," I thought, and I went to the door to call her.

She was singing a tune, petting Mrs. Roscoe's cat that had wandered into our yard. It was a quiet afternoon and the sky was clear, and I loved looking at her, loved seeing the beautiful, blessed creature that she was.

The cat walked away. My daughter made a half turn to follow it. The hem of her skirt caught fire.

FOR A YEAR *after she died, I did not leave the house.*

I couldn't tell day from night and didn't feel cold or hunger and I saw no one—not the well-wishers who called those first few weeks, nor the doctor who came to give me pills, nor even the Professor, who sat by me as if afraid I would never emerge from the darkness.

I remember being aware of his presence but not of his grief, wondering later at the strength that allowed him to put aside his own needs and tend to mine. Toward the end of that year Anne Pelton came to see me. She brought a plate of home-baked cookies and a Bible, knelt beside the chair in my bed-room and asked if she might pray for me.

I wanted to tell her NO, but I did not have the strength, or the courage perhaps, to turn her away. When I didn't answer she bowed her head and started to pray in that slow, melodic rhythm that moves the mountaineers' words, and after a while the very softness of her voice, the conviction with which she spoke filled the emptiness in my room, pulled me out of the silence, and made me want to hear more.

"Pray with me," she said, and I found myself kneeling next to her, looking down at the designs on the rug and repeating the words she uttered.

Maybe this is what faith is: a woman with a plate of cookies and an old book, a pair of hands that fold before you in the dark, a voice that asks you to believe.

———

I prayed that a man would ride into my town on a dark wind, bringing with him the dust of a thousand moons, spreading it by the handful through the narrow alleys of the labyrinth of longing I could no longer escape, setting to light a darkened passage that may lead to Hope.

BEFORE DAWN SHE MOVED AGAINST THE SHEETS, PULLED herself away from him, and rose from the bed. She had been lying on the right side of his body, her head resting between his chest and collarbone, and when she left, he felt a sting of cold air on his skin.

He kept his eyes closed and listened as she reached for her dress in the dark. He imagined the white fabric gliding across the front of her thighs and up around her stomach and her chest. He wanted to reach for her across the bed, run his hand over the places he saw in his mind, pull her back to him. She left without a word.

In the hallway below, Isiah Frank lit a lamp and talked to her in a whisper. Then he unlocked the door and let her slip quietly back into her life.

Adam lay faceup on the bed and smoked until the air became murky and his throat shut down with the bitterness of the to-bacco. He imagined Blue walking alone through the streets of Knoxville: her feet were cold and bare against the asphalt and her body moved effortlessly in the dark, and the color of her eyes changed from a deep indigo to an almost transparent sapphire with the rising light.

Without her, Adam's room seemed hollow and dark and hungry—an echo chamber where her words, the memory of her touch, hung like fireflies in mid-flight.

He got up and put on the first shirt he found, left his bed unmade, grabbed his car keys and money. He felt at once elated and lost, appeased and angry.

The Dutch boys were nowhere to be found. Isiah Frank was downstairs in the living room, wiping the dust off his glass animals and speaking to his cat as he worked.

On Gay Street Adam went into Nate's—the city's only deli—and bought a cup of coffee that he would drink in the car. He pulled into Henley, under the freeway overpass, and out toward Highway 75 going north. Behind him, mist hung low over the river, and the mountains were a thousand shades of green, and the earth was a bright, golden rust the color of Blue's hair.

He drove through the mountains all day and came back when it was dark. For a while he parked his car across the Gay Street Bridge and watched its lights reflected on the river, the shadows of people traversing it. Then he went back to the house and waited for Blue.

She came up to him from behind, stood so close, he could feel her chest rise with every breath. Naked, she pressed herself against his back, reached around him and unbuttoned his shirt. When he turned to face her, she kissed his mouth, the length of his neck, the edge of his shoulder.

"I always knew you would come," she said, and now he believed her.

In September the heat suddenly let up. The air, which had hung low and heavy through August, became crisp almost overnight, and the sky took on the transparent clarity of glass. The leaves began to turn, and the river rose from its lethargic state, and the light became vivid and sharp and animate.

The Dutch boys left their luggage in the boardinghouse and went on a monthlong drive through the American South. Isiah Frank unpacked two trunks full of costumes from Shakespearean plays he had produced at the university, and hung them out in the yard to air. Then he dressed up in a different costume each day, and acted the part.

"*Life* should be as grand as theater," he said as if to an audience in his thrall.

In the archives room of the *Knoxville News Sentinel,* Adam sat looking through stacks of microfilm on a badly lit monitor. He searched for references to Sam Jenkins and Blue, for a possible mention of his mother or Rose. He asked the attendant—a lanky old man with a faded green T-shirt—what he remembered having heard or read, whom he recommended Adam talk to. Mostly, he looked at the July 26 issue of the newspaper, where Little Sam's death and funeral were first announced.

On the very top of the page was a picture of Sam in his younger days. He wore a white shirt buttoned to the collar, stared at the camera with tiny eyes that almost looked frightened. His face was red and swollen from too much exposure to the elements and too many snakebites, and his ears were too large for his head, but there was nothing in the way he looked, nothing Adam could read in his face, to indicate the kind of man he was.

Below Sam's picture was a smaller one of the shed where he had been conducting services when he was bitten. It was a crumbling structure with a tin roof and board siding badly in need of repair, set in the midst of an empty field, with nothing else in sight.

A third picture, taken after Sam's funeral, showed the members of his family who had come to Florida to pay their last respects. They had driven all night, the newspaper said—four truckloads of relatives from Tennessee and beyond— just to attend the funeral and then drive home again to be at work the next day. No one had handled snakes at the burial, but a country music band had played and afterward, food had been served.

Adam had seen these pictures and the article several times, but he kept going back to them. With all of his power to conquer the souls of men and to resist the devil, Little Sam Jenkins had died in poverty and without much pretension. With all the sins he had committed against his family, he had been buried by two dozen loyal offspring.

The family portrait showed fourteen adults and three small children. They all wore neat clothes and church shoes. Some of the women bore the wide frame and the fleshy face of Esther Parker. One of them had dark wavy hair and looks reminiscent of the German wife with the Gypsy curse. A man in the back row, dressed in a light-colored suit and tie, had Sam's cauliflower ears.

One of Sam's daughters, herself a matriarch in a church in Kentucky, had recalled to the reporter present at the scene that her father had been so pure "he never even drank coffee."

***

Time and again Adam tried to guess which one of the women would have made such a remark. It was impossible to tell, of course, just as it was impossible to divine what any of those people thought at the moment directly following Sam's burial. What Adam knew for certain, what he kept wanting to remind himself every time he probed the papers, was that he had never belonged in that picture—regardless of his ancestry or the place or his birth—that he may have carried Sam's blood in his veins but had never shared his spirit or the dreams and desires of his other children, that he may have been conceived of Sam's flesh but would never perpetuate the legacy of lies and treason Sam had cast into the lives of his believers. Adam was, as Rose Watkins had often told him with contempt, a true bastard seed.

HE WENT TO see Anne Pelton again.

It was Monday, and he'd spent the morning driving through Lynch and its surrounding towns. Along the 63, the mountains jutted into and away from the road like jagged carvings of dense forest on a black diamond soil. Up the 25 and towards Cumberland Gap, the interstate grew wider, then narrow again. He had gone past Pineville, through Harlan, and into Lynch. He was watching the abandoned coal tipples, the empty barns with crumbling roofs, the slowly decaying crosses planted sporadically in the ground.

Lynch was a ghost town covered under an avalanche of dust and coal residue. Driving up its only street, Adam peered into the fronts of wooden cabins and homes, wondering what life had been like here in his own childhood, where Little Sam Jenkins had pitched his tent for the ten-day revival that had culminated in Adam's conception.

He was so engrossed in his search, so moved by the emptiness of this town where his own destiny had been shaped, he did not notice at first the silver pickup that had pulled up behind him and was now on his tail.

It was a wide and ancient vehicle, dented all over, its wheels smooth as skin. The driver wore a checkered gray-and-red shirt and leaned on his right elbow as he drove with his left hand. He stayed a hair's breadth away from Adam's rear bumper, and he had fixed his eyes on Adam's image in the rearview mirror. He must be a local, Adam thought. He had not recognized Adam's car as one of their own, figured it had to be a rental because it was new and had out-of-state plates. He was giving a warning, nudging Adam off the street and back toward the highway, where he felt strangers belonged. He stayed on Adam's tail until he had pulled back on the 25 and was heading south toward Harlan.

Anne Pelton lived in a one-bedroom house off an unpaved street across from the True Church of the Lord Jesus in Pineville, Kentucky. She was a tiny woman with a wide flat face marked with spider veins that loomed just under her skin. She had wrinkles around her eyes and her lips, but she looked younger than her seventy years, moved with a light step and an easy flexibility. Her hair, straight and shiny, was always tied in a ponytail that reached down above her hips, and she wore tennis shoes even to church. Her only downfall was her eyes: they were small and watery, forever squinting as if to bring the world into focus. Long ago, a preacher had told her that wearing eyeglasses might be interference with the work of the Lord.

Through her kitchen window she heard Adam's car approach, but she waited until he had walked up to the door before she responded. Even with her failing eyes she could see that he was paler, thinner, more intense than when she had seen him last.

"The Lord has blessed me with another visit from you," she said, and invited him in.

A tiny living room with faded green carpeting led to a small alcove that Anne used as her kitchen. There was a wood-burning stove, a refrigerator, a sink with a chipped surface revealing rusted metal underneath. Pale yellow curtains—hand-sewn with large stitches—hung at the window overlooking the road.

Adam sat at the folding aluminum table with a cracked vinyl top, and watched as Anne filled a kettle with water, set out two mugs, and prepared tea. She had her back to Adam as she worked, but her manner was easy and calm and welcoming in a way that disarmed him. Without asking, she put four spoonfuls of sugar in his mug, then put the tea in front of him and smiled.

"My husband only drank coffee," she said, easing into her chair, "but even when he was alive I never gave up my tea."

The table was so small, their hands almost touched when they reached for the tea. There was a phone on the counter next to the stove, but no radio or television—the devil's agents—in the house. On the window ledge, next to the yellow curtains, small glass bottles filled with liquid were lined up in the sun.

Anne Pelton was the child of a migrant coal worker, and of a Czech immigrant he had met at a coal camp in Virginia. Her parents had traveled everywhere by foot, living in the wild and bathing in ravines and lakes between jobs. Together they had borne thirteen children and put most of them to work in the camps. But in the later years of their lives, her father had become sick with black lung disease and her mother had lost the strength to keep working, and so they had given their four youngest children to strangers: they had placed each child in a different home, with elderly couples who needed a young body able to work.

Anne had been given away at age eight, but her new family had beaten her mercilessly and given her little to eat, and so she had run away after three years. From age eleven to thirteen, she had managed to work in the camps disguised as a boy, but when she was too old to pass undetected, she took to the road as her mother and father had done. One winter in Floyd County, she had spent three days walking alone, and she had nearly frozen to death when a man in his mid-forties stopped his truck and picked her up. She had traveled with the man to this same house, and married him a week later.

"I've been hoping you would call again," she told Adam. "I've been praying for you since you arrived, and I've prayed more since I realized who you are."

It bothered him that she was so direct, so presumptuous, almost, in extending her prayers. He took a sip of his tea and forced himself to push ahead.

"Blue tells me you knew my mother," he said.

Her name melted on his tongue like sugar. He loved the taste of it, the way it floated into the air and filled the space between him and Anne, the freedom to speak about her as if she—as if *they*—were real.

Anne must have been anticipating the question.

"Your mother was a few years younger than me," she said, purposely ignoring the reference to Blue, "but for many years I wanted to be just like her.

"She never came to church except to cause trouble, and that was all right by me, because I liked the way she dressed and talked and the way she wasn't afraid of the preachers or the church members or even Rose."

Anne Pelton had not been born to Holiness, Adam knew. She had been introduced to the church by her husband, and for a long time she had resisted the faith and refused to handle snakes. She was her husband's second wife, raising his children after their mother had run away and left them, and she had had time to have only one child of her own before Buford Pelton was bitten by a snake and died in Alabama. After that she had undergone a transformation, and in time embraced the church in earnest.

"The other women in these parts were jealous of her, of course: she was pretty, and she knew what to do with a man, and our husbands couldn't keep their hands off her. But I liked watching her. She was so different from Rose—almost like they weren't of the same blood, like she had landed in Rose's womb by mistake."

As she talked, the smile on her face widened and became more distant—as if she were transformed by her own words and the image she described for Adam.

Adam thought of the flowers Clare had in her hand that last time she came to see him in the orphanage: she had picked them off the side of the road, and they had wilted by the time she arrived, but their colors had been cast in his memory forever. Even after she had abandoned her child, Clare had continued to cling to an ideal of beauty and refinement so at odds with the reality of her life.

"People said Clare had taken after her dad," Anne mused, "but I think she was just different all around—not like anyone who should have been born in these parts."

Adam looked at Anne then and thought how gentle she was when describing Clare, how unlike the believers he had known in his childhood, who had judged Clare and her offspring so harshly. Anne, too, had been given away as a child, raised by strangers, brought into the church as an outsider who would have to prove her loyalty or leave. Still, her spirit had remained fluid and pure and devoid of judgment. She made it easy for Adam to turn around, to look back and see Clare and Rose and all the people he had once loved.

Anne was looking directly at him, not squinting at all, about to say something of consequence.

"I don't know why your mother gave you up," she said, "but I know why she killed herself."

On the windowsill, light was hitting the bottles with the clear liquid, exposing the tiny white flakes—feathers—that gave away their content: strychnine, mixed with water and ready to drink.

Anne caught Adam's eye on the bottles.

"My husband drank carbolic acid pure," she explained. "That's what Sam liked, too, but I prefer strychnine because it burns less going down."

She watched Adam's face for a reaction. He was thinking how strange it was that a woman as gentle and easy as Anne could inflict such violence on her own body, how someone as practical as she could buy into the preachers' lies. That's what he never could understand about the snake handlers, what drove him to condemn the faith and its practitioners.

She read his mind.

"It's not about the messenger," she said softly. "It's about the *message*."

He almost lit a cigarette right there in her kitchen, but he could hear the wheezing of her lungs—the result of breathing coal dust her whole life—and he stopped himself. He drank the tea she had poured for him, savored its sweetness, the simplicity with which it had been offered. She got up and poured more tea for them both. It was past noon, and she must have felt hungry or at least obligated to offer her guest some food, because she

221

went to the narrow cabinet in the wall and opened the door. There were cans of vegetables on the shelves, a box of oatmeal, a bag of rice. On the very bottom shelf were two snake boxes with wire mesh on top.

Anne took out a box of crackers and put it on the table in front of Adam. She caught him staring at the snake boxes—one painted a vivid blue, the other dark wood—noticed he was listening for the sound of the serpents inside. She went back to the cabinet, and instead of closing the door took out the blue box.

She placed it, still closed, on the table before Adam.

He held his breath and tried to stay calm, but he felt an almost primal fear—something larger and more devastating than he had ever experienced—and he threw back his chair and jumped to his feet. Through the wire mesh, he could see a yellow copperhead with a flat head, and a gray-and-black rattler next to it. He felt his heart race in terror, felt his body grow cold—a small boy asleep in a bed somewhere in the darkness of a derailed train car, with snake boxes under his bed and the fear of his mother's departure in his heart.

Anne Pelton saw Adam's reaction and became agitated herself. Wanting to prove he had nothing to fear, she opened the snake box, slipped her fingers under the copperhead's mouth, and gently pulled it up. She tapped the snake on the head, as if in greeting, then laid it back down.

She had miscalculated Adam's willingness to get close, and now, she realized, it was too late to win him back.

She saw that he was leaving, and she followed him to the door. She knew he would never return to see her again, and she felt sorry she had scared him off. Just before he left, she put her hand on his arm and stopped him.

"Your mother came into Sam's church one day with her new husband," she said.

She wanted to give him this—her last memory of Clare—whether he wanted it or not. It was like a keepsake she had guarded for too long, a duty she felt she should discharge.

"Sam was married to Peg then, who had a wooden leg, just like Clare's husband, except Peg used to take her leg off and leave it under her bed at night where she slept. I remember thinking how ironic that both your mother and Sam had run all their lives, only to end up married to people who could barely walk.

"She sat down and let Sam preach the whole afternoon. She'd been gone for a few years by then, and now she looked old and not at all pretty like she used to. Sam walked by her a few times, but he didn't attack her at all or even look at her in a special way. When the service was done, she stood up, and I saw that she was crying."

Suddenly, Adam knew how the story would end.

"He hadn't attacked Clare at all, you see," Anne said. "He hadn't said a word about her the whole time she was there. That's what killed her: that Little Sam, who never could look away from her, didn't recognize her enough to attack."

HE STOPPED asking questions.

It was a mistake, he knew—the kind of mistake he would live to regret, the kind that had cost him in the past, every time he had believed in his mother, or Rose, or all the seeming certainties of a life where, in the end, no one could be trusted. Maybe that's why he had been able to live dangerously for so long, why he had never sought the certainties of a conventional existence, why he was so drawn to Blue who gave herself so willingly to the unknown, who embraced death so easily, yielded to Adam so entirely.

Or maybe it wasn't the thrill of the unknown at all. Maybe it was her hands that were so small and frail and helpless sometimes, her smile that reminded him of all the lost children he had ever seen wandering the world, the impression he had that he was her last and only hope.

He called Chicago to say he would be staying in Knoxville for a while longer. He said he was still working on Sam's story, that he would write it in due time, that he would call again when he was ready. The silence at the other end might have meant he had already lost his job, but he did not stop to wonder. He wanted Blue more than anything he had ever wanted in life and he was willing to risk his job, give up the principles he had so far lived by, just to be near her, to turn a corner at night and know he would see her, waiting for him, her hands reaching toward him.

He didn't want to think that those might be a killer's hands, the hands of a woman who betrayed her husband and her God and all the laws of her church and her people. He didn't want to think that she belonged to another man, that Adam was crossing boundaries he had never imagined he would cross. Isiah Frank raised a sarcastic eyebrow at him every time Adam went by, and the old ladies at Nate's whispered to one another whenever he walked in for coffee, and Mrs. Roscoe bristled when he ran into her on the street, but all that, in the end, was irrelevant.

In mid-September Isiah Frank counted the weeks Adam had been a guest and handed him an invoice.

"Thirty-one days," he said, smiling triumphantly.

They had met on the staircase. Adam took the piece of paper from him and kept walking down. Isiah watched him descend the steps.

"Interesting town," he called when Adam had almost reached the door. "Grows on you like kudzu."

Adam hesitated, then started to leave again.

"The only trouble is," Isiah dug, "the kudzu can cover a whole lot. Even corpses."

HE HAD DINNER at Lucille's, walked back to the board-inghouse and tried to start the story he should have finished weeks ago. He sat with his tape recorder, dictating a line or two, stopped the machine and erased what he had said. He couldn't find the right beginning, couldn't remove himself from the story enough to see it for what it was. Around nine Isiah Frank came in and opened his window, mumbled that the smoke from Adam's cigarettes was giving the cat asthma so he might as well choke the rest of the neighborhood instead. He was wearing a gray cashmere robe and flannel pants, red leather slippers and a red ascot with tiny yellow and grey squares. He stared at Adam's tape recorder as if expecting an invitation.

"If you're going to mention me," he finally said, "make sure you say I was *well-dressed*."

She came in at ten o'clock. Adam heard the front door open and close, held his breath and waited until she had landed on his floor. When he could no longer contain his restlessness, he went to the top of the stairs and took her face in his hands, slid his fingers into her hair and kissed her. Back in the room he saw her reflection in the tall glass of the half-open window, closed the door behind her and pulled her dress off an inch at a time. She leaned against the dark wood, her hands locked behind her, her body trembling in his grip. He kissed her neck, inhaled the scent of unknown borders and unquelled longings on her skin. She was all he wanted, he thought, all he would ever want.

SHE DIDN'T GO home to her husband that night.

She stayed with Adam until noon the next day, slept in his bed and moved around his room as if she had lived there all her life. Intrigued, Adam let the hours pass but did not ask the question: he liked watching her up close, trying to unravel her mystery, find out for himself the reasons for her acts.

At noon she put on her dress and tied her hair back in a loose knot.

"It's Friday," she told him. "I'm going to church."

He stood still and let her feel the impact of her own words. She already knew what he wanted to tell her—that her time in the church was over, regardless of how much she wanted to belong and how hard she could fight a snake. She had been banned once and clawed her way back after her daughter's death, and maybe she wanted to do it again, to show the believers she had been stronger than Sam and still immune to harm, but it was too late because too many of them distrusted her and blamed her for Sam's death.

"What if they don't want you there?" Adam asked.

They walked to the train station on Central and Jackson Streets. She was going to ride a train down to Chattanooga, meet Anne Pelton at an evening service conducted by a man named Jimmy Ray Weston who had been Little Sam's disciple. The service would take up half the night, and afterward, she would ride home with Anne or stay at a church member's home.

On the street, Blue stayed close to Adam and seemed oblivious to the stares of passersby and to the station's small staff.

When the train arrived she reached over and kissed the side of Adam's face, put her arms around him and let her head rest for an instant on his chest. He felt the tremor in her bones then, sensed the fear—of the snakes, of the believers, of losing her way in the unknown—throb like a current under her skin. She was going back for the wrong reasons, he thought. The church members would sense her desperation and turn on her with a fury.

He wouldn't let her go alone.

He climbed on the train, took her hand and lifted her easily on board. It was a cargo train headed south, the kind Adam had ridden in his youth, when he had helped transport the tobacco crop he would sell on the open market. When the train started rolling, he lit a cigarette and watched the earth slide past him on the sides of the tracks, closed his eyes and imagined he was leaving Knoxville for good. He liked the illusion of departure, he thought—the seeming possibility of no return.

THE TRUE HOUSE of Prayer in Jesus' Name was a gray cinder block structure built in the middle of a lot cleared of trees and shrubbery but left unpaved. By the time Adam and Blue arrived, the service had started and the worshipers were gathered inside. From far away Adam could hear the sound of their music and singing, feel the reverberations of feet stomping the ground and hands clapping together in unison.

A hand-painted sign on the side of the highway read WORSHIP WITH US ON YOUR WAY TO MEET THE LORD. A second sign, carved in the shape of a cross, hung above the door leading into the church and proclaimed COME ALONG WITH US ON OUR WAY TO ETERNITY. It marked the beginning of a narrow dirt road that veered off the side of highway and into the woods, eventually leading to a space where cars were parked. Beyond that were three rows of wooden tables used for after-services meals, then the building itself.

Inside the church the floor was bare but clean, and light poured in from small rectangular windows carved high into the walls. A dozen pews were lined up on either side of the room, providing separate seating for men and women. An area in the back was reserved for children too young to stay on their mothers' laps during the long service. A kerosene heater provided warmth.

Directly across from the door, the pulpit was made of wood boards nailed together and painted white. It was mounted on a platform raised ten inches off the floor and also built of wood. A black cross was painted on the front of the pulpit, a second, larger one on the wall behind it.

Someone had brought in a microphone, but left it unplugged for lack of electrical wiring. Tubs of water had been laid against the far-right wall for those worshipers who indulged in washing one another's feet: It was a way for the believers to bond, for every man to retain his humility among the others.

On the pulpit were a jar of olive oil, two kerosene torches, and some Coke bottles filled with oil and stuffed with rags. In another bottle was a green, viscous matter Adam guessed was battery fluid.

In the midst of the singing, children as young as two and three ran up and down the aisles and climbed over the pews. Two teenage boys were clanging cymbals on the right side of the pulpit. Anne Pelton was dancing around with a tambourine in her hand, singing "Jesus Turned the Water Into Wine." Her arms were raised above her head, and her eyes were closed as her body swayed to the music.

Bob Reynolds's young bride, who looked pregnant, was smiling, as if in a state of grace. Across from her a thirtyish woman in a long gray dress stood mesmerized by an invisible sign. She was ghost-pale, her face thin as a razor, her hands skinny as chicken feet. She was the kind of woman who was used to tragedy and sought it out where she could, Adam thought— the kind who wouldn't know what to do with a bit of good fortune. She must have arrived at church early that day, remained by the door and kissed everyone who came in, wanting to suck out of them the joy they had brought, to instill in them the same sense of dread and foreboding she lived with all the time.

She was the first to notice Blue. Her eyes narrowed for a moment, searching her face and then Adam's. Suddenly animated, she turned to a bald man who had hung an electric bass around his neck but left it unplugged, and motioned toward Blue with her head. Then all at once everyone was turning to the door. The music began to level off, and mouths went limp in midsong. Even the children realized something was wrong and stopped their play.

Blue stood in the doorway with her revealing dress and her bare arms, looking nothing like the Holiness woman she had once pretended to be, and the very fact that she had dared come back was so overwhelming, barely anyone noticed her lover next to her.

Near the pulpit a tall man with stringy hair and bony legs stood up from his seat and cleared his throat. He had a bible in his right hand, a jar of olive oil in the other, and he came toward Blue as if to warn that she had ventured onto dangerous ground—as if he were motivated by concern for her and not by the desire to punish. From the way he was taking the initiative, Adam guessed this man must be the pastor of the church, or at least a deacon.

"Sister Blue!" the man said, and the very sound of his voice carried a thousand accusations he did not need to articulate.

Blue stood with her back straight and her arms at her sides. She looked serious but undisturbed, unafraid in a way that could have either disarmed or incited the man.

"Jimmy Ray," she said quietly.

They stared each other down—the pastor taller than Blue, his eyes and face laden with the conviction of his own power.

Just then Paul Kane, the newly appointed pastor of the Highway Tabernacle Church of God, appeared from the sidelines and took Adam's hand.

"Welcome," he said in a voice too loud to have been casual. "Welcome!"

One of the first people Adam had interviewed when he'd arrived in Knoxville, Paul Kane was younger and more open than most of his fellow preachers. He had taken Adam into his home and answered all his questions with as much sincerity as he could muster. He had told Adam about Blue's invulnerability to harm, sworn the woman would never be bit. All he had asked in return was that Adam write a story that was fair and accurate.

Pastor Jimmy Ray Weston studied Paul Kane and understood the meaning of his act. For a moment he considered the wisdom of standing his ground against another minister from the same faith. Paul Kane was slapping Adam's back as if they were old friends, and guiding him to a seat. Jimmy Ray Weston decided it was not a good time to fight.

Blue walked through the center aisle and sat in the front row on the women's side. Behind her Anne Pelton began singing "Amazing Grace." For a while hers was the lone voice in the church. Then others joined in, and instruments followed.

"Amazing Grace" flowed into a second, then a third song. Around eight o'clock the pastor signaled for the music to stop and invited anyone who wished to testify to step forth. There were a few minutes of nervous quiet—hands rubbing together and bodies shifting in the seats and children looking up from their play to see who would go to the pulpit first. Then an enormous man with a potbelly and very short legs stood up and began speaking. His name was E. Preston Pope, he said, and he had been visited by angels all week. They had told him he must testify in church and cleanse his soul, though he did not know just yet what purpose his testimony would serve. He was the grandson of a believer called "John the Baptist"—a handler known for his habit of standing in church with his arms outstretched in imitation of Christ. Rolling his eyes back in his head and leaning against a wall, John the Baptist had allowed women believers to touch him, thereby guiding the Holy Spirit out of his own body and into theirs. The women, E. Preston Pope now recounted, fainted onto the floor in ecstasy.

After him Paul Kane stood up to testify, and then a middle-aged woman with a scarred face and a strong stutter spoke of how she had been cured of "bad dreams and evil wishes" at the hands of a preacher in Georgia and how the preacher, himself a paraplegic who had been healed by Sam Jenkins in his youth, had promised to rid her of her speech impediment next. Her testimony was punctuated by cries of "Hear her, Lord" and "Help her, sweet Jesus" from the congregation.

They had been conducting their services in this manner from the start, Adam thought—since before Little Sam had picked up his first snake and maybe even before the Church of God had found its name. Still, he was struck by how different it was to be here, witnessing it all, as a grown man.

He had been terrified of these people in his childhood, resentful of Rose who had introduced him to her friends as "the child of my daughter's sins." Often he had sat through entire services with his fists hidden in his pockets and his head filled with visions of attacking the people who called his mother names. He had tried to imagine ways of destroying the entire congregation, hoped the snakes would kill everyone, that the

Coke bottles with kerosene would explode in their hands and burn the church down.

At the orphanage he had believed every derogatory remark anyone had made about holiness people, and memorized all the arguments against snake handling. The handlers, Mr. Harris said, were outlaws determined to spoil civic order, charlatans and circus performers who took advantage of the mountaineers' simplicity. The snakes they picked up had been defanged before they were brought to church; or they were milked of their poison; or rendered numb, and therefore unable to attack, by the loud music and the body temperature of the believers.

The poison used during services, Harris insisted, was diluted with water until it posed no danger; or it was not poison at all; or it had become so much a part of the believers' diet, their bodies had built immunity against it. It's true the believers stuck their face into the open flame of blowtorches, but they were careful to stay in the "cool spot" of the fire—the few millimeters of blue light where the flame was actually cold. When they put their hands into raging furnaces, they kept them away from the heat. When they picked up red-hot logs, they knew which areas to avoid.

Adam knew all of Harris's arguments, had heard them repeated countless times in the press. For years he had tried to believe the outsiders' logic. He had studied every bit of science he could find on snakes and their behavior, read accounts of religious sects and their practices in other parts of the world. But he knew—because he had seen his grandmother catch them, because he had slept with them lurking under his bed in the train car, carried them with Rose and her friends into church—he knew the believers did not defang or milk their serpents. Often, in fact, they handled snakes brought to church by hecklers and nonbelievers intent on revealing the handlers' tricks.

He knew also that snakes were deaf, and therefore could not respond to the loud music; that they did not behave differently because of a handler's body temperature.

He knew that the human body does not build immunity to poison, but in fact becomes more susceptible with repeated exposure.

He knew there are no cool spots in a flame, no right ways to hold a burning log.

Long after he had first set out to discover the lie behind the snake handlers' beliefs, Adam had come to the same conclusion that had forever baffled the reporters and scientists who studied holiness people: too often, for no logical, scientific reason, the snakes did not bite, the fire did not burn, and the strychnine did not kill those who believed.

About ten o'clock the music resumed, and the believers began dancing around the church. Suddenly the woman with the razor face stood up, cried "Judgment day is near," and fainted to the floor. Two men dragged her by the arms into the center aisle and knelt beside her in prayer. Pastor Jimmy Ray Weston was called to begin the process of revival. Praying loudly, he leaned over the woman and touched her forehead, first with his Bible, then with his hand. The music became louder, as if in celebration, and Jimmy Ray Weston rocked back and forth on his knees over the woman. She was writhing in ecstasy, her eyes still closed, her head moving side to side. He put his hand on her shoulder and her knees. He touched her lips, her stomach, put his fingers on her hipbones, then on her crotch.

She opened her eyes.

"Praise the Lord."

Her revival marked a turning point in the service. The air in the room suddenly felt thin, and everyone looked exhausted and ready to rest as they slowly returned to their seats. Jimmy Ray Weston started to pace in front of the pulpit with his hand crossed over his chest and his head bowed in reflection.

"My name is Jimmy Ray Weston," he began, "and I am here to receive the Spirit."

He spoke in a slow and halting pace, stopping every few words to run his hand through his hair and catch his breath. He had a burn scar over his wrist and the back of his hand, and a habit of rocking his torso back and forth as he spoke, moving faster as he became more excited. He was clearly not the kind of preacher who had spent much time in school, but he spoke with a fervor that was sincere and contagious in its fury, and he showed a passionate desire to communicate his faith that moved his congregation, and even Adam.

"All things work together for good to them that love God," he recited from Romans 8:28.

He spoke for over an hour, stopping every once in a while to allow time for a song, and he managed to capture everyone's attention so fully that they all seemed to have forgotten Blue and her presence. Then, all at once, Adam saw her standing in the far end of the church, and she had a snake in her hands.

It was a six-foot-long copperhead with a triangular head and a broken rust-and-coral–patterned coat. She was holding it from the middle, her elbows bent and slightly raised above her waistline, her palms turned toward her face. She looked calm but intent, focused only on the serpent in her hands, unaware of what was going on around her.

Adam bolted from his seat, horrified, and leapt halfway to the middle of the room. He was going to throw himself on Blue and the snake, wrench the beast from her hands if he could. Someone grabbed him from behind, and pulled him back.

"Easy," E. Preston Pope hissed in his ear, "or the snake will charge."

Adam wrestled free from the man's grip, pushed the others who had closed in around him. His instincts urged him to act, but he knew Pope was right—that any sudden move on Adam's part would only upset the balance between Blue and her snake and incite the animal to strike.

She was whispering to the copperhead. She wasn't fighting so much as seducing it, he thought, and now it had wrapped its tail around her wrist and was rising toward her face. She let it glide against her chest, up toward the center of her neck. When it had come to within an inch of her throat, she stopped talking and closed her eyes.

The snake rubbed its head against her chin, put its mouth on her lip.

She bristled, but that was all. She let the snake crawl over her face and onto her head, allowed it to wrap its tail around her neck. It went down the length of her back, through the opening in her sleeve, under her dress, and against her bare flesh.

Anne Pelton was singing about salvation in a voice that

shook with her tears. Hearing her, Blue opened her eyes and smiled. She looked as if she were far away—deep under a body of water that distorted all images and dulled every sound.

The snake circled around her waist—its colors and thickness visible under the fabric—then climbed up the middle of her stomach and chest. Its head rested in the spot directly between her breasts. It rose off her skin, pulled away, landed again.

She shook once, and her lips stopped moving. She looked stunned, as if faced with a question she did not expect. Pain washed over face and brought tears to her eyes. Her hands froze in midair. Then a single red spot appeared on the front of her dress.

She had been bitten. Bitten by a copperhead. Here in the middle of these woods, with nothing but dirt roads surrounding them and help hours away.

She brought her hands to her chest as if to take hold of the snake, but Adam saw that they were trembling and uncertain, and he realized that she was frightened. The woman with the razor-thin face had also noticed that something was wrong, and was examining the drop of blood that had now spread on Blue's dress.

There was no telling how much of its poison the copperhead had already dispensed, or whether it would bite again, Adam thought. With its head so close to her heart, a second bite might well induce cardiac arrest.

He went to her now, and pushed the razor-faced woman away. Blue's lips were chalk-white and her face was covered with moisture and now she was trembling all over. He knew it was only moments before she'd pass out.

He reached with both hands and ripped open the front of her dress, revealing her bare body and the serpent around it. The razor-faced woman screamed in alarm, but Blue remained still. The copperhead contracted around Blue's waist, turned around with lightning speed, rose higher off her body, and charged Adam. Instinctively, he grabbed it around the neck with the flat of his hand—his fingers pressing its neck. He held on, but the snake fought harder than he had expected, and now it was thrashing its tail at Blue's hip. Adam held fast, trembling and drenched in sweat, his arm aching from pressure. He saw that Blue was gasping for air, realized he had to free her quickly. He turned his wrist back and down—bending the snake's neck—and yanked.

The copperhead tensed up, then suddenly went limp. Adam pulled again, harder this time, and the snake came off Blue like a piece of rope.

She folded onto the ground as if made of fabric and string alone.

Coming down on his right knee, Adam brought his wrist with the snake still around it to the ground. He opened his hand, laid his palm flat against the earth. The copperhead loosened, unwound itself, and slid off.

Jimmy Ray Weston put the forked tip of a tree branch on the back of the snake's head and guided it smoothly into a cage.

"Praise the Lord," he said when he was done, but inside the church, everyone was numb and silent and deaf to his words.

ADAM GRABBED Anne Pelton's keys and ran outside to bring the car around. Driving back, he caught Blue in the car's headlights: she had been carried outside by Paul Kane and laid on a blanket on top of a picnic table. All around her on the ground, the church members had knelt in prayer.

Jimmy Ray Weston gave Adam directions to a clinic he thought might be open at that hour.

"She wouldn't need it if her soul had been clean," he remarked as Adam carried Blue to the car.

They drove up a winding road that rose through the woods and higher up the mountain, then slowly descended toward the opposite end of the highway that had brought them here. Above them the mountain cast long black shadows on the road and blocked out most of the sky. Blue was sitting in the front passenger seat with her head on a folded-up blanket placed against the window. She had become feverish and hot by then, and she was coughing as if to clear her lungs of something hard. Adam held her left hand as he drove, and told her to stay awake, not to be afraid, he would take her to a hospital soon and from there, they would go home.

She wasn't responding, and she looked more and more disoriented. When she coughed again, a narrow stream of blood poured out of her mouth and down the side of her chin.

Hang on, he thought, or maybe he told her. Hang on, and we'll be out of here soon, down on the flat ground with streetlights around us and signs showing the way. Down in a place where men put their faith in their own and each other's hands instead of God's.

Hang on, he thought, but he realized that they were completely alone—cut off from the church members and their music, surrounded by walls of rock and trees, alone on a narrow pathway he hoped would lead them out.

In the train car the day she died Rose Watkins had looked every bit as normal as Adam had ever seen her. She had died in mid prayer, the neighbors had deduced—which explained the engrossed but far-away expression on her face—but it wasn't until later that Adam realized what bothered him so much about Rose's appearance that day: she had looked no different in death than she did in life, and it seemed to him that this was wrong; that the line between the living and the dead should be clearly marked; that for all the physical and emotional turmoil it inflicted upon the body, life should assert itself differently from death.

"Hang on," he told Blue, but the mountain leaned so far onto the road, he could hardly see ten feet ahead of the car. He thought about he directions Jimmy Ray Weston had given in the church parking lot, reviewed in his mind every turn he had taken since he left. They were simple enough—the directions—but out here in the woods every road looked the same as the other and all at once he realized they had come to a dead end and were facing the mountain again.

He looked in the rearview mirror, out the side of the car. He must have taken a wrong turn, and now he was confused and had lost precious time.

Blue coughed again, and this time her eyes closed and her head fell limp to the side. He backed out of the dead end and turned the car around, found the road he thought had taken them here and this time took a different turn. He was driving fast but couldn't tell which direction he was headed in, couldn't find a sign or a marker to indicate the way out. Minutes later the road ended again.

He felt a panic he did not know he could feel—a blinding, suffocating fear that made his jaws lock and his fingers freeze around the steering wheel.

He put the car in park and killed the engine, jumped out the door and looked around for a cabin or house where he might ask directions. There was nothing—no people, no lights, not even the usual sounds of the woods at night.

Blue coughed blood again, and he saw that her skin had turned cold and cloudy as wax paper.

"Hang on," he told her, and opened the passenger-side door, knelt on the ground, and took both her hands in his own. Her pulse was beating erratically and her breath smelled like blood, and he realized there was nothing he could do now— nothing he could do but wait and hope she would beat the venom on her own.

"But to one is given by the Spirit the word of wisdom," he remembered a verse from I Corinthians, "to another the word of knowledge by the same spirit; to another faith by the same Spirit..."

Hang on, he prayed, and put his lips on Blue's forehead and her nose, kissed her eyes and her hair. He was speaking to her without knowing what he said, praying to her without knowing if she heard.

"To another faith by the same Spirit."

He wiped her forehead with his hand, caressed the sides of her face with the back of his fingers. He had failed her, he thought—failed to protect her from her own madness, to stop her when he knew better. He had failed her when it mattered most, and now he had no choice but to surrender to the darkness of the mountains and to his own human limitations.

Hang on, he prayed as his tears mixed with hers. His mouth burned with the fever on her skin. He opened the front of her dress and saw the two holes in her chest dug by the snake's teeth. They were red and turning black, the flesh around them a sickly white.

Hang on, he prayed, and put his lips to the wound.

ALL NIGHT LONG she lay feverish and trembling in the car. He wrapped her in the blanket and felt her pulse every few minutes, checked her wound for swelling and discoloration, tried to calculate the time left until sunrise, when he could attempt to find his way out of the mountains again.

Before dawn she stopped trembling, and he felt the fever slowly let go. He asked her if she could remember the events of the previous night, but she wouldn't look at him or respond at all. So he sat her upright in the front again, started the car, and began to drive. Down the side of the mountain, he could see bits of the highway through the thickness of the woods, and he heard Blue's breathing return to a normal pace. She was sleeping now, and he thought that the worst may be over, so he opened the window to let in the morning air and he let go of her hand and breathed a sigh of relief. He felt a dull ache in his arm, and realized it was a result of his struggle with the snake. Then he remembered Jimmy Ray's parting words, his buttonholes held in place with bits of rope, the way he had rocked back and forth as he grew excited.

On the highway toward Chattanooga, he turned on the radio and listened to a swarthy voiced announcer recite bits of the day's news, looked at Blue sleeping next to him, and he felt as if it had always been this way—as if the two of them had traveled in this car all their lives, sat next to each other as the sun rose over the mountain and illuminated the road that would take them away from their pain and home to each other.

I DID KILL HIM, it's true.

She spoke with her face turned away from Adam, her voice small and distant, devoid of conviction.

I killed Little Sam Jenkins with that snake, hours after we had entered the empty blacksmith shop in Altha and he started to preach his version of God's love, after he had lived almost nine decades and survived 446 snakebites, countless gallons of poison, a dozen knife wounds, electrocution, and jail.

It was either him or me, and I saved myself.

After my daughter died, I went back to church with Anne Pelton against my husband's wishes. I did not go to fight Sam. I went to seek the company of other humans, the peace that came with prayer, the possibility of finding hope.

The Professor was so alarmed by my return, he stood in the doorway and forbade me to leave when Anne came to fetch me. He had taken a leave from the university that year, and he spent most of his time at home, reading the Old Testament and writing down his thoughts and reactions in scholarly essays. He had stopped taking care with his clothes and his appearance, let the yard fall into disarray, abandoned the house to disorder. He talked to me with reason and explained why I did not belong in Holiness, why the mountaineers who had remained isolated for two hundred years would never accept an outsider, much less a foreigner like me, as their own. He said the snakes would kill me sooner or later or that I would kill myself, but that at any rate the harm I would do by handling would far exceed any relief the church might bring.

He may have been right, of course, but back then the church was the only place I knew to go.

Sam attacked me almost as soon as I went back, but for a while I didn't care enough to react. I had been wounded more deeply by my daughter's death than by anything he or anyone else could do to me, and it was easy, in those years when I hung between despair and the utter lack of feeling, to overlook him.

But the longer I stayed in the church, the more important it became to me, and after a while I found myself going back if only to prove I could, if only to beat Sam at his game. I began to fight him without knowing exactly why I wanted to win, and that became more essential than anything else the church had to offer and so I stayed, year after year, and the longer I resisted Sam's attacks and the longer I prevailed over the snakes, the more alive and in control I felt until he decided it was time to launch a different battle.

He started to look for evidence he could use to have me expelled. He asked a few questions, and found out about my husband's trips to Memphis. Suddenly he saw himself staring at the answer to the enigma of the Professor's life: the man was a Jew, of course—a Jew who had passed as a Christian. This made me a Jew as well, or at least half-a-Jew, but at any rate it made me a liar and a devil because I had kept the truth from the church. That's what Sam was going to reveal to the believers before I killed him.

Three weeks before Altha, we had been to Sister Mary's church in Mount Vernon, Kentucky, and Sam had spent the entire sermon talking about whores and adulteresses posing as Holiness women. He had not mentioned my name, but the members knew

*him enough to understand how he laid an accusation at some-
one's feet without naming them. Even as he spoke, I could hear
the whispers behind me, could see the slanted eyes and the side-
way glances, and the only thing that kept me from being expelled that day was the snake that bit Tess Bettis, and that
killed him on the spot.*

*Tess screamed when the animal bit him. He tried to drop the
snake, but it held on with its fangs and Tess had to pry it away.
Then we all saw the two holes left by the serpent's teeth and the
stream of blood that fell from them.*

*He turned blue almost immediately. Someone asked him if
they should call a doctor, and he said yes, get help as soon as
possible, because I am dying here and the Lord will not hear me
but by then he was already convulsing, and then he lay stiff—
twenty-six years old and the dead father of five.*

*Little Sam picked up the culprit snake and shoved it back
into a box, then tried to explain Tess's death: "Not enough
faith in the Holy Ghost," he said. "You must never handle if
you're afraid, or if you don't feel anointed."*

*On the ride home after Tess's funeral, Anne talked incessantly
about the Lord's glory and how Tess had died happy, knowing
he was closer to the Lord than at any other time in his life. She
spoke about her own family—her husband and his brother, who
had died within a month of each other—the brother from
strychnine poisoning, the husband of snakebite—and how that
had only strengthened her resolve to fight the devil through
prayer and do God's work.*

It was the first time I had seen someone die in church. All I could think of was that it could have been me lying in that coffin, dead at Little Sam's hands.

Then we went to Florida.

We drove twelve hours from Knoxville, through Albany and south, to Calhoun County, twenty-five miles from the Georgia-Florida state line. In Lester's shed, near Altha, we saw three dozen trucks parked outside in anticipation of Little Sam's arrival. I had not been to church since Tess died, but Anne had dropped by to see me every Monday afternoon, and she said that Sam had not handled snakes at any services. He said only that he had not felt the Spirit move upon him, but it was beginning to look like he had lost his nerve, Anne said, and now he was feeling the pressure to handle again: the worshipers expected him to set an example, and the local papers had been sending reporters to every meeting hoping that another accident would occur and that they could write about it first.

This was Sam's weakness, I thought: his fear, and the fact that he wanted to hide it.

In church that day Sam did not look at me at all. Tess's widow was there with all her children, and Sam gave her center stage to testify and sing and faint in ecstasy. But when his turn came up to preach, he chose a passage from I Corinthians: Know ye not that ye are the temple of God, and that the Spirit of God dwelleth in you? If any man defile the temple of God, him shall God destroy."

He spoke of the ways a woman might defile the temple of God and also the ways she could be punished. He was attacking me again, but now I could see the snake boxes lined up against the wall of the shed, and I knew how I was going to fight back.

Sam was winding down the service, ignoring the believers' desire to handle.

I saw the lard can in which he kept the rattler that had killed Tess.

I knew rattlesnakes are more likely to bite than the other serpents we normally handle. I knew Sam was afraid. I knew that snakes sense fear and attack the weak.

I opened the can, took out the snake, and walked it over to Sam.

I remember his wrist and arm swelled to three times their normal size, and his flesh turned black, and he started to vomit blood. George Guilford, who is the Calhoun County sheriff, asked if he could drive Sam to a hospital, but of course Sam refused. He lay on the floor, surrounded by worshipers in prayer, his eyes fixed only on me.

Some church members lifted him in their arms and drove him to a nearby house where they planned to continue to pray until he recovered. The mood then was still light. People were talking and eating outside the house, praying inside. Some newspaper reporters smoked on the steps, and even Sheriff Guilford, whose job it was to enforce the statutes against snake handling, was chatting amiably and drinking lemonade instead of arresting anyone. Nobody actually believed that Sam would die, and so they did not think about the fact that I was the one who had encouraged him to handle.

But Sam's body kept swelling and turning blacker before our

eyes, and he was getting more delirious every hour, and then all at once we all knew this was different——that he wasn't going to pull through as he had done hundreds of times before, that he was mortal and vulnerable and at last at the end of his fight.

The distance from innocence to guilt, I realized then, is the tick of a clock—quick, easy, impossible to undo.

When he knew he was going to die, Sam asked Sheriff Guilford to send for his children in Kentucky and Tennessee and wherever else they could be located. The sheriff obliged, and then everyone started to pray in a panic. Guilford came back from the station and said that a convoy of Sam's children was headed toward Florida. That's the way of mountain people, you see: most of the time, they put family above all, uphold the bonds of loyalty and kinship.

Hoping to avoid blame myself, I knelt with the others next to Sam, bowed my head, and sang:

"Faith, faith, it can cure anything."

He heard me singing and looked up. He raised a swollen arm, waved it in my direction and tried to speak, but his voice was barely a whimper and he coughed blood every time he wanted to force a sound out of his chest. So he looked again and found Sheriff Guilford in the crowd, motioned for him to put his ear to Sam's mouth. I knew then that Sam would manage to take from me in death what he had not managed to exact in life: my place in the church, the trust of the believers, the possibility of at last belonging.

"That woman brought fear into my church and handed me the snake to kill me," I later learned he had said.

"She's as guilty as if she had put a shotgun to my head."

ISIAH FRANK BROUGHT Adam a cup of Turkish coffee and a plate of pastel-colored sugar cubes arranged in the shape of a pyramid. He put the coffee on the table next to Adam, turned around, and surveyed the disorganized state of the room. He had taken to cleaning Adam's room in his absence. He made the bed, took out Adam's laundry, washed and folded his clothes and put them back in drawers instead of the backpack. He wasn't playing domestic, Adam knew. He was keeping an eye on his guest, a hand in Adam's affairs.

Adam had been dreaming of Sam all night. Sam was lying on a flat board inside a stranger's home, his face and body swollen black from poison, his feet bare and disfigured from too much abuse. Around him people knelt in prayer. They were waiting for Sam to get up, to raise himself from the dead as he had promised to raise so many others. He never did.

Adam heard Isiah moving around his room, and woke up. Sitting in bed, he forced the sleep from his eyes and slowly remembered the events of the last two days: the train ride to Chattanooga, Blue's getting bitten, the hours he had spent in the car waiting to see if she would live.

By the time they had found the clinic Jimmy Ray Weston had recommended, Blue had overcome the most critical effects of the poison. She had been admitted, observed, sent home a few hours later. Driving back to Pineville in Anne Pelton's car, she had said nothing and hardly looked at Adam.

After almost fifteen years of believing herself immune to snakes and poison, Sister Blue Kerdi had learned otherwise.

"I buy the coffee from an Armenian store clerk who runs his own business out of his boss's store," Isiah said as he opened and closed the dresser drawers across from Adam's bed. "He makes me a cup when I go in—cooks it with milk and sugar till it foams like cream—and then he reads my fortune in the lines at the bottom of the cup."

He stopped and threw a glance at Adam.

"You might try it," he said with exaggerated disdain. "It helps clear the mind."

Adam got up and went to the sink. He threw cold water on his face, lit a cigarette, fell back in the chair near the dresser. He felt exhausted and confused and overwhelmed by conflicting emotions—not at all prepared to tolerate Isiah's intrusions.

"Of course some of us *like* seeing things in a fog," Isiah went on.

Adam bounded out of his chair. He grabbed Isiah by the side of the collar, and turned him around.

"What is it you *want*?" he said. "What are you looking for all the time?"

Isiah was petrified. He stood with his eyes locked into Adam's, aware that the slightest move, a single word, might provoke further attack. A minute later he eased his collar out of Adam's fist and took a cautious step back.

It wasn't he that aroused Adam's rage, he knew. It was all the others—Blue and the Professor, Clare's memory and the snakes and yes, a dead man Adam had come back to understand and who was haunting him instead.

They remained facing each other for a while. Then at last Isiah gathered his courage and spoke:

"I'm looking for your *eyes*," he said. "Open your eyes."

THE PROFESSOR KNEW about them, of course. This much Adam was certain of. Blue had never acted in secret, never tried to hide Adam from her husband or from all those watching her. Her boldness had given Adam a sense of security—the impression that she belonged to him entirely, that her husband did not matter, did not exist. Night after night Adam had held Blue in his arms knowing the Professor must be waiting for her at home, that he must be going through their house looking for signs of the intruder in his world. He must search for fingerprints on every hard surface, Adam thought, must stand above his bed looking for the shape of Adam's body, asking himself if, in his absence, Blue had taken her lover into the places that were most holy to her husband.

He knew about them, of course, and yet, the Professor had done nothing to stop the affair.

It made no sense, Adam realized in the days after Isiah's warning—that a man who had worked so hard to build a home with his wife, a man who planned his every move so carefully, who guarded every word, every sound—a man as arrogant, as distant and frightened as the Professor, would so willingly allow himself to be robbed.

Doubt, like desire, had become second nature.

He went to find Isiah in his workroom behind the kitchen. He wasn't sure about allowing Isiah a glimpse of his thoughts— letting him play a part in an already tangled relationship. But Isiah seemed to know more than anyone else did about Blue, and he had wanted to tell Adam this—had offered a bait Adam could not refuse.

Tired of searching for perfect new pieces to add to his collection, Isiah had bought a book on making glass figurines, and was teaching himself the craft. He was bent over a large table in the workroom, holding a blowtorch to a piece of colored glass that melted and gave in the heat.

He saw Adam standing in the doorway.

"What about the old man?" Adam asked without coming into the room.

Isiah kept his eyes on the flame that was shaping his glass. He didn't answer for so long, Adam thought he hadn't heard him.

"Which one?" Isiah finally replied, still looking down. "The one she killed, or the one she has yet to kill?"

He looked up and winked playfully. His sarcasm made Adam's stomach turn.

"I mean her husband," Adam said sternly.

Isiah pulled on the melted glass until it was thin as a string, then swirled it around in the shape of a cone. When he was done, he turned off the blowtorch, put it down, and pulled off his goggles.

"Come on in." He motioned with his hand to the chair on the other side of the table.

In his late fifties, he was still fit and muscular—the lines in his face deep but still sharp, his manners affected but proud.

"What *about* the husband?" he asked once Adam had sat down.

"Why won't he stop her?"

Adam was uncomfortable asking the question—alluding to his own affair with Blue and, thereby, he felt, accepting the terms of Isiah's friendship.

Isiah looked pleased. He nodded at Adam in approval—a teacher, about to give up, suddenly discovering the light in his pupil's eyes.

"What makes you think he *can?*"

It was a tempting proposition: that the Professor was powerless before Blue, that he had not been able to stop her from going back to church or handling snakes, and he knew he could not separate her from her lover. Adam didn't buy it.

"Why doesn't he *try?*"

Isiah's smile widened. He started to say something, sighed instead and remained quiet. He was looking for the right words, Adam thought, for a way to reveal enough but not too much.

"People fight their battles differently," he offered at last with a shrug.

He waited to see if Adam understood.

"The young rush to confrontation," he said. "The old and the weak win by waiting. Sometimes by retreating."

They sat across from each other—two men worlds apart, similar only in their need to connect.

Isiah leaned toward Adam.

"Go to the house," he said. "Look around."

THE LOW WOODEN gate above the steps on Clinch Avenue was locked. Adam stepped over it without effort, crossed the front yard, stood at the door without knocking. It was ten in the morning, a time when the Professor was always at home.

Adam rang the doorbell once, waited, rang again. He heard no sound, felt no movement on the other side.

He imagined Blue and her husband sitting together in a room at the far end of the house. They had heard the doorbell and were looking at each other silently. They knew who had come to call. They were each wondering what the other might do, betting Adam would go away if they didn't answer.

He rang a third time.

A man's footsteps approached. A lock opened. The door creaked and gave.

The Professor was smaller and more anxious than Adam had ever seen him. He looked at Adam with a mixture of hatred and sadness, a plea for mercy, a promise to defend himself to the death. Facing him, Adam suddenly realized he did not know what to say, or how to explain the purpose of his visit. He felt ashamed of his own arrogance, the presumption that he had a right to steal another man's life.

The Professor's words sounded like a declaration of war.

"She's upstairs."

Adam sidestepped the husband and walked in without daring to look back. The hallway was dark, the doors to the rooms along it all closed. The wooden steps in the stairway were bare and clean and shiny. The landing was stripped of any cover, bathed in shadows from lace curtains that had been drawn against the light. The double doors to the master bedroom lay open.

He walked in with as much confidence as he could muster— aware that the Professor was watching him, hoping Blue was in the room.

She stood with her back against the bedpost, the sheer white mosquito netting draped behind her. When she saw Adam, her eyes moved. She raised her hands toward him, but pulled them quickly back.

He had not seen her since the ride back from Chattanooga. Her skin was still yellow from the poison, and her lips were drained of blood, and she looked as if she would fade into the white mosquito netting at any moment. He felt like going up to her, pulling her against him and holding her until he knew she was all right again.

Instead, they remained facing each other across the vast, empty room—their shadows reflected on the bare hardwood floor, their bodies drawn to each other but aware of the impossibility of union. Behind Adam in the hallway, the Professor stood guard.

"*Open your eyes,*" Isiah had urged, but Blue was all Adam wanted to see. The moment he was with her, he felt relieved and reassured, suddenly tired of his own doubts, unwilling to pursue the questions.

"*Look around,*" Isiah had said, but the room was empty except for the bed. There was no dresser table, no chairs. The mantel above the fireplace was bare, the freestanding closet open and hollow. Everywhere, the curtains were drawn.

"*Open your eyes,*" Isiah had said, but the longer Adam stayed in this house, the more he felt as if there was nothing for him to see here at all. He felt he had come here by mistake—wandered out of the boardinghouse and into his childhood dreams where he was always lost. He was locked alone in the boiler room; sleeping in Rose's train car. He was staying up nights in the barn, listening to the sound of worms plopping off the tobacco leaves and wondering where Clare had gone. He was vigilant, suspicious, always expecting to be let down.

"*Open your eyes,*" Isiah had said, and slowly Adam realized it was this—the very bareness of the room, the emptiness of the house, that he was supposed to see.

In her stories of life with the Professor, Blue had described a house filled with objects large and small—a place of quiet luxury and old pretensions, a cocoon packed with silks and linens and all the trinkets that would serve, the Professor had hoped, as proof of his own and Blue's existence.

This was not the house Blue had described, not the house Adam should have found.

"*Open your eyes.*"

Inside the house on Clinch Avenue, all the clocks had stopped and all signs of habitation had been erased and it was only them—the lover, the husband, and Blue—only them and the words that would save or damn them all.

"My husband has quit his job at the university," Blue said, but by then Adam had begun to understand. He could see the telltale signs of departure, could feel the separation he had so often experienced in the past.

He heard her without needing to listen, saw her without registering her image.

"He's been selling off everything we own." She paused.

Her voice was slipping farther away.

"He's going to leave town, and I have to go with him."

He didn't remember leaving the house, didn't remember turning away from Blue or bumping into the Professor on his way out. After that he drove for hours without knowing where he was headed or if he intended to leave or stay, pulled onto and off the highway looking for a place to have a drink and finding none. In Big Stone Gap off the 23, he parked at a truck stop and went in to buy cigarettes. Three men sat in work clothes and baseball hats, drinking beer and listening to bluegrass music on a scratchy tape recorder. He bought two warm beers and a pack of Marlboros, went back to his car, and sat drinking and listening to the radio. He hadn't eaten for two days, and now he felt his stomach churn from the effects of alcohol and the many hours of driving, so he rolled down the window and sat in the freezing night air until he started to shiver. The trucks that sped across the highway made the earth tremble under his car. He felt his head become warm and heavy from the beer, so he closed eyes to stop them from burning.

"*The old*," Isiah had said, "*win by waiting.*"

She had used him, of course—used him to detract attention from herself and Little Sam's death. She must have been planning to leave all along. That's why she had sought Adam out, given herself to him so readily, been so brazen in their affair. It was also why her husband had not tried to stop them: they had *wanted* the town to see the affair, *wanted* the believers to talk about her adultery instead of Sam's death. They had wanted Adam to stop searching, wanted to distract him and all the others.

She had been buying time in Adam's bed while her husband prepared for their escape.

Furious again, he turned the engine on and headed back toward Knoxville. He heard the sound of his own blood gushing through his head, heard his heart pounding in his ears. He was going back to confront her again, back to demand an explanation. But the truth was more readily evident than anything Blue could say.

Isiah Frank opened the door in his Shakespearean costume, and walked Adam upstairs. He fell on the bed, exhausted, pressed his eyes together, and hoped he could erase every thought from his mind. Next to him, Isiah was making grand gestures and saying words Adam could not hear, so he stopped trying to understand, let his head sink into the pillow, and gave in to sleep.

ADAM.

A thousand times these past weeks, I have awakened from a sleep in which I speak to you my last words.

I stir at night, feeling the touch of your hand, the tips of your fingers against my spine. It's like a child's touch: light and unthreatening and innocent in its intentions, and it sends white sparks through my veins and behind my eyes, and pulls me into that state between sleep and awakening, when all my sensations are sharp and my mind races, lightlike, in a sea of darkness.

I roll over and bury my face in the sheets, wanting the feeling to last, the ecstasy of knowing you are there, watching me, and that I can linger safely in your eyes.

Then I realize the tragedy that has happened: that we have parted without a chance to speak the truth, that I have stayed silent a day too long, that my words, like an invisible web, will surround me now and pull me to oblivion.

Lying in the dark, my sheets smelling like your skin, my body marked with your handprints, I call your name and pray that you will hear.

"Turn around," I say. "Hear me speak."

MY HUSBAND HAS *been preparing to leave for weeks.*

He heard her voice, but could not open his eyes to see her. He was still in bed, surrounded by darkness, and the more he tried to wake up, the deeper he sank into sleep.

He packs at night, with the lights turned off, the windows shut. He has packed all our clothes and all of my daughter's things, all the papers that may help us explain ourselves some-day, all the pictures we took in the course of our lives together. Everything else—his books, our bed, the objects that have for so long defined us—he has sold or will leave behind.

He had a life, once, he believed he could defend. He lost that life and in time, lost the conviction that he could build it again. His only hope now is to leave while he still has the legs to run—to leave and take with him the only thing—the only one—he has left.

"THERE WAS A MAN *who had a secret,*" *my husband told me in the days after our daughter died.*

"There was a boy who was born a mistake."

He knew this from the moment he became conscious of himself—before he had speech or understanding or a sense of his own place in the world. As a child he had felt like an outsider looking through glass at his own image, aware that it looked wrong—that he *looked wrong. He was certain he wasn't meant to be where his birth had placed him, that he wasn't meant to interact with and belong to the people who were his family. He felt removed from his mother, superior to his father. He had nothing in common with his siblings, and though he did love his grandmother, because he felt she came closest to appreciating his talents, he was aware that she was an old woman with little education and no real power outside her own family.*

The boy, on the other hand, was a great intellect in a small body, a refined spirit in an awkward figure, a burning ambition in limited flesh. He knew this without vanity and without excessive pride, with the same clarity as he knew any other fact of life.

He had been born in the port city of Basra on the Shatt Al Arab River, a few hours' journey from the Sea of Oman. His family had been merchants for many generations, and they had amassed a small fortune, which they used to educate their children and buy antique laces and European furniture for their homes. The city's position as a trading post brought its inhabitants into contact with people from all parts of the world. The Professor's family was cosmopolitan and westernized and aware of the ways of other peoples, but they were also bound by tradition: Girls grew up to marry and have sons. Boys were expected to enter the family trade and safeguard their fathers' wealth and good name.

The Professor had grown up speaking Arabic and French and English, learning to count on an abacus and to keep numbers and figures in his head. He was a good student—too good, in fact, for the liking of his father who saw the boy reading poetry and literature and quietly feared his son would become a homosexual. He had tried to discourage the boy from his studies, taken him to work instead, offered him every incentive to stop reading those books he liked so much. But even as a child the Professor had preferred the company of dead writers to the liveliness of the port and the sound of men unloading cargo from giant ships that had traveled a thousand seas.

All summer long he sat in the drawing room in the big family house overlooking the river. Warm, humid air blew in through the open windows and cast a sheet of moisture on his face and hands. With every word he read, the Professor imagined himself one step farther from his home and closer to the West.

He did not feel at liberty to share his feelings with anyone, because he didn't credit the others with enough largess of spirit to understand him. He had no relationship with his siblings and no friends at school. The other children thought him haughty and self-centered, but in fact, he knew, he was only following the direction of his own destiny.

And his destiny, he feared, had been less than kind to him. He was an Arab in a town that was ruled by Western men, a scholar in a country that measured success by other means, a Jew in a world that belonged to others.

He could have made peace with his Arab past by reminding himself of the great and illustrious history he had been a product of. The Arabs, after all, had one of the greatest empires in history, brought about an age of enlightenment that had transformed the civilized world.

He may have been able to accept his family's middle class mentality and their limited horizons, may even have taught himself, over time, to accept his body for what it was—frail and small and unimpressive, but commanded by a powerful mind.

What he could not reconcile himself to, what caused him interminable shame, was being Jewish.

He knew that his elders would condemn him for his thoughts, and so he hid them from his parents and later from his teachers. His father wanted him to grow up and become a merchant and his mother was planning his wedding even in his childhood, but secretly the little boy with the big ambitions was planning his escape.

He learned that the seat of power in the world had long ago passed from the East to the West, and that the source of civilization and respectability had been transferred from the old world to the new. So he gorged himself on every Western idea he could read about, and taught himself to speak French and German with as slight an accent as he could fake, and then he decided he would move—away from the humid little town with the rotting harbor and the small-minded merchants of silks and spices, and go to Paris, where men and ideas loomed larger than life.

In this new world, the Professor thought, he would reinvent himself as the man he was meant to be.

His only hope back then was his grandmother—the family matriarch and the person who controlled most of the wealth and, therefore, all of her sons. She understood and admired her grandson's thirst for knowledge like no one else in their family or their town, gave him the nickname "Professor" which quickly replaced his given name, and all through his childhood she protected him from his father's disdain and his mother's admonishments. She had selected him in her own heart as the heir to the family's legacy, the one among all the grandchildren who would take her place when she died. She willed to him her emerald wedding ring and a chest full of antique linens—her dowry when she had married at age nine. But she was not at all prepared, the day the Professor turned eighteen and walked into her drawing room in the house in Basra, to hear that he wanted to leave.

She sat that day in a wicker chair with pillows to support her back, a maid waving a fan behind her. It was in the years between the two wars. The West had already divided the Ottoman Empire and cast its footprints all over the Middle East. The grandmother listened to the Professor make his speech, then sat quietly and considered his request. She drank a glass of cherry sherbet—red as the paint that covered her lips and made her skin look even darker—then blew on a water pipe before she spoke.

"If I let you go," she said, afraid of her own wisdom, "you will not come back. The West will swallow you like a fish, and I will never see you again."

The Professor then got on his knees and kissed the old woman's hands, promised he would honor her in life as well as in death, that he would return home anytime she asked, and would come back to bury her. Even so, he had to wait a year before she relented.

HE TOOK HIS INHERITANCE *and her chest full of embroidered laces, then headed for the capital to start his journey. At the passport office in Baghdad, he bribed an official to write Professor on the line where his name was meant to be, then bribed him again to write Islam for his religion. It was easy, fair, and right.*

It was also practical—to go to the West with a new name and to pass as a Muslim instead of a Jew. Most people in the West were hardly aware that there were Jews or Christians among the Arabs. Muslims, like Jews, circumcised their boys, and most of them were dark like the Professor, so he had every expectation of being believed.

In Paris he spent the farewell money his parents had given him on a pair of dark suits and a hat, rented a room on rue de Ribe across from a tailor's shop, ate rabbit's foot marinated in white wine sauce every night. He studied at the Sorbonne and took walks in the Jardin des Tuilleries or on the Rive Gauche, visited museums on Sunday afternoons, drove into the countryside, and told himself he had arrived—that he had swallowed his secret and taken flight from his past, and had managed to become the man he wanted to be. He wrote home only once— to provide his address and to say he was well—and he did not feel the slightest bit of guilt for having left behind those who had loved and sustained him up to that stage. He knew he had never belonged to them. He expected they knew it too.

He had been at the Sorbonne for three years when his first wife started courting him. He had known other women before her—classmates, neighbors, girls who worked in the shops and cafés he frequented—but he had never looked at any of them with any level of interest, and he may have gone his whole life unaware of the influence of the opposite sex except for the teacher who called him into her office week after week and engaged him in long conversations that spilled into the night.

She was a professor of psychology at the school of humanities. She was older than he by twelve years, taller than he by four inches. She was not pretty, he thought—not now when she was in her thirties and wore drab clothes and dark lipstick, and not before when she had been younger and had long hair she washed in beer and curled with rollers. She had white-blonde hair, blue eyes, freckled skin that aged much too rapidly compared with that of Eastern women. Her hands were large and rough and full of veins—the hands of a woman who has never had a servant and who believes in keeping her kitchen floor spotless at the cost of ruining her health.

But she drank endless cups of coffee and chain-smoked filterless cigarettes while she talked, spoke in the confident, assertive manner reserved in the East for men. She motioned with her hands when she spoke, argued with male colleagues as if she were their equal. The Professor had seen her walk to her office early in the morning with a briefcase full of books and a cigarette in her hand, and he had thought that she looked lonely and lost and just a bit tired of her own strength. Then he would see her walk into class carrying a stack of students' papers, her glasses pushed up on top of her head, and he thought she was a formidable woman with endless confidence and an even greater intellect. Suddenly he was in awe of everything she said.

She was a disciple of Carl Jung's, he learned, an avid believer in his theories on the human mind, a great admirer of his writings in general. She agreed with Jung's views of American blacks as ignorant and incapable of analytical thought, shared his view of Jews as retrograde. She believed in the existence of a superior race—a better, more correct, more ideal version of humanity.

The more the Professor heard her speak, the more he found himself in agreement.

It never occurred to him that her views of the inferior people might affect the way she thought of him as well. He had never seen himself as part of that race. Wanting to impress her, he spent restless hours researching the works of Carl Jung and writing passionate papers, which he presented to her in class. She liked his enthusiasm, she said, his old-fashioned manners, the touching, almost eccentric way he wore nothing but dark suits to school. She observed that he was always alone and that he never appeared to crave another's company, that he seemed content within himself and his surroundings, and she liked this, because she was a woman who was growing too old and too lonely too fast.

When he went to her office to discuss a paper, she looked him straight in the eye, smiled when he spoke, touched her own hair as if to reassure herself that she was attractive. Years later she would confess to him that he was only her second lover. The first one, barely out of high school, had left her waiting in line outside a smoke shop.

All through his fourth year of university, the Professor went into his teacher's office and read and discussed the works of

Carl Jung. She helped him apply for a scholarship to pursue a doctorate, recommended him to the faculty of the school of languages. When he was accepted she invited him to her house to celebrate.

"Bring a bottle of wine," she said, "and we'll make love."

Suddenly the Professor was terrified that she might discover his secret.

He was thrilled that she had thought of him enough to want to seduce him, but along with the sense of elation came the fear that he may let her down, the suspicion that if she knew his true origins, she would see in him not the intelligent, sophisticated, self-made man that he was but the pathetic merchant's son, the Arab Jew, that his family had wanted him to be. He was so bothered by the possibility of being found out that he considered not accepting her invitation but in the end he went along, and after that he went to her house every week and then every night, and by the end of the summer, they spent all their time together.

It wasn't that he enjoyed making love to her so much, or that he found her company indispensable. She was the one who sought him, in bed and out, who clung to him like a teenage girl in need of approval, and who threw jealous fits every time he was less than responsive. What he liked about their affair was that she—a Western woman of refined origin—wanted him so much, that he shared such common ground with her, that in her eyes—she, who could detect the smallest of faults in people belonging to every race—he was a man worth loving.

THEY WERE MARRIED *on New Year's Day, 1930, in a church ceremony attended by members of the university faculty. He gave her his grandmother's emerald, certain it would impress their guests and even the priest, but afterward he heard her colleagues whisper that she had given herself to an Arab out of desperation and that the marriage wouldn't last.*

He moved into her apartment with his chest full of laces and his many stacks of books, continued his doctoral studies while she taught to support them both. They had three children in quick succession—girls with freckled skin and blue eyes and their mother's pale, thin lips. She dressed them in identical clothes, cut their hair short, and taught each to eat with a napkin on her lap. He watched them grow up from behind his desk piled high with papers, and wondered if they bore any hidden trace of his true origins—if they would betray him one day through their bodies or the workings of their minds. He wondered if they would grow to find him unacceptable, if they would be ashamed of having an Arab father.

Throughout the '30s, the Professor buried himself in his work, and let his wife raise the children and support the family. He let her invite friends into their apartment and sit with them drinking coffee all night and discussing the difference between the races and the ways these affected the development of mind and thought and language. When he sensed that the friends were uncomfortable discussing their views with him—because he was an Arab and by definition inferior—he went out of his way to stress his convictions and distance himself from his people. He put his arm around his wife and propped his daughters on his knees—look how blonde and white they are, he wanted to say, look how they love me.

Once he had earned his degree, he found a research job at the university and made it his mission to compare the origins of Romance and Germanic languages with those of Eastern tongues. Then the Second World War broke out.

The Professor and his wife kept the children out of school, ate rationed food, listened to the radio day and night. They watched Hitler march through Paris, up the Champs-Elysées, under the Arc de Triomphe. The Professor lost his research grant and was advised he'd best keep a low profile. His wife was recruited to aid in the propaganda effort.

She wrote articles and gave lectures affirming the superiority of the Aryan race and demonizing the Jews. She took her children to rallies in support of the German conquerors, and afterward spoke to her husband with breathless enthusiasm about everything they had seen and felt and envisioned.

She was not a bad woman, the Professor knew. She was a good mother and a devoted wife, a responsible citizen, a diligent teacher. She would not have hurt anyone directly. She was only dealing with ideas.

"The principle, you see, is what matters," she said.

But the principle led to acts of destruction, and the theories she voiced on paper found their way into the lives of individuals, and slowly the Professor's blue-eyed Aryan wife became part of the machine that destroyed Jews and Gypsies and Poles.

He might have spoken up then, but he was too afraid, too ashamed, too lost in the make-believe world of denial and longing to take a stand. He told himself he had gone too far to retreat, that any vestige of his Jewish past had washed away in *the oceans he had crossed to come here. He told himself it did not make sense for him to take a stand against principles he had believed in all his life, that he should defend, albeit only verbally, the races he had always held in low regard. He told himself it would be suicide, that his wife might suspect his origins if he spoke, that she might turn him over to the Nazis, who would haul him away in a cattle car with the others.*

He said nothing.

He looked away from the atrocities his wife applauded, allowed her to teach his children hatred and cruelty and crime. Slowly, the Professor watched his family become a monster that would annihilate him without remorse and without a moment's hesitation if the truth was known. They became strangers—he and those blue-eyed women—enemies behind the same line.

It was then—during the years of the occupation when news of the concentration camps spread through Paris and tales of German atrocities became common knowledge—that the Professor realized he must leave. He had given his youth to Europe and invested his time, if not his love, in the wife and daughters who never did become a part of him. But the secret he had taken away from the East had become too big and threatening for his small body to hold. It was spilling out in surprising and unpredictable ways—in arguments he had with his wife over the predicament of the Jews, in his dreams at night when he saw his daughters pointing to him and telling SS guards he was a Jew. He checked and rechecked his passport and employment papers for possible telltale signs of his origins, stayed off the streets as much as he could, for fear of being recognized by someone— anyone—as a Jew. He lived in fear of running into a friend or family member from the past, in fear of his anger getting the best of him and compelling his tongue to slip and let out his secret.

When the war ended, his wife lost her post at the university and came home to tell him they were going to starve. She said she had to keep a low profile and hope that she would not be targeted by vengeance-seeking Jews and anti-German French, that she could no longer write or teach or use her past work to obtain a job.

The Professor had spent his savings buying sugar and coffee and other necessities on the black market during the occupation. He felt no moral obligation to help his family, felt no pity for the children—fifteen, twelve, nine years old—whom he had feared all through the war. His wife wanted to sell her wedding ring, but the Professor would not allow it: it had been his grandmother's, he said, meant to stay with him for life. He offered to take a job instead.

He looked for weeks, but in vain. He had no training, no experience, no record of employment outside teaching or research. The city was in chaos and everyone was poor, and they would not entrust their affairs to an Arab man without a name.

That winter, the family had no money to buy heating fuel. The Professor's wife drank wine instead of coffee all day, and his daughters kept asking for things—food, clothes, books—he could not buy. He finally took a job washing glasses in a sidewalk bistro. He was paid in meals for himself and his family, and he got to keep the tips he received from the American soldiers who frequented the café. But his hands quickly became sore from being in water all day, and his back began to ache until he could not sleep, and he quit after only two weeks.

He told his wife he would rather die than do the common man's work.

She put on her best coat, and went on the street selling cigarettes and roses in sidewalk cafés along the Saint-Germain. She worked from dusk until dawn, counted pennies, and negotiated tips. Sometimes, she said, she accepted a glass of wine or Pastis instead of money for the cigarettes. Sometimes she agreed to sit down with a customer long enough to rest her legs, drink her wine, smoke a cigarette. She was fifty-three years old and holding on as hard as she could.

Back at home the Professor assessed his future carefully. Europe had betrayed him. He banked his hopes on America.

He went to the library and looked up the names and addresses of institutions of higher learning in the United States. He wrote letters, citing the university as a return address, and mailed them with money he took from his oldest daughter, who was fifteen and working in a bakery. She left home at three in the morning every day, came back at two in the afternoon, and fell asleep on the couch. The other two daughters stayed home and waited for her to bring day-old bread and stale pastries from her job.

In the spring of 1946, the Professor received a letter from the University of Tennessee offering him a teaching post at their campus in Knoxville. The university would pay for him to relocate to America, and they would extend credit to make it possible to purchase a home.

The Professor got dressed in his black suit and tucked his grandmother's ring into his inside pocket. It was early morning. His wife was still asleep. His oldest daughter was at work. The middle one had a fever.

His youngest daughter asked where he was going.

"For a walk," he said.

She wanted to go with him, she said. Maybe they could walk by the river, stop somewhere and buy sugar to sprinkle on their bread for breakfast.

He told her she should wait for him at home. He would be back soon, he said, and he would bring her fresh bread and sugar.

IN AMERICA THE *first few years*, the Professor kept his eyes on his work and tried to prove himself to his colleagues. He told everyone he was from France, with Arab origins, and they believed him. He said he had never been married. He joined a church.

He didn't think much about his wife and children back in Paris. He knew they would never find him in America, and he took comfort from this, felt safe from them at last. But the longer he stayed in America, the more he was haunted by the memory of his youngest daughter, and the more he began to wonder about the kind of cosmic justice that exacted retribution for long-ago sins left unpunished.

The Professor believed in cosmic justice, but he also believed in moving along, and so he decided he should marry again—because, in America, a man was expected to have a wife if not a family, and because he wanted to prove to himself that he could do this, find a girl who would respect if not love him, who would be a companion and not a judge, a source of comfort and not a threat. His experience with a Western woman had failed, so he went East to look for a girl.

By the time he found me, the Professor had searched far and wide for a wife and could therefore tell I would fit his purposes. It was true that I was illiterate and wild, but those were faults that he could correct. The fact that I was a half-Jew meant I would not be a threat to him like his Nazi wife had been. The fact that I was fair skinned and light eyed meant I could pass among Christians anywhere. The fact that my mother was mad meant I should never have children of my own.

This was crucial, you see—that I should not ask for children, that the Professor should not procreate again. He was not a bad man, so he couldn't be bad to his wife. He didn't understand my passions, it is true, but he could tolerate them well enough as long as I did not try to extend the bloodline that he so desperately wanted to stop. Every living child he left behind, he had decided after his experience with his first family, would be a witness to his sins.

It would have all worked out, he later told me. He would have died carrying the secret of his Jewish past, would have lived the rest of his life guarding the memory of his nine-year-old's eyes the morning he left. He could have justified his existence by producing exemplary work in his chosen field, could have left a trace of thought and understanding upon the world that his condescending colleagues would not be able to erase. It would have all worked out except for my daughter.

I had convinced him to produce her though he knew her fate, to bring her to life knowing she would die. It was the last thing he had wanted on his conscience—to have the undoing of yet another child, another girl, on his hands.

He couldn't sleep anymore.

In the weeks and months after my daughter's passing, the Professor reviewed his life—carefully and with as much objectivity as he could command—and tried to understand the source of his failings. He was being punished for his refusal to accept his blood and lineage. Never mind logic and science, you see: when all was said and done, the Professor knew there was an order greater than what civilized man had been able to define in books.

So he gathered his courage, looked behind at what he had so desperately wanted to deny, and for the first time, tried to understand why.

He threw himself into the task of studying Judaism, visited the old synagogue in Knoxville, and sat in on Friday night and Saturday morning shuls. He learned about the Orthodox Jews of Memphis, went to talk to their rabbis, attended their services. He did not admit to them that he was a Jew, pretended that his interest in them was purely academic. The rabbi in Memphis nodded at him quietly and said he understood. Nevertheless, he insisted on teaching the Professor to say the Sh'ma for his own peace, the Kaddish for the soul of his departed loved ones. Then he pulled the Professor over and told him that a Jew must be prepared to admit his lineage not only to himself, but also to those who might condemn him for it.

"It's a haunted man who runs from his own shadow," the rabbi said.

One morning shortly after another visit to Memphis, the Professor told me he was going to Europe. He was going to find the wife and children he had left behind, he said, to face them one last time and speak the truth he had never before been able to utter.

He was sixty-four years old and at last ready to face his shadow.

AT THE AIRPORT *terminal in Paris, the Professor watched three plane loads of passengers march past him through customs, and still, he did not have the courage to move. He had come prepared to face his family, to weather their hatred and the many expressions of their scorn. But in his attempt to get ready to stand before his judges, he had forgotten that he was also about to revisit the city of his youth, the place where he had experienced the greatest pain but also, before that, the only bit of happiness he ever knew.*

Paris was smaller, more crowded, less civilized than he remembered. The streets were narrow and overpopulated; the air and the river were polluted; the stores and cafés buzzed with an urgency that made him want to escape.

On his old block on rue Berger, the tailor shop was gone— replaced by a smoke-filled grocery store tended by an African man. Everything else—the apartment buildings, the bakery, the little booth where an old woman had sold newspapers and gardenias—was still the same.

He spent the night at a hotel two streets away. The next morning he accepted a glass of crème de menthe from the lady who owned the hotel, then went back to his room again.

On his third day in Paris, he gave himself the closest shave he had ever had, and dressed in his best suit. He took an umbrella even though there was no sign of rain, drank another crème de menthe. On rue Berger the old woman with the gardenias gave him a long, hard look before asking if he wanted to buy a paper. When he refused, she shoved the paper under his arm anyway.

"For old times' sake," she said, and he was horrified to realize that she remembered him.

His wife's name was still on the plate next to the button that activated the doorbell. He thought about ringing, then pushed the door to the lobby and went in.

A slim staircase led directly from the front door up toward the apartments. The building was narrow and deep, allowing only one unit on each floor and even then, the rooms within were stacked one in front of the other like hollow chambers of sound and clutter. On the third floor, his breath trapped in his stomach, the Professor stopped and stared at the black-painted door he had closed behind him so long ago.

It opened with swift and unprovoked force, putting the Professor on the defensive, as if he had been caught in midcrime. A woman in a tight skirt and heavy shoes frowned at him, then muttered something in French and pulled the door shut. She was on her way out, the Professor realized. She turned her back to him and struggled with the lock. Overweight and haggard, she had the flat, round hands, the square finger tips, the meaty elbows of women who have done hard, thankless work all their lives.

"Out of my way," she told the Professor, then nudged him with her body.

She was halfway down the first flight of steps when he found the voice to call her.

"Forgive me, Madame," he ventured, but she did not stop. He watched her for a moment.

"Madame," he called again. "One moment, if you please." She grabbed the railing with an angry hand and stopped.

"But hurry up, already," she yelled from the landing on the second floor. "What is it?"

She was looking up at him now with her light blue eyes, the freckles on her nose having turned with time into large brown blotches. Suddenly he realized he had come to the right place— that this woman he did not know and had not recognized must be one of his three daughters.

At that very moment the Professor grasped the enormity of his sin.

Slowly, one hand gripping the railing, he went down the steps to where his daughter waited. When he reached her level, he took his hat off and stood before her speechless. She must have known that he had something of consequence to say because she had forgotten her pressing business and was looking at him through narrowed eyelids.

"What is it?" she finally asked, but he could read the doubt in her voice this time.

He swallowed the bile in his throat and stood as tall as he could.

"My name is Professor Kerdi," he said. "I used to live in your apartment with my wife and three daughters."

Twenty years had passed since the Professor had walked out on his family. His oldest daughter, the one whose salary he had used to buy stamps for his letters to America, was still working at the bakery where she had started at age fifteen. His middle daughter had married a Portuguese singer and moved with him to South America. His youngest had continued to live in the apartment. She cleaned house for rich women on avenue Foch and wrote letters to the Bureau of Missing Persons asking them to keep her father's file alive, insisting that he had been mur-

dered or kidnapped or simply lost on his walk the day he left, but that he had not abandoned her.

Their mother—the blue-eyed professor of Jungian psychology with the Nazi sympathies—had hung herself from the ceiling fan in her bedroom three years after her husband had vanished.

HE CAME BACK *and told me he had run out of hope.*

He stood in our hallway with his hat in hand and his suit-case by the door—a pilgrim returning from a last-ditch jour-ney to the land of broken promises, sweating into his shirt collar and breathing the slow, scratchy air that surrounds dying men. When he saw me he opened his mouth as if to speak, but his lips were covered with cobwebs from all the years of silence, and it was all he could do to let out a sigh and extend his arm.

I thought then how odd it was that the end of our life—his and mine—had come in the shape of a pathetic-looking man dragging an old suitcase, and not, as I had imagined, in a spectacular inferno of rage and passion and wild, unchecked rebellion. I gave him my hand. He bent down and placed a tearful kiss on the tips of my fingers.

"You are my only link to the world of the living," he said.

NOW YOU SEE WHY *I cannot leave my husband, why I will have to go with him no matter how far he takes me from you.*

You see me now—the Jew's daughter from nowhere, my hands painted with the invisible colors of my mother's sorrow, my eyes filled with the longing for roads that might have led away but that instead took me to a place where I would drink poison and pray for a salvation I know will never come. You see me and wonder at the hollow promise of Hope.

This is what we all look for—the cynic with the restless boots who travels the world seeking justice, the preacher with the snake calling the name of the Lord, my mother braiding her hair with the gold of her father's betrayal, believing that if she kept the coins he may come back: we are all waiting for the luminous hands that will reach for us in the night, the eyes that will witness our pain, the voice that will whisper the possibility of a different truth.

I owe this to the Professor, you see. I have never loved him, but I long ago traded my life for the possibility of the one he offered, and I cannot leave him now that he cannot walk alone.

It's an even bargain—one in which we both lose.

ALL NIGHT LONG the wind howled in the mountains, and the temperature continued to drop. Adam dreamed that Blue stood above him in her transparent white dress. Reaching toward her, he ran his right index finger across the front of her chest, parting the fabric like water, laying bare the snake wound that was still visible, traveling down to the tip of her navel. Blue lowered herself onto him, seeped like a breath through the pores in his skin and into his muscles and bones. When she exhaled, he felt the weight of a thousand lives lift away.

Isiah Frank was shaking him by the shoulder. Adam opened his eyes and took a moment to remember where he was. Eight in the morning, late September, in a city he had come to conquer but which had entrapped him instead.

"Better get back over there," Isiah said quietly.

His face was grave, devoid of its usual irony.

He gave Adam a chance to sit up.

"And take your notebook with you."

MRS. ROSCOE ACROSS the street stood on the sidewalk in her gray-and-red terry bathrobe and her rubber rain boots. She had wrapped a blanket around herself, and she was shivering in the wind as she looked at the police and coroner's car outside Blue's house.

"Told you the devil's in that house," she said the moment she saw Adam. Behind him a second police car pulled to the curb and stopped.

Adam went up to the house with his knees shaking and his heart in his throat. He had been here less than twenty-four hours earlier and yet he could tell, without needing the police or the coroner to remind him, that disaster had come on his heels. The moment he entered the house, a pair of eyes fixed on him.

"Where is she?" he asked, his voice barely audible for its tremor.

A young woman in a bomber jacket came toward him and stopped half a foot away. He did not want to hear what she had to say, wouldn't accept the news he thought she would give him.

"Where *is* she?"

The coroner's assistant came out of the dining room with his hands still gloved, and nodded at the woman to let Adam in.

"See for yourself," he told Adam.

A body, wrapped in dark plastic, lay faceup on the dining room table. On one side of it stood a police investigator with Coke-bottle glasses and a thin mustache. On the other side Blue stood alone.

THE PROFESSOR, Adam learned from the investigator, had died after drinking a glass of water laced with strychnine. The coroner's report would estimate five parts poison to one part water. It was the same poison Blue drank at church services, the same one Holy Rollers used to prove the strength of their faith. The Professor, of course, was not a Holy Roller and had never participated in poison drinking. Nor was he—a man who had planned to leave the city and whose bags were packed and neatly arranged at the bottom of the stairs—a likely candidate for suicide.

He had died at approximately 2:00 a.m. following Adam's visit to their house the previous day. Blue reported having found him at 5:30. He had been sitting on the only chair in the dining room, and he had on his shoes and dress shirt, was well shaven and groomed. His hat lay on the table before him.

At six o'clock she had called the police to report the death. They had found Blue dry-eyed and calm—not the expected appearance, the investigator would note in his report, of a woman who has just found her husband dead.

The sheriff asked if Blue knew what killed the Professor.

"Strychnine," she said without hesitation, "and too many secrets."

"MY HUSBAND CALLED *me in the dark and said it was time to leave.*"

"*It's midnight,*" *he said.* "*Your bags are packed.*"

"*The church people would think we had left because of Little Sam's death. 'She killed Little Sam Jenkins,' they would say, 'and left to hide from the law.'*

"*Our neighbors would believe my husband took me away to hide from you—that he gave up his job to save his marriage.*

"*My friends would realize they never knew me at all—that I had never belonged with them and never deserved their trust.*

"*All the while my husband and I would be driving West— toward Memphis, he told me, and beyond it, to where Fate might take us.*

"*We had been outsiders, he and I, all of our lives. We had never belonged with anyone. It mattered little where we went now, as long as we did not lose each other, he said.*

"*I got up from the bed and put on the dress he had laid out for me. I washed my face, looked at myself one last time in the mirror above the bathroom sink. I remembered the day I had walked into that room for the first time, when I had wished I could flood the house with anger, float away and leave the Professor to die.*

"*He was waiting for me in the bedroom.*

"*I thought about a life away from you and your eyes, a life of silence and solitude and the never-ending need to speak.*

"*This is what I have learned through the years of living with the loss of my mother, then my child: the most real presence of all is the absence of those we love.*

"*I came back into the bedroom again and told him it was true—that I had loved you with my flesh and also in my thoughts, that I had told you what I was sworn never to reveal, placed his fate—my husband who had never done me wrong— in the hands of his enemy. I told him I would go away with him and leave you, but that I knew, just as he did, that we had run out of places to go and ways to reinvent ourselves. I told him it was not enough to pretend any more.*

"*It's not about finding the way out,*" I said, showing him my hands. "*It's about finding the way to live at peace* within the maze.*"

IT WOULDN'T BE easy to avoid being charged this time.

Blue must know this, Adam imagined, but she seemed strangely indifferent—resigned, almost, to the inevitable. She stood by the table with her hands crossed, answering the detective's questions in an even tone. She told him where she kept her poison, how she mixed it with water, why she had not bothered to hide it from the Professor. She kept looking at the outline of the Professor's body as she spoke: Inside the black plastic his frame appeared even smaller than it had been in life. His arms lay at his sides, and he looked more like a child than a man, and maybe that's what intrigued her, what made her look as if she weren't sure she knew the person inside the bag.

She had done this before, Adam suddenly thought. She had seen her daughter wrapped up and taken away, buried her and fought to keep the memory of what she was before death.

He went around the table and stood next to Blue, put his hand on her shoulder and asked if she wanted to sit down. She shook her head, and he thought she was about to cry, felt the cold in her skin and asked the detective if she could have a minute to get something warm to wear. The woman in the bomber jacket opened one of the suitcases in the hallway, and brought Blue an emerald-green raincoat with a wide belt.

Just then Isiah Frank burst in.

He was wearing a camel-hair overcoat with a fur collar. He had a cashmere scarf tossed around his neck, brown suede gloves tucked carefully into his pocket. He was carrying a cup of Turkish coffee he had brewed at home and brought along, and he was telling the junior detective assigned to guard the entry that he was out of line, interfering with a man who had urgent business with the police.

"Crime scene my eye," he told the detective when he found himself already in the dining room and before an audience. "There can't be a *scene* if there hasn't been a *crime*."

He raised his left hand when he saw Blue.

"*There* you are!" he announced, pushing back the detective.

"I came in the moment I heard."

He was in top form, Adam noted—as expansive and theatrical as any of the actors he had ever dressed. The detective seemed to have had experience dealing with him as well. He shook his head in dismay but did not try to interrupt Isiah or to force him to leave. Instead he humored Isiah, let him go through the motions without stopping him. It wasn't proper police procedure, to be sure. He may have acted differently in another house, with another victim.

Isiah walked up to the middle of the room and put his coffee cup on the dining-room table. Suddenly noticing the body, he twisted his mouth and drew back in horror.

"Ugh!" he muttered. "I didn't know *he* was here."

Adam wished the detective had kept Isiah out.

"Let's have a look," Isiah said, and opened the zipper on the body bag halfway. He peeked at the Professor curiously—careful not to touch any part of him—then closed the zipper again.

"That sure *is* a *vintage* tie," he declared.

He sat down on the chair where the Professor had died, and crossed his legs. Reaching for his cup, he drank gingerly, rested the cup and the saucer on his lap, and looked at the others.

"The news is all over town," he explained.

He looked from Adam to Blue and then back to Adam again.

"I thought for sure the poor girl is going to be harassed by these rogues in police drag. I figured I couldn't count on *you* to set them straight."

He wasn't smiling, but his eyes were filled with mischief—the awareness, Adam thought, that he could alter the course of another's life by his own words. He raised an eyebrow at Adam and spoke with a flat voice.

"I'm here to tell them she was with *you* all night."

He uttered the words as if they were true, waited, and fixed Adam with his eyes to dare him to react. He was betting on his own talent as an actor, Adam thought, on his ability to mold truth out of illusion.

Conscious of the gravity of this lie, Adam studied Isiah but did not respond. Next to him he could feel Blue's presence like heat, imagined the bright green raincoat against the white of her skin.

Isiah was getting braver by the minute.

"I saw her come in past midnight," he spoke now directly to the detective. "I heard them both from the bedroom until morning."

He sat back, took another sip of the coffee, and told the detective about the Armenian store clerk who read his fortune.

"Forget Tarot," he declared. "Coffee is most accurate."

Then he launched into a gossipy discussion of Adam's affair with Blue.

"Not that I blame the girl, you know," he offered. "Who could have stayed loyal to *that?*" he motioned with his head toward the body bag.

"Anyway. I let her out myself this morning."

He looked genuinely pleased with himself—triumphant in his performance.

"She left a few minutes past five."

Inside the Professor's dining room, all eyes focused on Adam.

"Go ahead and tell them," Isiah urged casually as he finished his coffee. "The truth, as they say, shall set you free."

Before him on the table, the coffee grinds had cast a web of black lines against the inside of the white porcelain cup.

IT WAS UP TO him now—to save her or to let her fall.

Adam had been moving toward this moment from the start, he realized—from the moment he'd read about Sam's death in the paper in Beirut and come back to find his own past. Blue had known this, of course, had warned him of it the first time they spoke. Isiah Frank must have known it, too. That's why he'd kept such a close watch on Adam.

He had left Appalachia hoping to overcome the loss and deception that had tainted his own and his ancestors' lives and had returned to lay them to light and instead, Adam Watkins had become a character in the very story he had intended to write.

He had come to bear witness—convinced of the importance of Truth, willing to accept its consequences. To do so now would mean to surrender Blue to her enemies—to tell them that she had confessed to killing Sam Jenkins, that she had not been with Adam the night the Professor died.

To save her he would have to buy into Isiah Frank's game of illusions, accept that they may never know the truth or their part in hiding it.

She may have planned to kill the Professor all along, may have conspired with Isiah from the start.

Or she may not have lied at all.

Maybe her only sin was in hoping that Jenkins would die, her only infraction was in confessing her thoughts to Adam. Maybe he hadn't been wrong, all those times when he had watched her next to him, when he had studied her every word and the very movement of her lips, when he had told himself he knew how to tell a lie from the truth, told himself that she was not lying.

Maybe that was why she had sought him out, why she had not been afraid to tell him the story she knew he might use against her: because, like him, she believed in the importance of Truth.

Adam had heard Blue's version of her story and seen its characters live and die. He had existed within the tale and outside of it and yet, he was no closer now to solving the riddle than when he had first arrived.

In the end, he realized, he would have to decide on faith.

He would have to close his eyes, let her voice, all the words she had spoken to him, play again in his mind, settle into him like a slow summer wind, and he would have to decide if he believed them.

Believing her, like making love to her, like holding a snake in prayer knowing it may kill or set one free—believing her would, in the end, have to be an act of faith.

He pulled a cigarette out of his shirt pocket and lit it without looking up. Inhaling deeply, he held the smoke in his chest, felt it sting the inside of his lungs, then blew it out in a long, slow breath. He saw himself turning to Blue, saw her moving toward him the way she had done that first day in August.

A phone rang in the distance and someone picked up. The investigator with the thick glasses shifted his weight on his legs and sat on the edge of the table. Next to him, Isiah Frank remained quiet and imperious and confident of his gambit.

The investigator looked as if he was about to ask a question, or warn Adam of the implications of his words.

"She was with me," Adam said, his voice so steady, it surprised him.

He let the realization of what he had done sink into him like a stone, felt the sadness, the sense of loss, spread inside his stomach and his chest until it had filled every hole. He wasn't sorry he had lied.

"She came in past midnight," he told the detective. "Left just after five."

THERE WAS A MAN *who had a secret, a secret so dark and frightening, he had sworn to protect it with his life or to die trying.*

As a boy he had buried the secret in the garden of his grandmother's house in a port city overlooking a wide and stormy river.

But the secret had crept into the roots of the roses his grandmother grew in the garden, and it had climbed up the thorny stems of each flower, and it bloomed a thousand times in a thousand colors every year. When he saw this the boy uprooted the rose bushes and scooped out the dirt, packed it in a locked box, and smuggled it onto a fishing boat with a prayer that it would sink in the estuary where the river poured into the sea.

But the secret had laced itself around every grain of dirt the boy had touched, and it had seeped under his fingernails and onto his clothes and the palms of his hands. He washed his hands in the river and burned his clothes, but then he went home to find that the water well had become contaminated with the dirt in the garden, and that the secret was flowing in every drop.

So he drank all the water in the well, and then he told his parents he must go away—to a place where no one knew his past and where his secret would not be recognized. For years he lived in this new world aware that the secret flew in his veins and traveled under his skin, and when he could no longer stand the weight of the water in his chest and stomach, he traveled again, to a still newer place.

As he got older the man watched the pores in his skin become bigger and more treacherous, and he felt the tears in his eyes flow more easily and in greater abundance. Then he realized he had devoted his life to a fight he was about to lose, that the secret was feeding off his body and getting stronger as the man grew weaker and that soon, his only choice would be to surrender. He tried to leave again, but he knew the secret would travel with him no matter where he went, and he was old and tired and unable to take chances alone.

So he found a poison stronger than himself, mixed it in a glass of water, and drank it to drown the secret for all time.

IN THE BOARDINGHOUSE, Isiah Frank had put away the garden furniture and covered his plants against frost. His cat was perched on the railing of Adam's balcony with its back arched and its eyes wide-open. The wind blew cold and furious, rattling the chimes and raising the cat's fur, but she seemed oblivious to the weather. She was watching Adam as if on a mission to relate his actions to her owner.

Adam packed his few belongings and picked up his tape recorder and the pieces of the story he knew he would never write. He had left Isiah and Blue at the Professor's house, promised the detective he would stay in town a while longer. With two witnesses and an alibi, a dead man no one had ever trusted or cared about, and the Professor's fingerprints all over the glass of poison he had drunk, there was little chance the DA would prosecute. Adam knew the penalties of evading police. He was going to leave anyway.

He pushed open the door to the Dutch boys' room and saw their luggage and the few belongings they had stored with Isiah. He remembered the day he had arrived in this house, remembered the boys' innocence, the comfort they seemed to take from one another's friendship.

Outside, the wind bit into him like ice. He saw the black woman who ran the antique shop across the street looking at him from behind the store window. She had on a yellow summer dress, a wide-brimmed straw hat with paper flowers and a ribbon hanging down the sides. He threw his bag onto the back seat and pulled away without looking back.

He drove along Gay Street, past Nate's and the Andrew Johnson Hotel, past the courthouse and the Bijou Theater. On the 158 on-ramp, he looked in the rearview mirror one last time and saw the city—its cobblestoned streets, its ancient cemeteries, the quiet river that emerged from the mist every morning only to reflect the colors of the mountains surrounding it. The thought of Blue tugged at him like a child's hand. He swallowed hard and pushed ahead.

Four hundred miles to the Washington airport, and beyond it he did not care where he went.

Merging into the James White Parkway, he hit the midday traffic and had to slow down till the I-81 split. Then he was alone again—the road before him white and empty in the murky sunlight, promising nothing, telling no lies.

Had she loved him—the girl who had painted herself to life? Had she loved him at all?

Near Bristol it began to rain, but Adam did not slow down. Large, heavy trucks, painted in bright colors and mounted on monstrous wheels dominated the road and hovered dangerously close to his car. The rain was so heavy, it blinded him in spite of the fast-working wipers. He peered through the bottom of the windshield—the narrow space just above the edge of the window—and followed only the white lines on the asphalt. Pulling up from behind each truck, he would push his car onto the edge of the road, then fight the urge to slow down and retreat. He raced the truck in this way, aware that he could be crushed at any moment—driven off the road or thrown into a tailspin if he so much as hit a stone at such high speeds. He floored the gas pedal and did not relent, kept the car parallel with the truck and knew it was a matter of time before he or the other driver lost their nerve and pulled back. Invariably, Adam prevailed.

It was like he had always known: the man with the least at stake won most often.

He had gone as far as Salem when he found himself thinking about Blue again. The rain had eased up, and the muscles in his head and neck were feeling looser, and he pulled into a gas station to load up and buy a cup of coffee. He though about the insides of Blue's arms—the way he used to run his lips, the very tip of his tongue, over the line that stretched from her elbow up into the side of her chest in a journey he had hoped would never end.

"Looks like rain all week." A brisk young woman with badly bleached hair and long painted nails handed him his change.

He wiped the rain off the edge of his car seat, drove out of the station with one hand as he held the coffee with the other. He was thinking about the Professor in his mortician's suit and his "vintage" tie, the way he had once brought Blue a box of colored marzipans, sat next to her before a mirror and a jug of clear water to start his life with her.

He thought how ironic it was that he had seen all the places of Blue's memories before he had ever found her, that he had lived in the places and among the people she had come from. They had switched places—he and Blue—switched worlds and continents and yet, in the end, they had arrived at the same truth.

He thought about all the years he had spent traveling through the mountains of Blue's childhood, how years ago he had already sailed the waters of the Sea of Marmara. He thought of Blue's mother turning around one day and offering a stranger her first smile, lifting the red veil that covered her face and letting him kiss her lips for the first time. He thought of the mad woman painting Blue's destiny onto the palms of her hands, the Professor laying a new dress and a dozen gold bangles on the floor of her father's tent.

He had seen them all, known them in his own time.

On the road before him, the black woman in the lavender suit painted her lips with a steady hand and arranged the paper flowers on her summer hat. Blue's daughter ran across the yard with her hair black as a raven's wings and her dress in flames. The Professor walked the streets of the Paris of his youth and imagined his first wife dangling alone from the ceiling fan in their apartment. They had raised their children in that apartment. They had entertained their friends, eaten dinner together, made love in that apartment.

Adam had seen all of this, and he had seen Blue's Appalachia as well. As a boy, he had sat in the same church alongside Anne Pelton and her friends, followed Little Sam Jenkins around the country as Blue would years later. He had repeated the same prayers Blue would in time learn, hoped that they would save him in spite of his lack of faith.

He saw Isiah Frank walk across the house of his own deception, watching the creatures he had helped create, saw John the Baptist stand like Jesus on the cross. A woman with purple eyes and golden-red hair rolled onto him in the dark, put her lips to his ears, told him tales he could not help but believe.

He was, in many ways, no different from the people in Blue's stories: like her nomad father; the Professor, who had died when he could no longer reinvent himself; like Sam Jenkins and the believers who forsook their lives on earth in order to live in the Spirit—like all of them, Adam had spent his life wanting to *leave*.

Somewhere out on the empty road, he saw the lines in the palms of Blue's hands etched before him and realized that he, too, had traveled through a maze that in the end, would lead nowhere.

LISTEN.

There was a woman who loved a man—a man so alone and unreachable, she saw in him her own longings and thought she could find her way into his heart. So she laid herself before him like a tale and let him see her as if she were made of glass, cried her tears into a jar and gave them to him like a gift.

Around you I spread my words like a wish, sprinkled the dust of all my dreams, the light of all the stars I had seen in my youth. I cast my story into your memories and onto your bed, onto the ground where you walked and into the night where you slept and all along, I prayed that it would keep you from leaving.

But the day came when I ran out of words and found myself alone, at dawn in a city where sleep was impossible, in a house full of sorrow and the ghosts of small children. You had freed me from my enemies and then left, walked out of my house and into the mid-morning autumn sun without so much as a glance for me to follow.

I stayed home and buried my husband. I opened his books, the small suitcase into which he had packed his clothes on the day he still believed he could escape. I hung the clothes back in his closet, spread his papers onto the desk in his study. I lit the lamp he used to read by, put his watch directly across from his chair where he always kept it. I wound the clock in the dining room, opened the drapes, returned his hat to the spot he used to set it when he came home.

I gave him his house the way I had known it first—a place that would serve as proof of his civility, witness to his Western ways, relic of his distinguished life. When I was done I took my daughter's suitcase and walked out.

Isiah Frank met me on the street.

"There's nowhere to go," I told him, "no chance to stay."

He smiled and took my hand, waved his arm against the dark night. Before us the street was covered with a film of shimmering silver dust.

"These are your words," Isiah said, "the ones you spoke to your lover, that you gave to him with your hope."

So I follow those words, walk along the edge of this translucent silver road that snakes through the night and glows like a promise in the dark. I think of a palace built entirely of glass, a song on the lips of a man who seduces every lover. I think of the gold in my mother's hair, the books on my husband's desk, the snakes in my own hands—how they were all one and the same, nothing more than the promise of a different fate, nothing less than the one path that shines in the dark. In my fist I press the handle of my daughter's suitcase and tell myself I should have shown her to you—should have shown you her pictures, should have let you see her eyes.

Isiah Frank walks with me until we reach the house where I first made love to you. Upstairs he shows me into your room. I see your empty bed, the sheets where I slept next to you, the mirror that until recently held my image.

"I don't know where he's gone," I tell Isiah. "I don't think he'll come back."

He smiles again and takes me to the dresser where he used to keep your clothes. I open a drawer and see that it's filled with

*silver dust—tiny grains of light, soft as the sand at the bottom
of a river, luminous as diamonds. I dig my hands into the
light, let it fall through my fingers in straight lines.*

*I open my daughter's suitcase and take out her pictures, the
tiny ribbons I once put in her hair, the satin shoes I put on her
feet when she was barely a month old. I arrange them all on the
dresser and stand back to watch.*

"This is my life," I say aloud.

*Isiah Frank goes to the window and opens it wide. The air is
cold against my skin. I hear the chimes ringing softly, see the
dust—my own words—falling off them when they move.*

"Make a wish," Isiah tells me in his director's voice.

*Already I hear the sound of your steps, feel the beat of your
heart against the silence of this house. In the mirror I see myself as if for the first time: a woman alone, separate from her
story, removed at last from the hopes and illusions of all those
who had painted themselves into her life. Then the stairs creak
under your boots and the walls give in your presence, and you're
standing in the doorway as if back from a thousand-year-old
war. Your eyes ache for sleep, and your body is uncertain which
way to turn, but I can read you by instinct, see your need as if
it were my own. I walk up and touch the fabric of your shirt,
close my eyes and feel the comfort of your presence, the weight
of your hands that will catch me, I know, in midfall.*

"Make a wish," I say, "and we will imagine it to life."

Acknowledgments

I wish to thank my agent, Barbara Lowenstein, for crusading on my behalf; my editor, the great Ann Patty, for unparalleled insight and calm guidance; publisher Dan Farley and editor in chief Jane Isay, for their faith.

Thanks to David Hough for his patience; to Claudine Guerguerian for her cover; to Jennifer Holiday and Tricia van Dockum for fighting the good fight.

I am grateful to my husband, Hamid David Nahai, who believed in this book from the start and blessed it with his vision and courage.

Thanks to my friends Adriane Sharp, who guided me through the maze, and Marilyn Stackenfeld, who reminded me I could write.

Thanks to my parents, Giti and Francois Barkhordar, who did not doubt.

And to my children, Alex, Ashley, and Kevin, who have painted their colors into my life and will cast them still onto a thousand distant skies.